ALSO BY GI

Unforgettable novels of

CHEROKEE . . . Nothin[...]
settling a score . . .

DEAD MAN'S POKER . . . Outlaw life is a deadly
game. But going straight is the biggest gamble of all.

GUNPOINT . . . There are two things more important
than money: honor and survival . . .

SIXKILLER . . . No one fights harder than the man
who fights for his kin.

HARD ROCK . . . Rough country breeds a rougher
breed of man . . .

JAILBREAK . . . When a man's got his back against
the wall, there's only one thing to do. Break it down.

AVAILABLE FROM JOVE BOOKS

"GILES TIPPETTE IS AN AUTHOR TO WATCH . . .
MUCH MORE THAN JUST A SHOOT-'EM-UP."
                                    —*The Washington Star*

"TOUGH, GUTSY, AND FASCINATING."
                                    —*New York Newsday*

"IMPRESSIVE AUTHENTICITY."   —*Booklist*

"HIS FICTION IS TAUT AND GRIPPING."
                                    —*Houston Spectator*

Books by Giles Tippette

Fiction

THE TROJAN COW
THE SURVIVALIST
THE SUNSHINE KILLERS
AUSTIN DAVIS
WILSON'S WOMAN
WILSON YOUNG ON THE RUN
THE TEXAS BANK ROBBING COMPANY
WILSON'S GOLD
WILSON'S REVENGE
WILSON'S CHOICE
WILSON'S LUCK
HARD LUCK MONEY
CHINA BLUE
BAD NEWS
CROSS FIRE
JAILBREAK
HARD ROCK
SIXKILLER
GUNPOINT
DEAD MAN'S POKER
CHEROKEE
THE BANK ROBBER

Nonfiction

THE BRAVE MEN
SATURDAY'S CHILDREN
DONKEY BASEBALL AND OTHER SPORTING DELIGHTS
I'LL TRY ANYTHING ONCE

THE BANK ROBBER

GILES TIPPETTE

JOVE BOOKS, NEW YORK

This Jove Book contains the complete
text of the original edition.
It has been completely reset in a typeface
designed for easy reading and was printed
from new film.

THE BANK ROBBER

A Jove Book / published by arrangement with
the author

PRINTING HISTORY
Jove edition / November 1993

ISBN: 0-515-11220-8

A JOVE BOOK®
Jove Books are published by The Berkley Publishing Group,
200 Madison Avenue, New York, New York 10016.
JOVE and the "J" design
are trademarks belonging to Jove Publications, Inc.

PRINTED IN THE UNITED STATES OF AMERICA

10 9 8 7 6 5 4 3 2 1

CONTENTS

THE BANK ROBBER

CHAPTER 1

Across a Rising River

We were robbing the bank in Carrizo Springs, a little south Texas town down by the Rio Grande River. I was behind the counter sacking up the money from the vault and the tellers' cages, and Tod and Les were out front guarding the bank employees and the few customers that had been unlucky enough to come wandering in just as we did. There were an awful lot of people on the street for it being the noon hour and we were in a hurry to get out of there before the place got completely filled up. I was working as fast as I could, but the money was nearly all in gold and it was taking longer than greenbacks would have.

"Let's go, Wilson," Les said. "You've got enough."

"Let him get it all," Tod said. "That's what we come for. Hell."

I could hear the edge in both their voices. They were both getting a little tense. That's all right for Les, because he's still a good man under pressure, but Tod's not that way. He loses his head sometimes. Right then he was feeling gunbrave because he was covering unarmed men.

"Just a minute," I said. There was only three of us, so we couldn't afford to leave a man to hold the horses. We had them loose-tied just out in front.

There was only one teller behind the counter with me, him and some officer of the bank that I had leaned up against the wall. I'd left the teller sitting on his little high stool. He looked so nervous and scared I didn't figure he'd do anything. I didn't have my gun out on account of my arms being loaded with the bags of gold. I shouldered the teller out of the way and sacked up what little money he had and then turned around to see if I'd missed anything. Just then I heard Les yell and I whirled to see the teller going for a revolver he had hid under the counter. I couldn't do a thing, but Tod was coming around and leveling right down on the clerk. I yelled, "No!" at him, but it was Les that saved the killing. He stepped over and knocked Tod's gun hand up. The gun went off, but the bullet went into the ceiling. By then I'd dropped all but one bag of the gold and I swung it and got the teller behind the ear and knocked him colder than a wedge.

Tod was cussing and getting red in the face, but we didn't have time to argue about it. I gathered up the gold and went running around the railing.

"Get the horses!" I said to Tod.

"Goddam him!" he said, meaning Les. "He better not—"

"Get out of here!" I said. "Get out there and get them horses! *Now!*"

He went off, still cussing, and I handed Les the money and pulled out my own revolver. The gunshot had made our prisoners nervous and they were moving around a little too much.

"Just take it easy," I said. Les and I began backing for the door. "Don't nobody move."

I paused at the door, giving Les time to get mounted and stow the gold in his saddlebags. Tod was already up, waiting to hand me my reins.

"First man out this door gets killed," I told the men I was covering. "Just think on that." Then I jumped back, jerked the door to, and leapt on my little filly. "Let's git!" I yelled. I still had my revolver in my hand and I fired a couple of shots into the air. Les and Tod were doing the same. As we whirled around in the street, the door of the bank suddenly came open and a man appeared in the doorway. I fired a shot over his head and he jumped back inside.

We got lined out, spurring up the street. People had come

running out of stores and houses at the noise of the commotion, but they went back inside just as fast when they saw us coming. I heard one shot ring out and a bullet sang over our heads, but that was all. In another second we were out of town and heading south over the prairie. The river and Mexico was about fifteen miles away.

Les was out in front and then Tod and then myself. I kept looking back, but couldn't see any pursuit developing. It would take them a while to get themselves collected and by then we'd be over the river and into Mexico.

Tod and Les are first cousins and they both have the same last name, Richter. My name is Wilson Young and we all three grew up together around Corpus Christi, Texas. We'd been riding together about four years, mostly engaging in bank robberies. The bank we'd just held up in Carrizo was the nearest to home country we'd ever worked, but we'd been down on our luck of late and needed a stake. I figured we'd got near four thousand dollars. It would buy us a lot of time in Mexico.

I felt good about not killing the teller. I've shot men before and probably will again, but it's always been my style to do it in a fair fight. There would have been no profit in killing that teller. It wasn't even necessary anyway. The way he was fumbling around with that pistol it was doubtful he even knew which end the bullet came out of. All Tod would have had to have done was leveled down on him and tell him to hold it. He'd have stopped. You kill a man, especially a respected citizen like a bank teller, and you're going to get folks a lot more stirred up than they'll get over just a bank robbery.

But that was the difference between the two cousins. Tod is a bully and a coward and ain't smart enough to pour water out of a boot if the directions are on the heel. But Les is a good man and he's been my friend ever since I was nine or ten years old. We're both about the same age, nearly twenty-eight, but Tod is a little older. You'd never think it, the way he acts; you'd think he was the baby of the gang.

We swept on over the prairie, gradually pulling our horses down to a fast gallop. That country is all sand and mesquite and cactus, but it's pretty flat and makes good riding. The sun was getting up, crossing over into the afternoon sky, and it was mighty hot. A little further on we pulled down to a lope and then finally brought the horses to a walk.

"We better rest these horses," I said. "Let's get down."

"Hell with the horses," Tod said. "Let's get on to the river."

I didn't say a word, just pulled up and dismounted. Les did the same and we strung out walking, leading our animals. Tod watched us, walking his mount along by our side.

"When you founder that animal," I told him, "don't look to ride double with anybody."

"Oh goddam!" he said. He got down. "All right, Mister Young. Whatever you say."

Les and I were walking side by side, but Tod was behind us. We could hear him cussing to himself. After a little he worked himself up and said loudly: "I'll tell you, hadn't nobody else better ever hit my arm when I'm about to fire. I'll just tell you that!"

Les nor I didn't say anything.

Tod wouldn't let it lay. "I mean it, goddamit! Next time I'll shoot the one that's doing the interferin'."

That done it. I turned on him. "Listen, you goddam harebrain! You ought to thank Les for what he done. He maybe saved your sorry neck from the gallows. That teller didn't need shooting and anybody with a lick of sense could have seen it. Now you shut up or I'm going to shut you up."

I turned back around and went to walking again. Tod's like that, you've got to come down on him every so often.

Tod's the tallest one of us, a little over six feet, and he's red-haired and he's got big, hairy hands. Les is dark, darker than me, and you sometimes wonder how him and Tod could be such close cousins, looking so different. Les is a quiet boy; he doesn't say much, but when he does it's generally worth listening to. At first you might think he's a little too serious, but he likes his fun and can be as wild as the next when he goes off on a drunk. Me and him have closed down our share of whorehouses over the years. There ain't neither one of us stingy with money when we've got it.

We got to the river about middle afternoon. We come sweeping up a little sandy rise and there it was on the other side. The horses had been smelling the water for the last mile or so, so we knew we weren't far.

But it didn't look a thing like it's supposed to. Instead of being a little, muddy, narrow stream that a tall dog could wade, it had turned into the Mississippi. We pulled up and stared at it. It appeared to be nearly a quarter of a mile across and the brown water moved along in a kind of whirling, rushing current.

"My God!" Les said.

"Yeah," I said. "What the hell is this?"

"Well, that rips it!" Tod said. "Goddam! Goddam! God-dam!" He was getting nervous, letting his gelding dance around and looking over his shoulder at the way we'd come. "You picked this crossing," he said to me. "Now what are we going to do? Hell of a crossing!"

I looked at Les. "What do you reckon?"

"I heard they'd had the heaviest rains in El Paso last week that anybody could remember. I reckon it's just now getting down here."

"It's a crest all right," I said. I turned my horse and rode back up on the ridge and looked back. The horizon was empty. I went back down with the others and let my filly go to the edge of the water and drink. The sand was soft and her front hoofs sank in up to the hocks.

"We've got a little time," I said. "But not much." It would take the town a little while to get a catch party organized, and they wouldn't gain on us on the ride down. We were all superbly mounted as befits people in our line of work and there wouldn't be two horses in the whole town that could stay with ours. I was riding a little mare about fourteen hands that was a real stayer and good for quick speed when you needed it. The Richters were both on big geldings, but Les's horse was the best of the bunch, a big black animal that was strong and fast and out of good blood.

"We got to do something," Tod said. "We got to get out of here."

I told him to take it easy. Les stood up in his stirrups and looked out over the river. He asked me if I didn't think that was a sandbar about midstream. "See how the water kind of banks up? Looks pretty long and wide."

I looked and agreed. "Water would have to be pretty shallow there. Couldn't be over a foot or two deep on top."

"Listen," Tod said. He sounded nervous and strung out. "We can't cross that! Goddam, we'd all drown. Let's ride upriver and see if we can't cross at the International Bridge in Piedras Negras. We've got to meet Howland and Chico there anyway."

Les and I looked at each other and smiled. We could see the authorities letting us across with our saddlebags full of bank gold.

"I believe I'll try it," Les said. He patted his horse. "This old pony needs a bath anyway."

It was his way of saying that he had the best horse and that it was right for him to make the attempt.

"Get upstream a ways," I said. "Give yourself plenty of leeway. That current's strong."

"I will," he said. He turned to ride off, but Tod stopped him. He looked sullen. "Just leave that kale with us," he said. "When you drown there ain't no point of you taking the money with you."

"All right," Les said. He turned around and untied his saddlebags. Tod was the closest and Les pitched the bags to him.

"If you get in trouble try to swing back toward the bank and I'll rope you if I can," I told him. He nodded and give me a little salute and then rode up the bank about a hundred yards and put spurs to his black and rode straight into the water. His horse never flinched as most will do when they don't know what they're getting into, but went straight into the water just like he was cantering up a country lane.

The water stayed shallow for a little bit, but then it got deep all of a sudden and Les's horse began to swim. Les slipped off his side, holding to the saddle horn with one hand and paddling with the other. For a second it looked as if they weren't going to have any trouble, but then they got out into the mainstream and the current caught them. Les's horse began to swim harder, raising his head up and fighting at the water that was foaming around his breastplate.

"Turn him out!" I yelled. I could see Les hadn't given himself enough lead on the sandbar. It was looking as if he'd be swept on past.

I don't know if he heard me or not, but he reached up and reined his good horse around and made him fight back against that current. The horse was getting frightened. He kept trying to get his head higher to get away from the water, but Les spoke to him and urged him on and, gradually, they began to gain. They got into a bit more trouble when they hit the end of the sandbar where all the turbulence was. The whirling water wanted to swing the horse around, but Les got up on his neck and just kind of led him back and forth until they found solid bottom. The horse got ground under him and then they were clambering up the sandbar, water streaming from both horse and rider.

Les looked back across at us. He had a big grin on his face and you could see his white teeth showing up in his dark face. He cupped his hands together and yelled across.

"It's easy! Come on!"

I looked at Tod. "You want to go next?"

"Hell no," he said.

"You've got to go sometime. That is unless you want to stay here and entertain that posse."

He was nervous and sulled-up. "You just go right on ahead. You just never mind me."

I looked at him. He looked so scared he was near white in the face. "What's the matter with you? Are you scared of that little bit of water?"

He looked down. "You know I can't swim."

I laughed. "Oh, hell, Tod, you don't have to swim. The horse will do that for you."

He didn't say anything. I waited a second and then turned my filly upstream to get a good lead on the sandbar. I'd seen Les hadn't give himself enough and I didn't want to make the same mistake. As I rode away I looked back at him. He was staring out at the water. "Come on up here, Tod. Just watch me."

"In a minute," he said.

"All right, but you're coming right after I get across. You'll be all right." I couldn't really believe he was that scared of a little water. I figured he was still pouting and playing the baby about the way I'd come down on him. He was wanting somebody to pet him a little. It didn't look good on a grown man.

I gave myself plenty of lead and put my mare into the water. After a little I done like Les and got off and floated alongside. I'd given my filly such a start that she didn't have to swim hard at all. We just floated along, letting the current do the work, and next thing we were hitting the sandbar. Les had waded out a little to give me a hand, but I didn't need it. We both got up on top of the sandbar and looked across at Tod. He was staring at the water, riding his horse slowly back and forth at the edge.

"Come on!" I yelled at him. "We're running out of time." A thought suddenly hit me. I turned around to Les. "Les, he's still got the gold. I forgot all about it."

Les was looking anxious. He didn't say anything to me, but cupped his hands and yelled for Tod to come on. "He'll do it," he said. "He'll be all right."

"He'd better," I said. "He's carrying four thousand dollars in his saddlebags."

Tod was still riding his horse back and forth along the bank and we yelled and waved for him to go upstream. "Hurry up!" I yelled at him. I was starting to get a little anxious about the time myself. We'd been fooling around at the river for I didn't know how long and only had it half crossed. If a party was to come up on the other side they could sit there and pick us off like ducks in a turkey shoot.

We kept yelling at him and he finally went upstream a little and kind of halfheartedly urged his horse into the water. The gelding went in willingly enough and we thought he was coming on, but, when the water got up to his horse's belly, Tod suddenly pulled him around and spurred him like crazy for the bank.

"Aw, hell!" I said disgustedly.

"Tod, you've got to!" Les yelled.

He stared back at us for a minute and then yelled something.

"What?"

"No! I said I wouldn't do it! I'm not going to drown!"

Les called back to him, "You've got the gold! You've got to!"

"No! I'm going to Piedras Negras! I'll meet you there."

"No, by God, he isn't!" I said to Les. I'd taken my pistol out of my holster and put it in my saddlebags to make the crossing, but I whirled around and ran to my filly and jerked my Henry repeating rifle out of its boot.

"Now, Will," Les said.

I told him to shut up and I run to the edge of the bank and went down on one knee and leveled on Tod. I didn't say a word.

"Don't shoot him, Will."

"I will if he don't come on," I said. I was right and Les knew it. That was our gold Tod was carrying and I wasn't going to lose it just because he was afraid of a little water.

Tod seen what I was intending and he stood up in his stirrups and yelled that I'd never hit him at that distance. It was a good long shot of near two hundred yards and his horse was dancing around.

"Maybe not," I yelled back, "but I'll damn sure get your horse and then we'll see how you like being afoot with that posse coming."

It hit home with him. He studied another second, with my sights leveled down on him, and then gave in. "All right," he called.

He rode upstream and then suddenly turned his gelding and charged the water. He had to do it fast before he lost his nerve.

But immediately we could see he hadn't given himself enough of a start on the current. As soon as the horse

had to start swimming we could see he was being carried
downriver too fast. To top it he wouldn't get off his horse
and help him. He stayed bolt upright in the saddle, even
drawing up his legs a little to try and keep them out of
the water.

"He's in trouble!" I said to Les.

"Get off your horse!" Les yelled. "Get off and hold on!"

But he wouldn't. He was too scared. Even as far off as
he was we could see the fear in his face. He was staring
down at the water, his eyes big in his head.

Les and I ran out as far as we could, but we could see
that the current was going to carry him on by. His horse
was trying hard, but Tod wasn't helping him any. A rider
and the current were just too much for the poor animal. We
could see from the way his head was drooping that he was
tiring badly.

"He ain't gonna make it!" Les said.

"Quick! The ropes!"

We whirled around and run to our horses and got our
lariat ropes and then ran back in the water. I went out until
the water was up to my waist and I could feel the current
sucking at my legs. I had to spread my feet to keep my
balance. It was an awkward position to rope from, but I
whirled my loop and watched as they floated along. His
poor horse had damn near quit swimming and they were
getting lower and lower in the water. Finally I threw. Tod
leaned out and made a grab for the rope, but it was short.
I reeled in as fast as I could and started down the sandbar
hoping for another try.

"Help me!" Tod was yelling. "I'm gonna drown."

Les had waded out even further than I had. He hadn't
thrown and then I seen what he was waiting for. There
was a little whirlpool about midway alongside the sandbar
and Tod and his horse floated into it. It flung them closer
in and Les whirled his loop and cast it. It landed neatly over
Tod's shoulders and the redhead grabbed on and slid out of
the saddle.

I put my own rope over my shoulder and ran to help Les.
The current was terrible to fight against, but we gradually

snaked him in. He got his feet and then stumbled up to the top of the sandbar and fell down to his hands and knees, coughing and gasping for breath. Les and I came on more slowly, coiling our ropes. I looked downstream. In the distance, and getting smaller and smaller, I could see Tod's horse floating along out in midstream. The poor animal was give plain out. He wasn't even trying to swim. The current had him and was turning him around and around. His head was getting lower and lower. I hated to see a good horse finish like that.

I walked up to Tod. He was still down on his hands and knees and I got him by the hair and jerked his head back. "Well, you've made a mess out of it. I ought to drown you anyway!"

I was mad as hell.

He jerked his head around trying to get loose from my grip, but I slapped him with my free hand. "That's four thousand you've lost us," I said. "You cowardly bastard!"

I slapped him again just for good measure and flung him away so that he kind of fell over in the shallow water. He scrambled to his feet.

"Look at that!" I told Les, pointing toward Tod's horse. He was just a dot in the water, way downstream. "There goes a good horse and four thousand dollars."

"I know it," Les said. He was feeling as bad as I was.

Tod came up. He had his head down. "This wouldn't have happened if you hadn't throwed down on me. I could have crossed at Piedras Negras."

I looked at him, disgusted. "Sure," I said. "Sure you could. Listen, Tod, don't always play the fool. What caused it was you being such a coward."

"My cartridges are wet," he said. "And you know it." The poor fool hadn't even thought to put his revolver in his saddlebags. It was a wonder he hadn't lost it.

"Listen," I told him, "I've backed you down before and your cartridges weren't wet then. And when they get dry I'll still back you down. You're quick enough to kill little bank clerks, but you ain't much against a man."

Les asked me to take it easy. He could see I was mad

enough to kill. "I ought to shoot him," I said. "Drowning a good horse! Fool!"

"Maybe my horse'll wash ashore," Tod said lamely. "Maybe we can get the gold back." He didn't want any more from me. I've always noticed a bully will stay mad just so long as you let him. Once you put it on him he'll get calmed down right away.

"Not a chance," I said. "That horse will end up in the gulf. And if he did come ashore it would probably be on the Texas side anyway."

"Then we better get out of here," Les said. "We've still got half a river to cross. And that posse could show up at any minute. Not a lot of cover out here in the middle of this river."

"You're right," I said. "We better get moving." Things were in a pretty mess. There we were, in the middle of the Rio Grande, a horse short, and all our work for nothing. The only thing good was that we'd actually made it better than halfway across the river and the water on the side we still had to cross didn't look anywhere near as bad.

Me and Les walked out in it a bit. It stayed shallow and the current wasn't too strong.

"I could swim this," I said. "Tell you what, you ride your gelding and pull me across on your rope. I'll let Tod take my filly."

I took off my gun belt and boots and put them in Les's saddlebags. He got up on his mount and took a dally around his saddle horn and handed me the end of his rope. I opened the loop and put it around my waist. Tod had gotten up on my filly and I looked over at him.

"You drown that mare," I warned him, "and I promise I'll drown you. You get off and give her some help."

He didn't say anything and I followed along behind Les as he rode his gelding into the water. It got up to my chest and then I began to swim, having very little trouble with the current.

It turned out to be easy. We made it to the other side and then looked back for Tod. I don't know if our easy crossing had braved him up or if he was ashamed of himself, but he rode into the water without hesitation and made the crossing all right.

I put my boots back on and reholstered my gun and sat down to blow a minute. The posse still hadn't shown up, but we weren't going to linger.

CHAPTER 2

Villa Guerro

We were due to meet two of our partners in Piedras Negras in a few days, but I knew we'd never make it riding double with our mounts as jaded as they were from the long run and then the river. Piedras was a good sixty miles away and we were still going to need another horse even if we got there. We had a job planned with these two men we were to meet.

"There's a little town up the road a bit," Les said. "Place called Villa Guerro. I've been there some and it ain't much, but we might pick up a horse."

"How far?"

"About four miles, I'd make it. I'm not sure, though."

"We might as well," I said. "At least we can get something to eat." I was hungry, not having had time for lunch what with the robbery and all. And I can never eat breakfast before I go in on a job. I'm too nervous. A mess of tortillas and beans would go good, with maybe a little shot of tequila to boil the river water out of a man.

We mounted up, or at least Les and I did. I made Tod walk. Les was willing to carry him double, but I wouldn't let him. I was still pretty sore at him and I figured a little walk in the sun would do him good.

It was a long, hot four miles. There hadn't been any rain down in that part of the country and the ground was dry and caked. There was cactus and some mesquite and piña,

15

but that's about all that'll grow in the poor soil.

After a while I relented and we swapped off walking. Tod's a fool and that's just a fact you can't do anything about. He's not going to change no matter what you do to him. If he'd of killed that bank clerk he would have still been going along just the same as he was. Les was letting him ride his gelding and that was good enough for him at the moment.

Killing is a thing that somehow just seemed to slip up on me. It makes me feel bad when it happens even though I know I've give the man a fair shake. I have never in my life set out to kill a man. When it's happened it's happened because it's been forced on me, just as it was the first time I ever got into a shooting. That'd been when I was punching cattle up in Carson County, Texas, up in the Panhandle. A grand jury had bound me over, but I was acquitted. The brother of the man I'd killed had been kicked by a horse the day before the hearing and knocked senseless. He'd been the only witness against me and the judge had let me go for lack of evidence. It'd been an act of God as the judge had said and I must therefore be innocent. I was, but I'd been in big trouble if the brother had gotten a chance to testify. He'd of lied and I might have spent some little time rotting away in a jail somewhere. They'd been deviling me and I'd finally went to giving them a little back. I was just a kid and they'd been giving me a hard time for days. When I come back at them the little game had turned serious. We were in the bunkhouse and I'd shot the man just as he'd gone under his pillow for his gun. It had given me a bad feeling seeing him fall by my hand.

The only other time I'd been lawed over killing had been up in Arkansas. Again it had been a fair fight, but the man was very popular and his friends had all testified against me. I'd had to break confinement while they were transporting me up to the state penitentiary at Little Rock.

Villa Guerro was just another dusty little Mexican town of about fifty adobes. There were some kids and goats along its only street and an occasional old man sleeping in the sun, but, other than them, there wasn't much stirring. We searched around a little until we found what passed for a cantina and then pulled up in front of it and dismounted.

The front door was open. They had a big, heavy door that they barred at night, but it was swung back and there was only a little curtain of beads across the front. We brushed through that and went on inside, our big roweled spurs clanking against the hard-packed dirt floor. Nobody much looked up when we came in. There was a bartender about half asleep behind the bar and a couple of Mexicans drinking in the back, but they just gave us a little glance and went back to their business. That close to the border Texas cowboys aren't too unusual.

"This'll do," I said. We walked over and took chairs at a table. The bartender come awake enough to yell toward the back and a big, fat Mexican waitress came out and came over and asked what we wanted.

Les spoke the lingo the best and he asked if they had any beer. She said no. Tod asked for American whiskey and she said they didn't have any of that either. We all ordered tequila.

"And bring us something to eat," I said. "Whatever you got and make it snappy. Pronto!" I was hungry.

Tod was leaned back in his chair and he reached over and give the woman a pat on the ass. He had a big grin on his face. "What's your hurry, Will?" He patted the girl again, but she didn't pay it no mind. I guess she was used to it. "Don't rush this mamacita off so quick. Me and her look like we'd get along."

I didn't say anything, but Les looked over at him. "You better cut that out. We ain't quite got the lay of the land here, yet."

Tod let out a big laugh. He still had the waitress by the ass. "The lay of the land ain't the kind I want."

She was just a big fat pig and it disgusted me seeing him taking on over her so. She had a great big moon face that was covered with sweat and her arms, coming out of the loose blouse she was wearing, were near as big as Tod's. Tod had her by one cheek and he was squeezing it like it was a big grapefruit.

17

"You ought to feel the ass on her!" he said. "It's as big as any two I've ever got hold of."

I motioned at the waitress. "Get the drinks," I said.

She suddenly jerked away from Tod and took off for the back. He made a pass at her, but missed and leaned back to the table laughing. "Boy, that's a piece!" he said.

Les asked me if I thought the posse would cross on over and try to pick up our trail.

I shook my head. "The river will stop them." I looked at Tod. "All we did was rob their bank. Luckily."

But me saying that didn't bother Tod any. He didn't give a damn.

The place was cool, or at least it was cooler than being outside. I looked around. At one time the walls had been whitewashed, but they'd long since got dirty and stayed that way. They had a lantern hanging from the ceiling and it put out some light, but I expected the place was pretty dark during the night custom.

The girl came back with a bottle of tequila and some glasses and we poured out all around and made a toast to luck and then knocked them down. Tequila's hell on the taste, but it does a good job in the belly. I could feel it spreading around and relaxing me. We had a couple of more drinks and then the girl brought our food. It was beans and rice and tortillas and some dried beef. I rolled up a tortilla and dug in. I was feeling pretty low about the gold and I didn't know quite what we were going to do, but the drinks and the food were making me feel a little better. While we were eating Les asked what I thought.

"First thing, we've got to get a mount for this fool here. Unless we figure to leave him."

Tod was wolfing his food down and didn't pay me any attention. He was sweating like a pig from the heat and the tequila. But then we all were. The sun had dried us off after our dip in the river, but we were near about as wet again from sweat.

Les said: "There's some pretty big ranches around here. We might be able to pick up something from one of them."

Of course we didn't want just anything. When you rob

banks for a living you want to be damn sure you've got a good gun and a good horse. Generally, you try to buy for blood, because blood is the only way you can assure yourself of a stayer and you've just got to have that in an animal.

We didn't have much time either, not after losing the gold. We had to get to Piedras Negras and meet Chico and Howland before they pulled out without us. When I'd made the deal to meet them I hadn't been too sure we'd go through with it. In the back of my mind I'd figured to wait and see how it went at Carrizo Springs. Well, I was sure now, and we needed to get high behind and get on to Piedras.

I sat there, ruminating on how to get Tod a horse. Suddenly it hit me that we didn't have much money. I guess it hit Les at the same time, for he suddenly set his glass down and asked what I thought we had between us.

"I don't know," I said, suddenly worried. "Let's get it up and see."

We went to our pockets and anted up everything we had on the table. In American money it come to about thirty-five dollars.

"Well there it is!" I said. I hit the table with my fist, making the coins and glasses jump. A good horse would cost at least seventy-five or a hundred dollars if not more. And, if we were going to pull a job, Tod would have to be as well mounted as the rest of us else he'd slow up the whole party.

I stared at him, but he wouldn't look back at me. "How you like that, Tod?"

He didn't answer, but Les said: "Lay off him, Will. He feels bad enough already."

"No he don't," I said. "He ain't got that much sense."

"Well, it ain't going to do any good. It don't change nothing."

I leaned back in my chair and put both boots up on the table. Les was right. Getting mad at Tod is like whipping a dead horse. "All right," I said, "but there it is. What are we going to do?"

Les was thinking on it, but Tod said, "We could steal a horse. Slip out to one of them big ranches Les was talking about and take us one." He had his mouth full of beans.

"The hell with that," I said. "We ain't doing nothing in Mexico. I don't want law from both sides of the river chasing us. I done told you—down here we walk the straight and narrow."

Les was still eating. After a few more bites he pushed his plate away and said he thought if we could just make it to Piedras Negras that Chico and Howland might have some money and we could borrow enough off them to get Tod well mounted.

"They might," I agreed. "Though they couldn't be holding too considerable a stake. When I saw Howland in El Paso he didn't act like he was flush. Besides, I hate to borrow from Howland. You know how he is." I looked over at Les.

"You got any of them little cigars?"

He shook his head. "I been out a week."

Tod said he had tobacco.

"Keep it," I said. I didn't want nothing off him. I didn't quite know what to do. We were in a mess. Just then Tod had another big idea.

"We could sell them spurs of yours," he said.

I just looked at him.

Les said: "Will don't want to sell them spurs."

I had a pair of gold-mounted silver spurs that were about the prettiest things I've ever seen. I'd bought them in Durango during a flush time and had intended on wearing them on a trip I'd planned back home. I'd paid over a hundred dollars for them and I intended they should tell folks I was doing pretty well and hadn't turned out so bad after all. But the trip had fell through and, other than when I'd tried them on, I'd never worn them. I was saving them for the day I did finally get back to Corpus.

I told Tod: "Maybe we ought to sell your guns. I believe we'd be better off all around."

He flushed and looked down. "I was just trying to help."

"Them spurs is special to Will, Tod," Les said.

Just then the fat waitress came back over to clear away our meal and I lifted my boots so she could get my plate. I asked Tod why he didn't inquire of his girl where we could get a horse.

"I just will," he said. He grabbed her by the waist and pulled her over to him and tried to run his hand in under her dress. He had a big grin on his face. "I'll ask her in sign language."

She wasn't liking it. It looked like playing with her ass was all right, but she didn't go for nothing else. She was jerking around, trying to get loose, but Tod had a good hold around her waist. She wasn't saying a word, but I could see she was getting mad. Tod was laughing and talking to her in Spanish.

"You better let her go," Les warned. "She don't like that."

"Sure she does," Tod said. "Sure she does."

About that time he succeeded in getting his hand up her dress and she let out a little shriek. She'd been holding an armload of dishes, but she suddenly dropped them and slapped the hell out of Tod. Her big fat hand hit his face with a wallop you could have heard in Denver.

"Goddam!" Tod roared. His face flushed and he jumped up and hit her right back. He hit her hard, with his fist half closed, and it knocked her back into the middle of the room though she didn't go down.

"None of that!" Les yelled. He jumped around the table and grabbed Tod and pinioned his arms.

Tod was yelling and struggling to get to the girl. "No greaser bitch gonna slap me! I'll by God—"

"You started it," Les said. He was having trouble holding him, Tod was so mad. I'd got up too and, out of the corner of my eye, I saw the bartender suddenly duck down. I swung around, but he was already up leveling down on us with an old shotgun that looked to be about ten gauge. If he let that thing off there wouldn't be enough of us left to fill a pipe.

"Watch it!" I said to Les and Tod. "Goddamit! Hold it!"

The bartender looked like he was fixing to use his cannon. "No, no, Señors!" he was saying. "No, no!"

Just then Les got Tod swung around and they both seen the shotgun pointing at them. Tod calmed right down and Les let him go.

"Just take it easy," I said quietly. "That gent will blast us all to hell if we're not careful."

I raised my hands very slowly. "Many pardons," I said to the bartender. "*Mi amigo es borracho.* He meant no harm."

The bartender didn't say anything, just kept watching us from behind his big shotgun. "Les," I said, "ease up there and tell that gentleman that everything is under control. Tell him we'll behave ourselves."

Les went up and talked quietly to the man behind the bar. After a second he lowered his cannon. The girl was still standing where Tod had knocked her. She had her head down and I thought she was crying, but, when I looked closer, I could see she had a wicked little dagger all clutched up to her breast. She'd been all ready for Tod to come charging up to her.

I scooped up a couple of dollars from the table and went up to her and held the money out at arm's length. I wasn't going to give her a chance to carve me up with that frog sticker of hers.

"Many pardons," I said to her. "Your beauty caused my friend to forget his manners."

I don't know if she understood my bad Spanish, but she understood the money right enough. As soon as she seen it she put her dagger away and went all smiles. I never seen such a change in a person in my life. One minute she's ready to kill and the next she's giving me and Tod little bows.

All of a sudden she turned to the bartender and called out something to him in Spanish that was just a little too rapid for me to follow. The bartender said something back to her and then he said something to Les that I couldn't hear. I went back and sat down at the table and motioned for Tod to do likewise.

"You damn fool," I told him when he got seated.

"She slapped me," he said. "Hell!"

Les was still at the bar. The bartender had put his shotgun away and he and Les were talking and Les was laughing. The waitress had come up and was standing behind Tod. She laid her hand on his shoulder. He looked back at her, but I told him to take it easy. I didn't know what the hell was going on.

"Les," I called, "come on back over here."

He came back with a big grin on his face. When he sat down he motioned at the girl and told Tod that she was all ready for him.

Tod asked what he meant.

"She's a whore," he said. "A *puta*. She got mad because she thought you were trying to get some free."

"Aw, hell!" Tod said. He looked around at the fat waitress.

"Go ahead," Les said. "She called across after Will give her that money and said your friend had paid for you and was it all right to take you on back to the room."

Even I laughed a little at that. It was just like Tod to be getting into something of that nature. "Go on, Tod," I said. "She's all ready for you. About your speed, too."

"Aw," he said, "I wouldn't screw that for half interest in the Katy railroad." He'd flushed a little. "What do you think I am?"

"Never mind that," I said. I motioned the woman away. "Bring us another bottle," I said.

"We're still here," Les said.

"Ain't we," I agreed. Tod said something low that I couldn't hear. I asked him what he'd said.

"I said there's still them spurs of yours."

"Tod . . ." Les said.

"Well, he could always get them back after we pull that job. Hell! What else we gonna do? He won't let us steal no horse."

I picked up a coin from the table and turned it over and over in my fingers. They both got quiet thinking I was mad. Well, what the hell difference did it make about the spurs anyway? We couldn't sit in Villa Guerro and rot and my spurs looked like the only way. I was kidding myself if I thought I was going to impress anybody back in Corpus, spurs or no. They knew me and a little dressing up wasn't going to change anything.

I pitched the coin back to the table. "All right," I said.

"Now, Will," Les said.

"No, it's all right. I don't mind. We've got to get to Piedras. Question is—where do we sell them? Not in this town. I bet there wouldn't be a hundred dollars cash in the whole place."

"How about one of them big ranches Les was talking about?" Tod asked. "Maybe you could ride out and make a swap."

I laughed, but it wasn't good-natured. "I ought to just let you do that. You ever met one of them patrons off one of them big ranchos?"

"I might have," he said.

"No you ain't," I told him, "or you wouldn't talk so foolish. For just plain snobbery and proudness, they're the champions. I just got a big picture of me riding up to one of them like a saddle tramp and asking him to swap me for a horse. I think a little more of myself than to be shamed like that."

The girl came back over with our bottle and put it on the table. She stayed right beside Tod. Les and I were watching him.

"Aw, hell," he said. "She ain't so bad. Are you, Mamacita?"

Now she was giggling and helping him move his hand around. It was irritating to me to see it. We were in a mess of his making, but he didn't give a damn. He figured we'd get him out of it.

"There's still Howland," Les said.

I sighed. "The hell with it." Who was I to worry about being high-hatted. "Go on up to the bartender, Les, and ask him directions for the nearest ranch. And while you're at it, ask him where there's a livery stable. We've got to get these of ours grained before we start out."

While he was gone I poured myself a drink and tried not to get mad about the way Tod was fooling around with the girl. Hell, I didn't care what he did. It was his business. I just thought he ought to have a little more class than that.

Les came back over and sat down. "He says there's the rancho Fernando about six miles southeast of here toward Villa Union. Big place. Says he thinks they got good stock."

"What about the livery stable?"

"There's a blacksmith shop up the street that stables horses."

I stood up. "Let's get at it." I scooped up the money and put it in my pocket, leaving two dollars to pay for what we'd eaten.

"What about me?" Tod asked.

"You stay here and you stay out of trouble."

"Well, leave me a couple of dollars to drink on."

I pitched a dollar on the table. We were already short, but Tod wouldn't understand. "Make out on that," I said. "You and your girl friend."

Les and I went out and mounted up and rode down to the livery stable. While they grained our horses we done what we could to clean up, but we were still pretty dusty and travel-worn.

It was odd, in a way, how Les and Tod and I had hooked up together to go on the scout. Even though we'd grown up together there'd been such a break in years after I'd left home that I hadn't even recognized them when we'd met back up. We'd all grown up around Corpus and we'd been the best of friends from about the time we were ten years old. My daddy and Les's had had big ranches out from Corpus, but Tod's parents run a mercantile store in town. We'd gone to what school there was together and rode together and fished and hunted. Then, when I was about sixteen, I'd left home and gone up to north Texas and went to punching cattle. My daddy had held a considerable spread, but, in the years after the Civil War, Yankee land-grabbing politicians had come down and done him out of the biggest part of it. Most of his titles were old Spanish grants my ancestors had gotten from Mexico and some of the records weren't too clear. Out of almost forty sections they'd done him out of all but about a thousand acres, and you just can't make a living running cattle on that little land, it being as poor as it is.

Anyway, I'd gone up into the Panhandle for a few years and then drifted north into Idaho and Wyoming and Montana. It'd been in the Panhandle that I'd got into that first shooting scrape and that had been what caused me to move for new country. I stayed up north for a while and then worked my way down into Arkansas. Of course that was where that other business had taken place, so I'd kept on running south. Finally I'd come on back into Texas and found that my mom and dad had died whilst I'd been gone and that the ranch had been taken over by the state on account of there being no heirs on record.

Hell, the place wouldn't have been worth the fight it would have taken to get it back and, besides, I was on the scout by then and didn't want much truck with the law. I'd never turned an outlaw dollar until I'd busted jail in Arkansas, but after that I'd just kind of drifted into the road-agent business out of hunger and necessity. Coming south through New Mexico, I'd found myself broke and hungry and it had been a rancher family's misfortune to meet me as they were coming along in a buckboard. They'd looked pretty prosperous and I'd suddenly rode up to them and threw down on the old man that was driving. He had his family with him, but I never gave them no bother other than scaring 'em a little while I was relieving the old man of about fifty dollars.

So there I was, wanted for robbery and murder, and I figured I might as well make it pay so long as it lasted. Being alone, I couldn't rob no banks (that being pretty risky on the lone scout) but I done my share of road-agent business until I drifted back into home country and rode into Rio Grande City.

It was there, in a saloon, that I got into a tussle with a great big redheaded fellow over a saloon girl. Course I didn't know it was Tod at the time. About eight years had passed since we'd seen each other and folks do change.

Anyway, he had come over to this girl that was talking to me at the bar and asked her to come sit with him at a table. Naturally I got my back up a little at that and I'd told him just to bide his time. The girl wasn't much, being about as ugly as homemade sin, but I didn't like nobody pressing me too hard and I told him so. Then, one thing led to another and nothing else would do but I got to jam my gun in his belly and offer to blow a hole in him for his trouble. Of course that had settled it, Tod being the way he was, and he'd backed off and gone back to sit with a dark-complected fellow at his table. I hadn't known that was Les, either, but I'd turned around and put my back to the bar and watched the redhead just in case he felt it wasn't over. They'd put their heads together and had a talk, all the time giving me looks. Finally, this dark-complected fellow had come up and asked me if I wasn't Wilson Young. Hell, I didn't know who he was—he might have been a lawman or a bounty hunter for all I knew—so I didn't say, just asked him what business it was of his. He said if I was then I'd know who Les Richter was and put out his hand with a big smile.

Well hell, I like to have fell over I was that surprised. We went over to their table and me and Tod apologized to each other and said we'd never had no trouble if we'd known who the other was and then I sat down and we fell to talking over the years that had passed since we'd seen each other last. It took a while for it to come out, but they finally let on they were on the scout too. They'd had some trouble with the law about a herd of cattle they'd been driving back from Mexico and one thing had led to another and Tod had shot a deputy sheriff. After that they'd done just like I did, just kind of drifted into the business.

We sat up late, drinking and talking, and before the night was over we'd decided to throw in together. Tod's all right in his way but you don't want a better partner than Les. He's a man to go down the road with.

CHAPTER 3

Rancho Fernando

The ranch house at Rancho Fernando turned out to be a big yellow adobe building with many breezeways between the sleeping quarters and the cook house and the main structure. Me and Les had done our best to shave and clean up at the livery whilst they was graining our horses but we still didn't look very good. We rode up and hallooed the house and a peon came out and asked us what we wanted. I said we'd like to see the patron about buying a horse. Well, this peon give us a look like we ought not to be soiling the dust of the place but he bid us get off our horses and went on back and reported to the head man.

Pretty soon this old gent come out and greeted us with stiff, formal courtesy. He was getting along, but he was straight as a board and had a great big handlebar mustache and white hair and was wearing good hand-made boots.

We got our hats off in response to his and told him we were looking to buy a good blooded horse if the price was right. Well, you'd of thought we come with a letter of credit from the bank the way the old gent acted. You can't beat a high-bred Mexican for manners. He invited us in and we sat down and put our hats on our knees and he sent a servant to fetch us a cool drink. It was papaya juice and it was very refreshing, but, after that, a servant came in with cognac and cigars. It was real French cognac too. I didn't know where he'd got it, probably had it shipped in from one of the coastal

ports like Tampico, but I didn't much care. I was just content
to enjoy it. I tell you it was fine sitting there in that beautiful,
cool room enjoying the patron's hospitality. It almost made
me feel like a gentleman myself. I was conscious of the
dusty condition of our dress, but the grandee was such a
gentleman that he didn't seem to take any notice.

I'd made up a story to tell him. I told him we were cattle
buyers from Fort Worth and that we'd lost a horse and
needed a replacement and that we'd heard he had the best
stock around.

It pleased him and he sat there drawing on his cigar and
nodding. He said that he did indeed have some fine stock
and that there was a chance some of it might meet with our
approval.

I allowed that I had no doubt of that, but I was a little
worried about us being able to come to terms.

"We're but poor strangers, Señor," I said in Spanish, "and
had no thought that we'd be riding up to such a magnificent
hacienda when we set out for your ranch." And indeed the
place had been finer than I'd expected. I was trying to set
him up to spring the spurs on him. It was making me feel
a little uncomfortable.

Not to be outdone by my humble politeness, he said,
"Señores, I extend the welcome of this poor place to you.
I know it does not meet with the elegance to which you're
accustomed, but perhaps you will find my horseflesh pass-
able. I can assure you it will be within your means."

The old man made me feel like a lying thief. He was being
so polite and treating us like equals and we'd come to him
with a mouthful of lies and were about to soil our dignity by
trying to barter with him. Les wasn't saying anything and I
could see he was feeling uncomfortable himself. Well, I'd
known it was going to be the way it was. Even though
I didn't know what else we could do, I almost felt like
thanking the patron and getting up and walking out. I felt
so shabby sitting there in that fine room and being treated
like a gentleman when I knew I wasn't. It give me a twinge,
the first, I guess, that I'd felt in years.

We were on our second glass of brandy and I almost

hated to finish it. I don't mind robbing a bank, but I hate to steal from a man like the grandee and I was stealing his brandy just as sure as if I'd had a gun on him.

Finally he proposed that we go out to one of his remudas and see what he had on hand that we might like. He stood up and Les and I did the same. We got up slowly, giving each other looks. I didn't know if I was going to be able to come out with my spurs or not.

Just as we got ready to go out the door, a young lady of about twenty years suddenly came sweeping into the room. I was heading right for the door she entered and the sight of her stopped me dead in my tracks. She was of a size that would just about fit under a tall man's arm and she was dark and lovely, with high cheekbones and black flashing eyes and red lips and black shimmering hair.

She gave a little start when she almost ran into me, but then she regained her composure and went around me with a little nod and went up to the grandee and said something.

He took her shoulder and turned her. "We have guests, my dear." She turned and faced us and he introduced her. We bowed and she dropped us a curtsy.

She was the most beautiful woman I'd ever seen. While the don was introducing us I stared boldly at her. I couldn't help myself. She was slim and small, but her hips and breasts were putting a strain on the material of this pretty gold and white dress she was wearing. She had one of those jeweled combs set back in her hair with a lacy white mantilla just hanging loose from it and it kind of framed her face and set off those big, dark eyes and her big, red lips.

"This is my niece," the patron said proudly. "Come to bring joy to a childless old man's house. She is Linda Fernando de la Piña De Cava."

Or something like that. Mexicans don't arrange their names the way Texans do. They generally end up with the mother's name and work in all the ancestors somewhere along the way.

But her calling name was Linda and that certainly fit her, for Linda means something more than beautiful in Spanish.

I had forgotten all about the horse. I was trying desperately to think of something to say when the patron indicated that we would excuse her. The Spanish are very protective about their womanfolk and I might have known she wouldn't have been allowed to stay and talk, especially to a couple of dusty strangers like Les and myself.

"Con mucho gusto," she said. *"Adios."* We bowed and she dropped us a curtsy and then headed for the door where she'd entered. I watched, hardly aware of what the patron and Les were saying. Then, just as she was about to go through the door, she suddenly turned and looked right into my eyes and made another curtsy. It was a long look she gave me, and it took me so by surprise that it was a second before I returned a bow. Then she was gone and I could hardly believe it had happened. But she had looked at me and it had been a special look just for me. But what would a beauty like that be wanting to pay attention to an old dusty cowboy like myself?

Not to say that I haven't had my share of women when I've wanted, but none of them had resembled this little Spanish beauty any more than a sow's ear resembles a silk purse.

But the patron was bidding us go and Les and I followed him out the door. He said the girl had been sent up from her parents' ranch in Sabinas Hidalgo because of bandit trouble in that part of the country. I took the name down in my mind, vowing to remember it, and we walked out of the house, him telling us the details about the girl and his ranch and the country in general.

As we walked along he asked us how the cattle business was up around Fort Worth and that give us a little trouble, me and Les not being too well informed on the subject. We told him it was a little slow. Generally I don't mind lying and, generally, I'm pretty quick with a good story when the occasion demands it, but I was starting to feel a little pressed inside. I don't know whether it was the sight of the girl, or the great courtesy the old man was showing us, or what, but I was beginning to feel bad embarrassed. I've sailed under other colors from time to time, but generally I like to fly my own. My life ain't been much and I've done a fair job of messing it up, but I'm not all that ashamed of myself.

The old man led us over to a corral full of big, clean-limbed animals and went pointing out this one and that and what was particularly good about this horse and what sire and dam that one was out of. I was feeling worse and worse and getting a little tired of leaning up there on the fence, smoking that good cigar and playing the country gentleman. I'd known it was going to be this way, but that only made me feel worse. Finally, I blurted out, "Let's get down to business here, Don. How about giving us some prices on these animals? Them pedigrees and all is very good to listen to, but we ain't buyin' paper."

Well, it was a rude thing to say and I was immediately ashamed, but I was feeling mad and mean and I couldn't help it.

The old don never let on, just nodded gravely and pointed at one with his cigar and said this one was so many pesos and that one so many and so on.

They was all out of our reach. Translated into dollars, the least of 'em was somewhere around a hundred dollars. I looked over at Les, but he didn't say anything, just kind of shook his head. He was about as embarrassed as I was. I took the cigar out of my mouth and looked at it for a second and then threw it on the ground and stalked over to my horse and got my silver spurs out of the saddlebags. My face was burning, but I was beyond thinking. I went back over to the don and thrust them spurs out at him.

"Here," I said, "here's a pair of silver spurs I give two hundred dollars for. We're down on our luck and broke and we've got to have a horse. What will these buy?"

Well, it startled him, but he was so well-bred he like to have covered up. The way he took those spurs, so graciously, made me feel even more like trash than the way I was already feeling. He got them by the rewels and turned them this way and that and said they were certainly fine examples of silversmithing.

"That's all well and good," I said. "What will they buy?"

He smiled very gently and gave me a kind of sad pitying

look and handed the spurs back. In Spanish he said: "I had understood you were cattle buyers. Have you no letter of credit from your bank? That would be acceptable to me."

Now, by God, it looked like he was trying to make me squirm. "No," I said, "we ain't got no letter of credit. I've told you we're down on our luck and needing a horse. Now what about it?" Out of the corner of my eye I could see Les kind of hanging his head, but I was past caring. I tried to hand the spurs back to the old gent, but he wouldn't take them. He was high-hatting us all right, but I don't guess I blamed him. I guess if we'd have come up and told a straight story, it would have gone different, but we'd come up with a mouthful of lies and misled him and now he was set on shaming us.

"Let's go, Will," Les said, lowly.

"No," I said. "I'm trying to do some business here." I looked at the old grandee. "Now, how about it? Will you give us a fair shake on these spurs? Maybe you don't want 'em. I'm sure you've got much, much finer up in your big ranch house there. But will you do a favor for two strangers on the road? Or maybe they don't understand hospitality in Mexico."

He looked at me for a second, kind of sighed, and then walked off toward a little building at the other end of the corral.

"We better get out of here, Will," Les said. "We've played the fool enough for one day."

"Listen," I said, whirling on him, still mad, "I told you it would be this way. But now that we're here we'll play it all the way."

"Hell, he's left. He's walked off on us."

"No, he hasn't. He ain't the kind that would do that. Let's wait and see what happens."

Pretty soon the old patron came walking out of the building he'd gone into, give us the barest kind of nod and went on up to the house. We watched him step up on the porch and go in. Les said: "See? What'd I tell you?"

But before we could make a move, an old peon came down toward us in a kind of shuffling run and asked that we please wait patiently, that a horse was being brought us. I thanked the old man and looked over at Les, but didn't say anything. We leaned up against the fence and spit and I rolled a cigarette and pretty soon another peon came around the stable, a-horseback himself and leading an old grey that had been fitted out with a rope bridle and one of them wooden, high pommeled saddles you'll see the peons using. Me and Les pushed away from the fence and the rider brought the grey up and got down and said the horse was for us.

Well, that grey would go about seventeen hands, and he was near that old in years and the most hamhocked, swaybacked critter I had ever seen. In addition he had about the longest neck it's possible for a horse to have and still keep his balance. It damn near swung from side to side when he walked. I'd been standing there kind of idly tapping my spurs together, but I put them in my back pocket and just shook my head at the peon who was holding out the grey's reins to me.

"No thanks," I said. "We may be broke and out of luck, but we ain't lost our head. I ain't about to give you no two-hunnert-dollar pair of spurs for a plug like that."

"He is not for your spurs," the peon said to me severely in Spanish. "He is for twenty-five dollars American and you are to pay Don Fernando when you have the cash. He will trust you."

"I'll just bet he will," I said.

"Do not criticize the horse, Señor. It is clear that he is old and not pretty, but he is strong and well and is a good traveler. He will take you forty miles in a day."

Well, I ain't used to having peons stand around and read me off, but this one was making a good job of work out of it. I walked around the horse a couple of times and looked in his mouth and it was true that he was clean-limbed and pretty solid and his teeth showed I'd been about three or four years too high on his age. I looked over at Les and he shrugged.

"Get on your horse," I told him, and then I mounted up. The peon was still holding out the reins of the grey and I reached over and took them. Then I reached in my pocket and drug out our little stake and counted out twenty-five dollars and pitched it to the ground. "Tell the don we won't bother him for his trust." I wheeled, taking the grey on lead, and put my horse into a lope out the front gate.

CHAPTER 4

A Need to Travel

The grey led all right, but after we got out of sight of the ranch house I got down and tied his reins to the pommel and took a turn through his halter with my lariat rope so I wouldn't have to snug him up so close. I was still feeling pretty bad.

"Say," Les said. "That girl, that Linda, she was really something, wasn't she?"

"Yeah," I said shortly, getting back up.

"You reckon on a young girl like that would know anything? I mean about a man, in bed."

"I don't know," I said. "Why don't you clam up."

He looked over at me, a little startled, 'cause he and I always been able to talk pretty freely together. "What's eating you?"

"Well, you really are trash," I said, "if a man treats you like it and you don't even know it."

"What do you mean by that?"

I started to kick my little mare into a lope, but drew back on her. There wasn't any sense taking something out on my good horse that was none of her doing or her fault. "I'll put it this way," I finally answered. "If he'd known what we was after in the first place and what kind of quality we was, do you reckon he'd of introduced that little niece of his to us so nicely?"

"How the hell do I know?"

"Well, you're a damn fool if you can't see what you are, Leslie Richter."

I was still boiling when we got back into the little village, and the sight of Tod still pawing around on that damn fat old whore didn't do a thing for my temper. He was sitting at the table and, from the look of his face and the sweat on him, you could see he'd been getting better acquainted with the tequila. We clumped in and sat down and I told the wench to move off.

"Hell," Tod said. "What's biting you? This here hot tamale ain't so bad." Then he looked up at her and run his hand in under her dress. "Are you, Gordo?"

"Get her outa here, I told you. I bet you've even had that pig in bed. Wouldn't put it past you."

The tequila had made him whiskey-brave. He sulled up and give me a defiant look. "Well, so what if I have. You was the one that paid for it, so I reckon that makes it your business, don't it?" He looked at me, getting braver because I was being calm and quiet. "Hey, don't it? Don't it?"

I guess it was the thought of that girl still on my mind and then coming back and seeing that bitch and him pawing around on her. Hell, I don't care what he sticks. It ain't none of my business, nor my concern, but he was pushing me a little hard. Normally I would have let it pass. I got up. "C'mon outside, Tod," I said.

"Go to hell," he said. "You go outside."

Leslie was looking at me narrowly, but my being so calm was putting him off. "No, come on. I got something I want to show you. Got you a horse."

Tod looked at me and then Leslie, and his cousin nodded. "C'mon," I said. "He's right out here." I walked around the table and I could hear his and Leslie's chairs scraping as they got up and followed. I went out the door and then Tod came out. He seen the horse and pushed his hat back on his head and asked me if I was playing a joke.

"No joke," I said. "That's your horse."

"Well, I'll just be goddam if I'll be caught—" But he got no further because I suddenly wheeled into him and hit him in the face as hard as I could with my fist. It got him right in the nose and he went backward, blood already spurting, and hit the wall and fell down and bounced back up, a little dazed but more surprised, and I hit him again just as he began to cuss. This time I got him on the side of the jaw and he went down hard and just lay there.

Les jumped in between us and put his hands on my chest. "That's enough!" he said. "That's enough, Will! Now, dammit—"

But I pushed him out of the way and stood over Tod, my chest heaving a little. "Don't you push me no more," I said. "Don't you ever push me again. You hear me? *Do you hear me?*"

He was up on his elbow by then, shaking his head and looking a little bewildered. "Hell, Will . . ." he said, and paused to wipe the blood out of his mouth. "What the hell did you go and do that for?"

"I ask you did you hear me?" I was getting my temper back and was already beginning to feel ashamed. I knew why I'd hit him and it really had nothing to do with him or that whore or anything he'd said. Les knew it too, I could see it in his face.

"What'd you hit me for?" Tod asked me again. "I never said that much."

I heaved up a deep breath. "I know it," I said. I reached down and got him by the shoulder and helped him up and leaned him against the wall. "I guess I'm just getting nervous. Guess I need to travel."

Les got Tod's hat for him and put it on his head. A little crowd of curious kids and old folks had kind of gathered up, but we shooed them away and went back into the cantina. Les said something to the Mexican woman and she went into the back and returned with a pail of water and some dirty rags. She was almighty curious about what had happened, but wasn't none of us going to enlighten her. She helped Tod clean up his face and then brought us another bottle of tequila and sent her away. We poured out all around and knocked the drinks off and I told Tod, again, that I was sorry.

"Hell, Will, sometimes you're too quick. Was it about me

sayin' you paid for it? Hell, I was funnin'. I know why you paid her."

"Forget it," I said.

"Maybe you're still sore about the gold?"

"I said forget it. I told you I was sorry." He was starting to irritate me. Now that he'd gotten me to apologize he wanted to bleed me for all I was worth.

"Let's drink up and forget it," Les said.

"Yeah," I said. It ain't much sign of a man that he'd pick out something like Tod to let his spite out on. Les would have probably shot me if I'd of come that on him.

"I'm just needing to travel," I said. "Tell you what, we'll lay over here tonight to give them horses a good rest and then start out fresh tomorrow. Les, you go see about us a place to stay. Mind we ain't got but about two dollars left."

Next morning, early, I was standing in front of a piece of mirror in the livery stable trying to shave with cold water and lye soap and making a pretty good botch of the job. I've got a little scar that runs along just under my jaw from where a whiskeyed-up cowhand had tried to interfere with my breathing. Fortunately, he'd used a clean, sharp knife and it hadn't left much of a scar. It don't generally bother me except when I'm shaving, but, what with the cold water and dull razor and all, it was giving me considerable trouble. I stopped and went to examining my face and I guess that put me to thinking about the girl. I'm Creole-dark from my mother's side, she being out of a good Louisiana family, and, in a way, I guess that was what put me onto the girl, Linda, so strong. I've got that same dark skin and black hair and dark eyes. Just like her.

I stood there, looking at myself, the razor still in my hand, but making no move. The face that looked back at me was getting older. There were no lines or bags or nothing like that, but I could see it maturing and the thought came to me that I was suddenly pushing thirty. The thought kind of shocked me. You start out on your own and you're sixteen or seventeen and somehow you get the idea that you'll stay that way. But you don't. You get older. I stood there, looking at myself, wondering just what kind of pass I was going to come to. I don't reckon the thought had ever entered my mind before, but suddenly there it was. I guess the thing that really started crowding my mind was the idea that I'd never really give no thought to nothing, had just simply kind of drifted along. At sixteen I'd just shucked out and from then on it don't seem like I ever give five seconds to reflecting where I was going or what I intended on doing. Seemed like everything I'd picked up had come from just incidental moments.

I remembered riding back into Corpus after I'd been away some eight years and finding my mom and dad dead and the ranch confiscated. There'd been an old aunt of mine still living there and, for want of somebody better to talk to, I'd gone by to see her. She'd received me in her old house that was set just back from the harbor and asked me if I wanted coffee. It being the middle of the afternoon I'd told her I didn't care for none. I was sitting in an old rickety chair that had some kind of velveteen covering on it, and me, being dusty and trail-worn, I'd felt a trifle out of place. After a little talk about my folks we'd sat looking at each other. Finally she'd taken note of the gun on my hip and said: "I see you've gone bad." She said it mean with a kind of sneer in her voice and I'd brindled up. At that age I wasn't ready for someone to tell me I'd gone bad. Sure, I'd done some things that folks might consider bad, but all in all I didn't think of myself that way.

"I've done my best," I said to her. "With what I had."

"Yes," she'd said. "I see that, Wilson."

It didn't take me long, after that, to make my adieus and get the hell out of there. I don't know how that old lady had made my face burn the way it had, but she'd done it somehow.

Wasn't but a day later, me still hanging around Corpus, that I'd run into a deputy sheriff I'd known before when I was a kid. Had run into him in a bar and we'd stood together, drinking quietly, until he'd said: "Got a dodger a while back from Arkansas on you."

Well, that had taken me up short. I kept on sipping my

whiskey, trying to be casual. Finally, I'd said: "A wanted notice? On me?"

He'd nodded. "Murder. Said you kilt a man in cold blood in Jonesboro."

I didn't say anything for a minute, just kind of edged around until my rightside was clear of the bar and then asked him what he reckoned to do about it.

"Nothing," he said.

"Nothing?"

"Naw. Ain't no reward attached and I ain't going to the trouble and bother of gettin' you back up there, which, from the looks of you, might be a job, for nothing."

"What would you do if they was money involved?" I'd asked him.

He'd shrugged. "That's another story. But they ain't. Besides, I knowed your pap and I recollect the way them Yankees did him and others."

Yes, I'd recollected that myself. From about the time I was ten it didn't seem like he was ever at the ranch. Seemed like he was always in town at the courthouse. He'd come in, his face flaming, cussing and swearing, and me and Mom would try to lay low from him. I never knew what was happening but I was able to guess when I got a little older. One by one he laid our hands off and little by little our pasture shrunk. I remember once him and Ma in the parlor and him sitting in a chair, having a whiskey, with his big fist knotted in his lap. "They've got the power!" he'd said. "The power and the money! The money, goddamit!"

So that's the way some of my recollections laid out. The only fault in that is that you don't go into bank robbing for your health; yet there I stood, in a ramshackle livery stable, in a dirt-poor adobe town, standing in front of a busted mirror trying to shave with cold water and lye soap without a dollar in my pocket. Well, something had gone wrong somewhere. Something had gone bad wrong. Tod picked the wrong moment to come sashaying by and ask me what I was prettying up for.

"Get the goddam horses saddled," I told him. "We're moving out."

"Still on the prod, huh? Les told me you was mighty upset about some Mex girl."

I whirled on him. "Mister," I said, and my throat was so tight I could barely get the words out, "you better do what I told you. It was just my fists I used on you yesterday."

"Okay," he said, backing away. "Okay, okay, for God's sake."

We rode out about ten. There wasn't no hurry, us not being due in Piedras Negras until the later part of the week and having no sure way of knowing that Howland and Chico would be there on the exact hour we made it.

Howland was Howland Thomas, a cowboy out of Kansas who'd drifted down into the Southwest. Way I had it, Howland and a few others had made a specialty of meeting the smaller herds being drove into Kansas City by Texas drovers and relieving them of all or most of their herd somewhere after they'd crossed into the state. That must have proved a little warm because he'd apparently give it up to come south and go into the holdup business. I didn't know a hell of a lot about him except he was give out to be pretty dependable in a tight place, but a little mean when he'd been drinking or not drinking. Him and me had never had no kind of run-in, but I'd seen him pistol whip a half-drunk cowpoke near to death in a saloon in Albuquerque, New Mexico. But then, in our business we don't generally ask a man for his membership in the Baptist church before setting out to ride with him. It's a pretty rough and pretty risky business and it don't generally attract Sunday-school teachers.

I'd seen Howland in El Paso a spell back and he'd let on that he knew a bank in Uvalde, Texas, that was just begging to be robbed. Said we could open it up like a can of peaches. Uvalde being just north of Piedras Negras some sixty miles, we'd made it up amongst ourselves to meet in that town and talk about it. I hadn't much liked the idea of going too far into Texas, but Howland had said there wasn't enough law there to put in your eye and that we ought to do it before somebody else did. He'd been riding a spell with a Mexican boy named Chico Rodriguez and he said he'd bring him along. Said the five of us wouldn't have no kind of trouble, that we might, if we wanted to, set up in the town and take turns electing each other mayor.

Well, it had sounded pretty good—though I wasn't taken in by believing it would be as easy as he'd said—so I agreed that me and Tod and Leslie would meet them there.

Tod bitched a little at first about the grey, but quieted down after we'd been on the trail awhile. I could see myself that the old horse was a good traveler and Tod himself finally come out and said the animal wasn't near as bad as he'd thought. "Got a good gait. He cross-hammers a little, but it ain't too bad."

Well, that was that damn high-born Mexican for you. He wouldn't even give me the satisfaction of feeling cheated.

We rode along, the sun being plenty high and burning down hot. Les was to my left and Tod was quartered off to the right a bit. I figured we'd make it in two days easy, taking it slow in order not to work the horses too much and making it a little light on ourselves as well. We had us a big mess of beans in a crock in my saddlebags as well as a good supply of tortillas. Also, I'd spent the last dime we had on two bottles of tequila, the bartender being good enough to make me a special price as I was a little short on the second bottle.

I tell you I didn't much like going down a strange trail with such a few provisions and no money at all. We were taking a straight shot to Piedras Negras and, so far as we knew, there were no ranches of any size on the way, so we wouldn't be enjoying anybody's hospitality.

In spite of our slow pace we made about forty miles the first day and turned in that night in the lee of a big rock. Bandits are pretty bad in northern Mexico, so we built our little fire up under the rock, heated the beans and made a supper. After that we passed the bottle of tequila around until we'd killed it and then turned in. It being snake country and season, we each took our lariat ropes and encircled our bedrolls. Snakes won't cross a rope, they say. I don't know if that is true or not as I've never seen a snake try. I do know I ain't never been snake-bit while in my bedroll and that's good enough for me. Me and Tod and Leslie grew up knowing to do it and we just did it.

Next morning there was a Gila monster in bed with Tod. I was first awake, it just coming light, and I reared up in my blankets and looked around. First thing I seen was what looked to be a crooked stick lying just beside Tod's leg, on top of his blankets. Then the stick moved and I seen it was a Gila. Without making too much commotion I eased my hand back to my saddle horn where I had my holster looped and come out with my pistol. The Gila made as if to crawl across Tod's stomach, but just then the cousin stirred and the Gila turned around and started down his leg. He was a big one, maybe two feet long, and I was surprised the weight of him didn't wake old Tod up. Out of the corner of my eye I noticed Les had woke up also and was watching me quietly. I let the lizard crawl a little further, till he had his head clear of Tod's thigh, and then thumbed off a shot.

Well, it blowed that lizard's head into about nineteen pieces, but it acted even worse on Tod. He come out of his bed screaming he was shot and carrying on like I'd never seen. Of course I hadn't hit him, but I had blowed a nice little hole in his blankets. Les and I were laughing so hard we couldn't get breath to explain. All Tod seen was me sitting there with a smoking gun in my hand and I guess he thought I was gonna shoot again because he flang himself sideways and laid flat on the ground and yelled for Leslie. "Get his gun! He's gonna kill me!"

I was about to say something, but Les finally got himself together enough to point at what was left of the lizard. Tod seen it and come to his senses and began to look sheepish. We all got up and he grumbled around during breakfast and then finally said to me that he guessed I was expecting a thank-you. I said no, that I wasn't, and he said that was good because he wasn't offering none. He said that while it was true I'd got the Gila, the scare I'd give him could easily cost him several years of his life.

"What'd you want me to do?" I asked him. "Let him get in under the covers with you?"

"Well, you could have called out or something. Warned me somehow."

"Yes," Les put in, "and you'd have reared up and that lizard would have bit you and there we'd be. If it hadn't kilt you outright you'd have been sick a week and then what would we have done? No, Will did right."

"You always side with him," Tod said. "And it ain't natural. Not against your own kin."

"I side with him because he's generally right," Les said.

I told them to knock off the argument. "We've got tracks to make," I said. I rolled my gear and tied it to the saddle and went off to bring in the horses. "Kick that fire out," I told Les, "and put the beans in the grub sack."

The horses had found themselves a little water seep down in a draw and they were easy to catch. I got down on my belly and had a drink with them. The water was sweet and pure and cool, probably coming from an underground spring and being washed clean by all the limestone rock that's in that northern Mexico country.

I took the horses in and we saddled up and rode out. Les said the only thing for Tod to do was get him a bigger rope. "Something a Gila can't step over."

It was a fine morning, the night coolness still in the air, and we urged our horses on and made good time. Before we knew it, the steeple of that big Catholic church there in Piedras Negras was rising up in the distance and we rode on in good style. Tod made some noise about coming in on such a sorry-looking animal, but we shut him up mighty quick about that. I told him the animal had done a good job of carrying him there and he ought to think about that instead of being ashamed of the way the horse looked.

I'd made it up with Howland to meet them at the Gran Nacional Hotel and we headed for there as soon as we hit town. It was the siesta hour, it being midafternoon, and the streets were quiet and near empty with only an occasional peon asleep under his serape.

We put our horses up at the livery stable next to the hotel and clumped on into the lobby carrying our gear and bedrolls. I'd half expected to see Howland or Chico sitting around, but they wasn't, so we went on up to the desk and got us a room. Naturally we didn't have no money, but we slung our saddles over the desk for the clerk to hold as security. I told him we had pards riding in and were expecting some money in a day or two. That being custom in that country, the clerk didn't make no commotion, just took our two saddles (we hadn't brought Tod's, it being not worth much) and stacked them in the corner.

"Let's go up to the room and wash up," I said, "then go in the bar and have a drink. Maybe Howland and Chico is there."

We did, but our partners weren't there. We got a table but didn't order anything on account of being broke. It was a bad feeling and I didn't like it.

"Well, what the hell are we going to do?" Tod demanded. "They's liable to not show up for two or three days and what do we do meantime for eats and drink?"

"Oh, shut up, Tod," Leslie said, but the redhead had a point. I wasn't much liking sitting around broke any too much myself.

"Why don't you sell them spurs?" Tod said. "You'd get enough to at least grub-stake us."

"All right," I said. "But we'll have to wait until siesta's over and them shops open back up. Meanwhile we've got most of that second bottle. Let's go up to the room and finish it off."

I tell you we'd been in the brush a mighty long time and I was sure feeling blue about being in a town and not having money for a blowout. All the way up the trail I'd been looking forward to getting to Piedras and getting drunk and having myself a woman. Les had felt the same way because he'd said, "Listen, let's let our hair grow a little when we get to town. We owe it to ourselves, don't you reckon?"

I'd reckoned, but there we sat in a broken-down hotel room passing around a greasy bottle of tequila. There were two beds in the room and Tod and I were sitting on one apiece while Leslie was hunkered down on his bedroll where he'd spread it in the middle of the room. The Gran Nacional didn't quite live up to its name; the room we were in was dusty and worn and the plaster walls were cracking and the window was dirty. The beds had rawhide thongs for springs and no sheets and the water basin was near as cracked as the walls. Still it was some better than we'd been enjoying on the trail. I sat there on the side of my bed, nipping at the tequila bottle and getting lower and lower in spirit. It was a fine comedown for a boy who'd set out to be free and rich and who'd determined he'd kiss no man's boot nor follow any man's orders.

God, I was hungry for a woman. It had been a long, long time and I guess the sight and sound and smell of that girl Linda had just brought it all to the front of my mind. I felt horny, like a young bull does in spring, and I wanted me one of those soft, smooth-skinned Spanish girls with big breasts and hips and red lips. Nothing like that sow back in Villa Guerro but a sweet-smelling, sweet-kissing, soft, clean little beauty. Money could get that for me, but nothing else. And meanwhile, all I could do was sit there, drinking that hot, gut-burning, throat-searing tequila. I tell you, every drink made me feel worse.

About six I went down and got my spurs and we sauntered out of the hotel and walked down to a saddle shop. The town had woke up by then and people was going about their business and tending to others' and generally raising a little dust in the street. Occasionally, a Mexican woman would go by, her head low and her shawl pulled down to hide most of her face, and even the sight of these shapeless figures made the breath kind of catch in my throat.

The owner of the saddle shop wasn't in and his clerk had no authority, so we hunted us up a silver shop and propositioned the head honcho. He was a little Mexican with a bald head and gold-rimmed glasses. He got behind a counter and took my spurs and turned them this way and that and then looked up at me and said he'd give two hundred pesos.

Hell, it was an insult. He was offering barely thirty dollars and I'd give over a hundred for my silver spurs. I looked at him and shook my head. Les went into a barrage of Spanish on him, knowing better than any of us how to bargain, and the owner took the spurs back and commenced looking at them some more.

I tell you I wasn't feeling too good about selling those spurs. I'd been willing at first, but the more I got to thinking about it the more I didn't want to. Like I say, I'd bought them spurs during a flush time just before I'd been about to set out for my last trip to Corpus. I don't know whether I was intending to "show" anybody or not, but I'd bought them spurs and a new hat and new boots and got myself just as fancied up as I could. It had all happened just after me and Les and Tod had commenced riding together and just after my visit back to Corpus after running down from Arkansas. I guess I was feeling a little bad about the way folks had treated me and determined I'd go back and show them. But it was all good intentions gone to waste. I hadn't made it. Still, what would them spurs have proved except that I had a little money which I'd made robbing banks?

"Three hundred," the little silversmith said and made as if to open a drawer where he kept his cash. "And that is all."

"Why, you bandit," I said in English. "You're worse than us. Why don't you get yourself a gun if you mean to hold folks up?" I was mad.

"I don't believe he's going to go any higher," Les said quietly. "Do you want to take that?"

"Hell no," I said and reached across and took my spurs. "I wouldn't take nothing less than a thousand pesos." I turned around and walked out, the others following me, and the little silversmith adjusted his glasses and went back to his workbench like we'd never been there.

We stopped at the street.

"Well," Tod said, "now what do we do? I thought you was going to sell them things."

"I'll sell them," I said. "But I won't give them away."

"Meanwhile, what are we going to eat and drink on?"

I looked at him. "I don't know," I said. "I never took you to raise. Look out for yourself." And I walked off, leaving them both standing there.

49

CHAPTER 5

A Good Time

I went on back to the hotel and sat around the lobby for a while, but Chico and Howland didn't show up. I went up to bed after a little and Les come in about eleven. I'd been asleep but I woke up as soon as I heard his step in the room. He was down by his bedroll, getting his boots off, and I raised up and asked him where Tod was.

He was evasive. "Aw, he's out somewhere."

"On what?" I asked him.

"Hell, I don't know."

"Listen," I said, "is he up to something? I done told ya'll that I didn't want to do nothing this side of the border. Now what's he up to?"

"Well," Les said lamely, "you'd find out anyway. He sold that grey horse."

I didn't say anything. Just lay back for a minute. Finally, I asked, "How much did he get for him?"

"Fifteen dollars," Les said. He'd got in bed by then and drawn the blankets up to his chin.

I was trying to keep my temper under control. "Well, that rips it," I said. "Not only do we lose ten dollars on the horse, but now we don't have no horse. What do we do now?"

"I tried to talk him out of it, Will," Les said.

"Good for you," I said.

"I told him you'd be mad."

"That's the stuff," I said. "I bet that slowed him down."

"Well, hell, Will, he figured Chico and Howland would show up with some money and then we could get him a decent mount. He said he wasn't about to ride that grey out of town anyway."

"Your cousin thinks good," I said. "What if Howland and Chico don't show up? Or what if they show up without any money? What do we do then? How did your smart cousin figure that one?"

Les didn't say anything for a minute. "Well," he finally ventured, "I ain't trying to excuse him, you understand, but we had been out a considerable spell."

"What's that supposed to mean?"

"Well, goddam, Will, he was hurting for a little good times. He said if he didn't get himself a woman he'd just about bust."

I reared up in bed and looked at him. "Goddam you!" I swore. "Goddam you and that baby cousin of yours to hell! Goddam you both to hell and perdition! What makes you sonofabitches think you was the only ones wanting a little good times! What makes you think that! Huh! *Answer me, goddammit!*"

He didn't answer me because there wasn't nothing he could say. "Goddam him!" I said. "Who said that grey was his to sell? I'm the one laid out the money for that horse. I was wanting a little stuff as bad as all of you, but I wasn't about to sell that horse!"

I was so mad I couldn't even see. I got my legs over the edge of the bed and sat up. "Where's he at?" I asked.

"Now, Will . . . Now, Will, let it go now." Les was up on his knees, holding his hands out at me like a man trying to stop a runaway team.

"Where is he?"

"I ain't gonna tell you. You'd kill him tonight. Let it go until morning and just whip his ass. You'd kill him tonight."

I looked at him. "You gonna tell me?"

He shook his head. "Let it go until morning."

I suddenly rolled back into bed and pulled the covers up.

"All right," I said. "But if you get in my way then I'll cut you down as well."

"I know it," he said.

If I didn't kill Tod the next morning I was gonna come mighty close to it. I was damn sick and tired of his hare-brained pranks. The idea of him out laying up with a woman using money I could have used myself if I'd wanted was near more than I could bear. I was past anger, I was in a killing rage. I set my mind to come awake at the slightest sound. My pistol was under the old corn-shuck pillow I had and I was ready for the lightest step. I wasn't going to shoot him unless I had to—that would have been a waste of good lead and powder—but I meant to pistol whip him within an inch of his life. Maybe more.

It was a little after first light that I heard the door open softly and I slipped my hand under the pillow and set myself. The floorboards creaked once and then twice and I came up and threw down on the figure I could see in the half gloom.

"Right there!" I said. "Just hold it right there!"

There was a laugh. "Aw hell, Wilson," a voice said, "can't a man slip up on you no how?"

It was Howland Thomas. Right behind him was the grinning face of Chico, peering over his shoulder. Les stirred and I sat up on the bed, feeling a little foolish, and nudged him with my foot.

"Look here," I said. "Look here, Les. Come awake and see who's here."

Howland had a bottle of rum in either hand and Chico was carrying an armload of cantaloupes. They come on in, laughing, and Howland uncorked a bottle of the rum and poured a little in Les's face to wake him up.

"Here, boy," he said, "git up there. It's damn near noon!"

Howland was a medium heavyset man in his middle thirties. Neither he nor Chico was shaven, but it didn't show up so much on the Mexican. They looked tolerable clean, not as if they'd just come in off the trail. I was mighty glad to see them and, from the looks of the rum, they might have a little money.

"Hell," I said, reaching out for the rum bottle. "Give me that. Don't waste it on no lie-a-beds."

"Who the hell was you fixing to shoot?" Howland asked me and I realized I was still holding my pistol. I dropped it on the bed and shrugged and took the bottle he was holding out. "Anybody," I said. "Hell, I ain't particular." I could see that Tod still hadn't come in.

Howland and Chico got chairs and we sat around passing the rum bottle. It was a little raw, first thing in the morning, but Chico outed with his frog sticker and sliced up the cantaloupes and we sat around eating and drinking. It made a fine breakfast, one that would wake a man up and settle his stomach at the same time.

"Where the hell ya'll been?" Howland asked me.

"Us?" I said. I had my face buried down in a half a cantaloupe and I raised it and looked at him. "Hell, we been here since yesterday."

"Is that a fact! Well, we'd have never knowed it if we hadn't seen Tod out on the street just a bit ago." He laughed. "Drunk as hell and had lost his shirt. Hadn't he, Chico?"

"*Si,*" Chico agreed. "No shirt."

"Bare as a jaybird above the waist. And drunk as hell. He said ya'll was up here, but said he believed he'd go on down and fall in a horse trough somewhere. Said you was gonna be mad. What'd he mean by that?"

"Nothing," I said. "But where ya'll been? We looked all over this hotel for you."

"Hell," Howland said. "Name of this joint plumb slipped my mind. Me and Chico bunked at a place just up the street. Figured we'd find you anyway."

Well, I was that glad to see them. At least now we could get down to business and get out of the bind we were in. And maybe, just maybe, they'd have enough dough to pull a good time on.

We sat around having a few more drinks and then the door cracked and Tod stuck his head in. He had a sheepish grin on his face and roved his eyes all around the room without ever coming to rest on mine.

"Howdy," he said.

Chico and Howland shifted their chairs around. "Well come on in, boy!" Howland said. "You'll catch cold out in that hall as wet as you are!" And then he gave a great gurraff, for Tod was wet as well as being shirtless.

"Aw," he said, edging in and taking little glances at me. "Ya'll don't hooraw me."

I watched him, not saying anything. He'd got in the door by then and he kind of slid along the wall, all the time watching my face. I still hadn't said nothing.

"What the hell's going on?" Howland asked me. I didn't say anything, just watched Tod. Howland turned to Les: "We ain't about to have a killin', are we? If so, me and Chico wants time to get under the bed."

"No," Les said. "I don't think so."

I was still watching Tod, just sitting on the side of the bed and watching him. Finally he couldn't stand it any longer. "Well, just go to hell!" he said defiantly. "I done what I did and I don't care."

"Come here," I said. "Right now."

"No," he said.

I picked up my pistol and laid a shot just to the right of his shoulder. "I said come here."

The gun crashed, sounding like a cannon in the small room, and everybody jumped. Tod's eyes walled out like a frightened steer. Instead of moving toward me he flattened himself against the wall.

"Listen," I said, "I ain't gonna kill you. Ain't even gonna hit you. But you pull something else like this again and you're through with this outfit. You got that? You're through!"

"All right," he said.

Howland was looking back and forth at me and Tod. "What the hell!" he said. "What's going on?"

"Nothing," I said. "Forget it. You got any money?"

The very first time I'd ever seen Howland Thomas had been in Crystal Springs, Texas, some three years back. I'd been sitting out on the sidewalk just taking the sunshine and watching a bunch of cowboys sporting up and down the street on a Saturday afternoon. Finally, they'd got a little rambunctious and commenced riding up on the sidewalk. One of them had come along, shouldering me out of the way with his horse and I'd taken offense at it. The cowboy had got off his horse and come swaggering back up to me. He was drunk and mouthing around and I calculated to let him get so much off his chest and no more. A man had come out of the saloon and was standing up against the wall watching us. I'd worked around until I was facing into the building with the cowboy in front of me. He was a young kid and about three quarters drunk, but he was really letting his mouth off. The man who'd come out just lounged there, grinning and seeming to enjoy the exhibition. Finally, he'd turned to the cowboy and asked him if he knew who it was he was fixing to get kilt by.

"What?" he asked.

Howland had indicated me. "I was just wondering if you was acquainted with the gent that's fixing to put a bullet through you."

The cowboy had blustered. "Damn if he is!" he said. "Ain't no man—"

"Ain't?" Howland had said (for it was he) and laughed. "Reckon you don't know this gent. This here is Mister Wilson Young."

"Who?" the cowboy had asked, but it had given him pause. A little of his drunken bravado had left him.

"Mister Wilson Young," Howland said. "I know he's got six and them is just the ones been actual counted. You'll make number seven."

The cowpoke had blustered a little bit more, but then one of his pards had come up and talked low to him. I reckoned he was glad to be out of a bad scrape, so I let his friend lead him off. After they were gone Howland came over and stuck out his hand and offered to buy me a drink.

"Been wanting to meet you," he said. "I've heard about you all the way from the Arkansas River."

"That's all right," I said. But I went along to the saloon with him and had a drink or two. We didn't talk no business then, just had a visit. I don't generally like to preen and I ain't too proud of what I've done, but Howland can be damn friendly when he wants to be. Of course he ain't ever gonna be any way but that way with me, for at heart he is a coward and we both know it.

We seen each other off and on after that, but it was a year later before we got around to doing any business. I'd joined up with Les and Tod by then and Howland came along and helped us with a bank in New Mexico. We hadn't taken out much cash, but he'd impressed me as being a fairly cool hand and a pretty steady man to have around. After that we'd tried to set up one other job together but it hadn't come off and then we'd got together and set up this meet in Piedras Negras. Like I say, Howland knew who I was and I knew who he was.

"Money!" Howland said. "Hell, we got a sight of money! Near three hundred dollars. Why? Ya'll broke?"

"Something like that," I said. "Anyway, we need money for a horse for Tod. He's afoot right now." I give Tod a look and he hung his head. I went on, "I mean if we're gonna pull that job . . ."

"Pull that job? Hell, we can't afford to pass that up. Can we, Chico?"

"No," Chico said.

"It's a cracker box, ain't it, Chico?"

"*Seguro!*" Chico said.

I leaned over the bed and located my boots and commenced to pull them on. I hated to ask any man for anything. "In that case, Howland, I wonder if you might be willing to bankroll us to a little good times. You know I'll pay you back and I'll be willing to put up my silver—"

"Why, pard," he said, "hell yes I will! Hell, I didn't know you was busted. Been that way myself. Yeah, we'll have ourselves a blowout and then go rob us a bank."

I done a little figuring in my mind. "Can you let me take about seventy?" I asked him.

"Why not?" Howland said. He dug down and came out with a pile of coin, both Mexican and American, and began counting me out my sum. "You care for pesos or dollars?"

"Don't make a damn," I said. "Either one."

He counted the money out for me and laid it on the foot

of my bed and I took twenty-five for myself and pitched Les twenty-five and then took the balance and handed it to Tod.

"What's this?" he said. "Ya'll are taking twenty-five apiece."

"Not only that," I said, "but you are going to get that grey back out of that money. Anything left and you can spend it on yourself, but you better have a horse when we get ready to ride out or you ain't going."

He seen I meant it. "Listen," he said, a little worried. "I ain't sure I can get that grey back. I mean, twenty ain't much of a price."

"You let him go for fifteen, didn't you?"

"Well, yeah . . ." he said. "But that was kind of different."

"Yeah, different," I said. "Different because you gave him away. Well, you just figure to have a horse that can keep up when we get ready to leave or you just figure to stay here. Knowing you, you'll lay here and rot."

"That's harsh, Will," he said. "That's mighty harsh." I was shaming him in front of Chico and Howland and he didn't like it. I couldn't say I blamed him, but then he'd brought it on himself.

"Just mind what I say," I said, not backing off an inch. Hell, I wasn't going to save any of his face. He was the biggest part of the reason we was in the mess we was in. I don't like to go to another man for money and he'd been the one that caused it. Hell with his face, I had my own to think about.

We started out slow. For the balance of the morning we sat up in the room eating cantaloupe and drinking up the rest of Howland's rum. Then, about noon, we wandered downstairs and took dinner in a little café a piece up the street. They had tamales and some enchiladas and I had some of both as well as a little stewed chicken. Them Mexicans do know how to stew a fowl. They get him in there with all kinds of herbs and spices and hot stuff and then fire him over a grill and bring him out with a kind of cheese sauce all over the meat which is just falling loose from the bones.

It was mighty good. After that we located a cantina and knocked off a few drinks. The place had a little Kentucky bourbon, which I was mighty glad to see, not having had any for a time, and I got in my share of that. After that me and Les went back up to the hotel for a short siesta and the rest of the bunch went wandering off looking for a card game.

Me and Les slept longer than we'd meant to, what with the good feed and the bourbon and all, and it was good dark by the time we got downstairs. We checked by the livery stable just to be sure the horses was okay and then set out to hunt down the rest of the bunch. We found them in the Texas Bar, it being pretty close to the International Bridge and catering to an American trade. Chico and Tod was at the bar, the latter being drunk and showing it. They were watching Howland playing poker with several cowpokes at a table just a few feet away.

"He's whipping 'em bad!" Tod said to me when we came up to the bar. The sweat was shining on his face and soaking his shirt. He was really drunk. "He's taking the hide off 'em!"

"All right," I said. Me and Les got a drink and then turned to watch the play. "Who's he playing with?" I asked Chico. They didn't any of 'em look like house men.

"Cowboys," Chico said with that accent of his. "From Eagle Pass."

Eagle Pass was just over the bridge and they were probably cowboys from a local ranch come over to try their luck on a Saturday night. I could see they was drunk and Howland was having a pretty easy time with them. While we watched he caught one of them in a hand of five-card stud and sucked him in with two pair. The cowboy had had kings with one showing, but Howland had fours and jacks with a four in the hole. He was looking down the poke's throat all the way and leading him on. With his final bet he drawed the cowboy all the way in and then cleaned him out on the show of the cards.

"Jacks and fours!" he said, laughing that loud laugh of his and raking in the money.

They didn't like the easy way he was having with them and after a few more hands, when he up and quit, they made a loud noise about it. The saloon was smoky and hot and we was all sweating a little. Howland picked up his money and came to stand with us at the bar. We could see the cowboys watching him and considering what they ought to do.

Howland was counting his money. "Won fifty-six," he said. "Which is near about what I let you have."

I knew what I'd borrowed off him and I didn't think I needed reminding. I thought it was poor milk on his part but didn't say anything.

"Let's have a drink," he said. "I'm dry." He signaled for the bartender to pour and then held his glass up in my face. "Here's luck," he said.

"All right," I agreed. I had to drink to that. It would have been bad luck not to. I downed mine and set it back on the bar just as one of the cowboys came up. He was drunk and looked to be spoiling for a fight.

"Say," he said to Howland, "I think you cheated. What do you say to that?"

Howland just laughed. "What do you want me to say to a drunk fool?"

"That'll get you killed," the cowboy said. He was so drunk he was reeling back and forth. No wonder Howland had had such an easy time with them.

"Yeah?" Howland said. "And how you gonna do that? You're so drunk you couldn't hit a barn door with a handful of buckshot."

"Never you mind," the cowboy said. "They's three of us. What do you say to that?"

Howland jerked his thumb at me. "I say this here is Wilson Young and he can put a bullet through your brisket before you draw another breath."

The cowboy looked uncertain. "Wilson Young? Wilson Young?"

"The same," Howland said. "The very same. Now, what do you say to that?"

"I say to hell with it," I said. I wasn't fighting no man's

fight for him. There was a little whiskey still in my glass and I drained it and turned away.

"Listen, wait!" the cowboy said. "Hey wait, I said."

When I wouldn't he run a few steps and grabbed my arm and whirled me around.

"That's a good way to get killed," I told him.

"Listen here," he said, "are you really Wilson Young?"

The bar had suddenly got quiet. I looked at him. "What's it to you?"

"Well . . ." he said. "Well, just this." He was breathing hard and trying to think what to say. Finally one of his friends at the table called to him to say I wasn't. "Yeah," he said. "You ain't. You ain't no Wilson Young. I knowed him. Knowed him over at Arkansas Pass and you ain't him."

I looked at him. Everybody in the damn place was staring at us. "Boy, get away from me. I'm tired of this foolishness."

"Yeah," he said. "I bet you are. Tired and scared. That's what you are. Tired and scared. Scared mostly."

He was just a young kid, twenty at the most. Kind of blond and skinny. He was even wearing his hand gun wrong, all up to the front and out of place where he'd have to draw and then aim. Over his shoulder I could see Howland enjoying himself.

"You kill him," I said to Howland. "I ain't got the heart."

Howland just laughed. It was all a huge joke to him. Me, I felt sick. There I was, a man who'd wanted to make something of himself and had been fooled by his own reputation, being faced by a kid in a low saloon in a Mexican border town.

I looked at the young cowboy. He was edging closer and closer to me. "Your fight's not with me," I told him. "I wasn't playing at cards with you."

"That's all right," he said, getting braver by the minute and pushing me harder. "That's all right for you." He was so drunk he couldn't even think up a good remark. "I seen you helping that fellow. I seen you and don't you try to lie."

"Boy," I told him, "you better get back to your table before you get hurt. Now go on." Les and Tod was watching us. Tod with a kind of silly grin on his face, but Les with the kind of look that told he understood. I didn't want to kill the boy.

"You cheated me," the kid was saying, "and now you're going to give me satisfaction." He backed away like he was going to make a play for his gun. I didn't even shift, just watched him. I'd seen the move a number of times and it wasn't nothing new to me.

There had only been them two times I was brought up on charges for men I'd shot, but there had been a number besides that. Howland was wrong that time he'd said six. Actually there had been nine at the time and the count had grown. Mostly I was in rough country and if men didn't have beast or nature to pit themselves against they'd try the man next to them. In the early days I'd had a hot temper and a disinclination to back away from any man. Fortunately I'd had a hand fast enough to match and so had avoided getting killed. Of late, however, I'd grown to the point where the whole business had commenced to sicken me. I'd got to where I'd rather walk away.

I looked at the kid. "The hell with you," I said. "Go back to your table."

"Wilson Young," he sneered at me. "You ain't Wilson Young."

"Suit yourself," I said. I turned away and went for the door. The kid wouldn't shoot me in the back, Les would see to that. The quiet got so low I could near about hear it as I went out the door. Then, just as the doors brushed together, there came a little laugh and then the talk picked back up again.

What I should have done, I guess, was to have shown that kid some quick iron and then let him back off, but that would have been playing the show-off and I don't like to do that. Hell, I didn't care about what had happened. I know who I am and I ain't too worried if anybody else does or not. But I hadn't liked the way Howland had acted too much. He was starting to get just a little big with that "This here is Wilson Young" business and I resolved to have a little talk with him. To me, that kind of stuff is just plain foolishness.

Why in hell should a man want to brag on somebody that had killed folks? Sure it made a name for you, but with who? Drunks and outlaws and that ilk. They was the only ones that cared or took notice of a man like me. Not good folk; not that don or his goddam beautiful niece. I bet she thought I was dirt. Sure, I'd told myself she'd give me a long look, but I was lying to myself. She'd seen me all right and taken a long look, but it was probably just to fix me in her mind as someone she wanted to steer clear of.

I heard a step behind me and looked around. It was Les, coming along quietly, a little cigar burning in his mouth and making a glow along the dark street.

"Damn dark out, ain't it?" he said, coming up to me.

"It'll do," I said, "until they figure out a way to get inside a cow."

We stood there, in the dust of the street, just kind of looking around and not saying much. Except for a few saloons that were going full blast the town had gone to sleep. The saloons threw light out their windows and it made little golden patches in the dark of the street.

"Well, Will . . ." Les finally said. "You done right. That kid was drunk and stupid. I seen you do right."

"That Howland," I said. "Sometimes I wonder about that man. He seems to get a positive pleasure out of meanness. I don't know that I can figure him. I'm like you, I'll shoot if I have to, but that Jacob's coat seems to enjoy it."

"Well, you done right."

We stood a moment more and then I kind of half turned away. "I reckon I'll go on," I said.

"Where you headed?"

I studied a minute, but Les is my good friend. "Les," I said, "I'm just about froze for a pretty woman. I think I'll mosey along till I find a place that specializes in 'em and try a little sample."

"You want company?"

"No," I said. "I reckon I'll try it solo. May not find nothing. You go stay with the rest of the boys and keep 'em out of trouble."

I turned away and took a few steps and Les called to me.

I looked back and could just make out his dark form lit up by the glow of his cigar.

"Listen," he said. "You're letting that girl ride your mind."

"What the hell you mean by that?"

"You ain't been yourself. You've been bothered. You ought to get her out of your mind. Hell, Will, she ain't your kind."

"I don't know what you're talking about. Anyway, it ain't none of your goddam business."

"I know that. Just thought I'd say it."

"Well, don't."

I turned around and walked off. I didn't know what a man can find in a whorehouse, but I was damn sure going to give it a try.

The bordello I finally went into was a two-story adobe-brick affair. Downstairs was the bar and some chairs where you could get to know the girls, and upstairs was the rooms you took 'em to once you'd made your choice and settled on the price. It was hot and smoky and busy. A good body of what I took to be drovers was in the place and they was mostly drunk and loud. I went in and went up to the bar and watched them for a while. They were yelling and laughing and sporting with the girls and I envied them. I still had the feeling of ice in my belly and a bad touch in my mind that I couldn't get rid of. I took several drinks trying to loosen up, but they didn't help much. I felt sour and on edge and a little angry, not at all the way I like to feel. Standing with my back to the bar, I watched the cowboys sporting around the room with the girls. The whores wasn't much, being mostly dogs, but the pokes didn't seem to care. I wanted to get in the kind of mood they were in, but I couldn't. All I could do was stand there and think about how I'd come from a good family with extensive holdings and yet there I stood, in a whorehouse in Mexico, drinking cheap whiskey on borrowed money and watching a bunch of forty-dollar-a-month cowboys blowing a month's wages on a passel of cheap bitches. Had even made a botch of bank robbing. It sure looked like a man who'd decided to go bad could make a better job out of it than I had. Hadn't even been able to hang on to what we'd taken, which is a pretty sorry comment on bank robbery.

Finally I got so down on myself I decided to hell with it and took a bottle of whiskey and walked across to a table where the prettiest girl in the place was sitting with a young cowboy. He was pawing around on her, trying to get his hand down her blouse, and she was laughing and giggling and asking to see his money. He was a young kid, about the same as the one in the Texas Bar, and I just walked up and kicked his chair and told him to move it. They both looked up at me in some surprise and the poke asked me what I'd said.

"I said move it. Didn't you hear me?"

"Well now, mister," he began, but I kicked his chair again and set the bottle down on the table so as to have both hands free. "Boy," I said, "you get up and move it and do it pronto or I'm gonna eat you alive. My name is Wilson Young and if you don't think I can't kill you before you can wink you just set there another second."

He hadn't had much to drink and he looked me over a second, taking note of the way my gun was set up and the look on my face. Finally he kinda swallowed and stood up. I hadn't been too loud, so nobody else was paying us any mind. He seen that and seen he wouldn't have to get killed over his pride, so he took a step or two backward.

"Hell," he said. "I don't care none anyway, I didn't have no more money, so I didn't care. Besides, she's got the clap."

He said that last and looked quick to see if it made me mad, but I never said a word, just took the chair he'd vacated. The girl looked about as bored as one can get. She'd seen it before and, hell, with me coming up the way I'd done she knew she had a sale. I made sure the kid was gone, then poured us out a drink and knocked mine off. Maybe if I got us both drunk enough I could have some fun.

"What's your name?" I asked her in Spanish.

She giggled and said it was Louisa.

"Well, Louisa," I said and poured myself out another

drink, "you better lay in your powder for a long siege. Me and you is going to war." I downed my drink and got out some coin and spilled it on the table. "Pick that up," I told her, "and get me another bottle of whiskey and let's go on upstairs. I got a lot of catching up to do."

"Ah," she said, "you're *muy rápido*."

"Yes," I said, "I'm fast with everything—guns, mistakes, whiskey, even girls. Let's go."

CHAPTER 6

A Cactus Has Sharp Thorns

We all met a little before noon in the bar of the hotel. All of us, that is, except Tod. I asked Les where he was.

"Far as I know he's out trying to get that grey back. That's what he said when he left out this morning."

"Well, he better have it," I said, "or he'll stay right here. I'm through with his harebrained pranks."

We were all sitting around a table in the center of the bar. Chico and Howland were eating a dish of eggs and chili, but me and Les, having already ate, were having beer. I was feeling a little better in my mind, but not much. The girl had been all right, as whorehouse girls go, but she hadn't helped and, after the first trick, I seen I couldn't go on and I'd got up and dressed and went back down to the bar downstairs. A poker game had been going on and I'd sat in on that.

I sat there, ruminating, until Howland wiped his mouth on his sleeve and called to the bartender to send him over a drink of whiskey. He looked at me.

"Well, you about ready to get down and talk some business?"

"I reckon," I said, but I had something else on my mind. I had that "This here is Mister Wilson Young" business on my mind. "Look here, Howland," I said, "I want to get you to do me a favor."

He leaned back in his chair and grinned at me. "Need

67

some more money, pard? Did you use up all your luck on them little señoritas?"

That made me a little angry, but I let it pass. "No, that ain't it. I'm much obliged for the loan and don't figure to want no more. No, what I had in mind was something on the order of you not being so quick to tell folks who I am."

He tilted his hat back at that and looked at me with a big grin. Howland is a thickset man with powerful arms and a big, heavy face. His grin never seems so much happy as mean. His mouth may smile, but his eyes don't.

"What's the matter, pard, you don't like being famous?"

"Well," I said, "that may be all right for you, but it ain't my style. And I don't much like you using the word 'famous.' Don't get cute with me, Howland. Just play it straight."

He seen I meant it. "Aw, I was just funning you."

"That's all right," I said, "but I think you're wearing the joke a little thin. If I want people to know who I am I'll be quick enough to tell 'em without no help from you."

"Well, I see that you're getting everybody straightened up around here."

"What do you mean by that?"

"First Tod, now me. When do you go to work on Chico and Les?"

The grin had kind of frozen on his face. I just kind of straightened up, which let my chair slide back from the table a few inches. Howland seen the movement, but he never budged. The grin did, however, kind of fade from his face. I just looked at him, knowing he understood I was getting a little touchy.

Finally he laughed. "Hell," he said, slumping over the table and propping up on his elbows. "You're too edgy, Wilson. You know I never meant nothing by a little kidding."

"Just so we understand each other," I said. "Now, what about this bank?"

"I like to rob one Mexican bank first," Chico said. I looked over at him. In the little set-to between me and Howland I'd forgotten about everybody else in the room and it kind of surprised me to hear him speak.

"What?" I asked him.

Howland laughed. "Chico said he'd like to rob him a Mexican bank. He wants him some of them gold pesos. That's all he's been talking about."

I shook my head. "No," I said, "we ain't robbing no banks on this side. That's out. We're going to Uvalde, Texas."

Howland laughed again, but this time it had a different sound to it. "Well, then I reckon I ought to tell you there's a little dirt out on you over in that state."

Les hadn't said anything, but now he asked Howland what he meant.

Howland was enjoying himself. "Why, I reckoned ya'll knew you'd kilt a man in that little job you pulled over there in Carrizo Springs. An important man too, big rancher and state senator or something."

I looked over at Les. His face looked as blank as mine. We hadn't killed anybody on that job. I knew we hadn't and so did Les.

"You're crazy," I said to Howland. "We didn't kill nobody on that job."

"Then me and the man's widow and half the state is mistaken. I beg your pardon. Why don't you step over to the telegraph office and get 'em off a wire telling 'em the straight of it. I'm sure that'll get all them rangers off your tracks."

Well, I didn't know what to say. I didn't see how anybody could have been killed. There hadn't been a straight shot fired while we was inside the bank. True, once we got outside we'd wheeled back and forth and fired a few shots into the air just to hold everything in place and keep folks from rushing out the door after us, but I didn't see how none of that could have killed anybody unless he was sitting on the rooftree of a building.

Les said: "We never fired on nobody."

"Well, it's all the news on the other side, ain't it, Chico?"

We looked at the little Mexican and he nodded solemnly. "*Si*, we hear of it in three, four places. You have shot a state senator. A big man."

"Where? Where was we have supposed to killed him?"

"Right there in the door of the bank," Howland said. "It's said he run to the door to see which way ya'll was heading and one of you gunned him down in cold blood. They say he wasn't even armed."

"That's a lie," I said.

"Sure it is," Howland said. "I just made it up to entertain of a morning."

I studied over it a minute. "How do they know it was us? Who says we was even at Carrizo Springs?"

Now Howland leaned back in his chair and really began to enjoy himself. "Well, that's what comes of being famous, Mister Wilson Young. Ya'll was all recognized. Especially you."

"Did they say who done the actual killing?" Les asked.

Howland shook his head. "They's a wanted notice out on all three of you. The way I had it they was so much shooting and commotion that nobody got a clear idea."

I had a clear idea. It hadn't been me, for the couple of shots I'd fired had all been right straight for the sky. And I'd gotten a glimpse of Les wheeling his mount around and shooting. He'd had his gun aimed straight up.

I sat and studied over it again. Finally it come to me that Howland had known all along. I asked him why he'd waited until just that moment to tell us.

"Who's had a chance?" he came back. "Besides, I figured you knew it." He grinned. "I generally know it when I kill a man. He's generally standing right where I'm pointing."

"So?"

"So I figured you knew it. I was just telling you you was wanted and that they've give a warrant to the rangers. I reckoned you didn't know that."

Well, we hadn't known it and Howland knew we hadn't. He'd just saved it up until he could spring it on us when he chose. I was getting a little tired of Mister Howland Thomas and his idea of a joke.

"We never meant to shoot nobody," Les said. "If it happened it was an accident."

"Oh sure," Howland said. "Wilson Young is known all

over five states for never meaning to kill nobody. Everybody knows it's always an accident."

I didn't even feel like getting into it with him. I felt pretty bad. As a matter of fact I felt real bad. I slumped back in my chair and called for a whiskey and put my boots up on the table. When the drink came I knocked it off and just sat, staring. Les didn't say anything either.

After a long time, Howland said: "So I wouldn't be too concerned about nothing this side of the border. I hear tell them rangers will come get you, legal or not, if they's enough reward money involved." Me nor Les said a word. Howland waited, then went on. "I hear the family has put up five hundred dollars a man." He still didn't get any reaction out of us. He went on, pressing: "That's near a year's pay for them rangers. Some of 'em would be willing to go to hell and try to bring back the old Nick himself for that kind of money. What do you say to that?"

I didn't say anything. There wasn't much I could say. Legally, rangers can't come into Mexico for you, but that don't often stop them. They'll carry you back over in a load of hay if they have to. The job we'd pulled in Carrizo Springs had been as close to home as we'd ever worked. I hadn't like it, but we'd done it and now it looked like we were fairly in for it.

"What do you say to that?" Howland asked me again.

I turned my look on him. He'd been holding this, waiting to spring it on us. "I say we're going and rob a bank. Are you going? We're pretty well wanted right now. Maybe you won't want to be seen with us."

"Oh, don't make me a damn. Me or Chico. Does it, Chico?"

"I like to rob one Mexican bank," Chico said. "They have much gold and I don't like the people that are in the bank."

"No," I said. "We're going to Uvalde. Are you coming?"

"Sure," Howland said. "Ain't that what this is all about?"

"What about Tod?" Les asked.

I stood up. "If he don't show up before we pull out he's gonna get left. I ain't waiting."

Howland yelled for the bartender. *"Cuenta,"* he said.

"No," I told him. "I'll get the bill. And, by the by, here's your seventy greenbacks." I reached down in my pocket and got a handful of currency and counted out the money I owed him. "Wouldn't want to be beholden to you."

He looked at me. "Well, well, well. Flush again, huh?"

"That'd be my business," I said. "Let's move." I turned around and went out the door without bothering to see if they were coming.

Tod was not there when we got ready to ride out. We sat, mounted, in front of the hotel and looked around for him. It was near two o'clock and I wasn't going to wait any more. I looked at Les.

"I told him," I said.

He answered, "I know it."

"We're going to ride out and leave him. I warned him."

"I know it," he said.

I reined my horse back in the street a little and looked at him. "Well?"

He seemed to study a moment. Finally he kind of shrugged and turned his mount out beside mine. "I reckon it's right," he said.

"Let's go," I said. I turned my horse into the street and kicked him into a lope toward the International Bridge. Howland and Chico strung out behind us. Howland and Chico would cross the bridge, but Les and I would cut north for a mile or so, make a fording, and then rejoin the others on the Uvalde road. I'd done checked the river and had been glad to see it had gone back to being a shallow, muddy little stream. Apparently we'd just had the bad luck to catch the crest of the rise that afternoon downriver. Nearing the bridge, Les and I cut off to the left and Chico and Howland went on ahead. Wasn't much stirring at the lower end of the town, it being siesta, but me and Les made no sign to the others, just cut off and left them. Probably we could have crossed the bridge ourselves, customs along the border being what they were, but there wasn't any point in taking the chance. So Les and I rode along, feeling the heat from that Mexican sun on our backs. My little mare was feeling pretty frisky from the several days of stable life with the good grain and hay and all and I had to hold her back she wanted to go so bad. I patted her on the neck while she kind of danced sideways against the check rein and told her she'd get plenty of chances to run soon enough. Les looked over at me. He was riding out a few yards to the right on his big, noble-looking gelding. His old pony carried his head high with his ears peaked up and just kind of cantered along very stylishly. They made quite a sight, Les in his chaps and big hat and being what I reckoned the ladies would take for a handsome man.

"How you doing, pard?" I asked him.

"I'm all right," he said. "Didn't drink enough last night to feel real bad. How about you?"

"I'm okay."

We rode along a little further, both with his own thoughts, and then Les asked me, a little slowly, if I was back to being myself. I asked him what he meant by that and he said I knew. "You ain't been yourself, Wilson. You just ain't. You haven't been satisfied with nothing and you've been ornery and mad and, well, I guess just down on everything, yourself included."

"When did you take up the ministry?" I asked him.

"All right. Never mind then. But don't tell me I'm wrong. I been knowing you a powerful long time."

"Yes, you have. Long enough to know I don't like nobody butting into my business."

He looked back at me, but didn't say anything, just pulled his hat down a little lower over his eyes and hunched up in his saddle. The road we were following had slung us over next to the river and we rode along by it watching how the brown waters just kind of slugged along down toward the gulf. A man could go to the coast in that water if he could find a boat with a shallow enough draft to float in it. After a little I pulled my horse up and Les followed suit.

"This looks pretty good," I said. The river had narrowed to about a hundred yards and had got real shallow. I put my little mare forward and made the crossing. Les came right behind me and I pulled up on the other side and got down

and took my chaps out of my saddlebags. As I did I pulled
one of my silver spurs out of them and it fell to the ground.
I picked it up and put it back in the saddlebag and tied the
flap down. Les watched me while I put on my chaps. We'd
be cutting overland as soon as we caught up with the others
and you've got to wear chaps in that country else you'll
get your legs tore up by the cactus. There's one cactus
they make a pretty good drink out of, but most of 'em
ain't good for nothing except ripping up horses and cattle
and men. I got remounted and rigged out and we rode on.
After we'd gone on a little piece Les said he was surprised
to see the spurs.

"How's that?"

"I figured you must have sold 'em last night. You had
money to pay Howland back."

"So?"

"So where else would you get money?"

"How you know some whore didn't pay me? How come
you figure I sold the spurs?" I was starting to get angry.
I was starting to get very angry. I knew the reason why,
too.

"Well, hell, Will, you don't have to take that tone. It's
none of my business. I was just asking."

"Well, I'll tell you. I played a little game for that money.
You keep sticking your nose in my business and I'm going
to play that same little game with you." As I said the last
I looked straight at him. I guess it was the first time I'd
ever really offered him what you might call a challenge.
Les ain't Tod and he ain't Howland. He's a good man.
The minute I said what I did I began to feel bad. What
had happened and what was making me mad was none of
Les's doing. Hell, I wasn't even mad at him; I was mad at
myself.

He took the words and the look with never a quiver.
Finally I turned away and went back to riding for the Uvalde
road. Les hadn't said anything but after a few hundred yards
I heard his horse's gait quick and he went on by me in a slow
lope. I wondered where he was going, but then he wheeled
around and pulled up facing me.

"Will," he said, "you've read me out twice in the space of an hour. Maybe I was butting my nose into something that was none of my business, but we been together so long that it gets hard sometimes to tell where one or the other's business leaves off."

He was right and no doubt about it. It just made me feel worse.

He went on: "But you read me off. I just wanted to let you know that would be the last time I'd take it." He looked at me narrowly. "I can't draw with you, Will. Can't anybody else I know." He paused. "But you come this again on me and I will. I sure as hell will."

I put up my hand. "Now just take it easy," I said. "Just hold up there."

But he wouldn't. He said: "I just wanted you to know." Then he wheeled his horse and loped on off ahead. I followed, not trying to say anything or catch up to him. For the moment I was content to just let him cool out.

Howland and Chico were waiting for us under a shade tree about three miles the Texas side of the bridge. To my great surprise Tod was with them. He was sitting under the tree holding the reins of a pretty good-looking black gelding. We come clattering up and they asked if we'd had any trouble on the crossing.

"No," I said, my eyes on Tod and his horse. "Did ya'll?"

"Not a bit," Howland said. He got up and stretched and walked around to his saddlebags and got out a bottle of rum and offered it up to me. I uncorked it and took a swallow of the fiery stuff and passed it along to Les.

I nodded over at Tod. "Where'd you get him?"

Howland laughed. "He was waiting for us. Setting right here taking it easy." He jerked his thumb toward Tod's horse. "Looks like the boy would make a horse trader. See that black he got for twenty dollars?"

"Yes," I said. I dismounted and walked over to the horse. Tod never stirred other than to cut his eyes up at me for a second and then go to ground again. I walked around the horse and found he was well set up and clean-limbed. I raised one of his hoofs and saw that it was trimmed and well shod. There was a brand on his hip and I patted it and then looked over at Tod.

"Mighty good horse for twenty dollars," I said.

He never said a word, just stared at the ground.

The horse was easy worth a hundred dollars and I knew Tod hadn't had no hundred dollars. Everybody stood around watching me and Tod, waiting to see what I was going to say or do. I'd told Tod I didn't want no trouble on the Mexican side, but anybody with one eye could see he'd stole the pony.

I just looked at Tod. Finally he said: "I bought him. I couldn't find the guy with the grey, so I bought this one."

"Who from?"

"A cowboy," he said vaguely. He had a little sullen, defiant thread in his voice. "A Texas cowboy off a ranch."

That stopped me. After what had happened at the whorehouse with the foreman off the Texas ranch there wasn't a hell of a lot I could say to Tod.

Howland seen me pause. I think he wanted to egg a fight on. "What'd you buy him with, Tod, twenty dollars and a six-gun?"

"I bought him," Tod said back to him.

"Yeah," Howland said, "but did the old boy want to sell?"

"I'll handle this, Howland," I said.

Howland laughed that irritating laugh of his. "I see you are. Hell, it ain't no skin off my nose. I don't care if the boy steals the whole damn country."

Tod got up and came to stand in front of me. I think he sensed I wasn't going to do anything. "Listen, Will, it wasn't like I done nothing to no Mexicans. It was a Texas cowboy, I swear it. Them Mexicans don't care if we steal off one another." He was talking very earnestly. I looked at him for a second and then turned away and told everybody to get mounted up. "Let's ride out. We've got tracks to make."

No, I guess the Mexicans wouldn't care if we stole from one another. I guess nobody would care except the man that was robbed and the man that had done the back-alley bushwhacking. Back-alley bushwhackers are a sorry lot.

When a man comes down to that he's gotten mighty sorry. He's got way off his trail—a hell of a long way off his trail.

We rode until good dark, then turned into a little dry stream bed and made camp. On the off chance that somebody might have scouted out our trail I told off watches, giving myself the first and Les the second. We were now in territory where we were wanted and somebody might have picked us up when we made the crossing. It wasn't going to hurt to be careful.

We made a supper out of beans and a little dried goat, had a drink all around and then everybody else turned in while I took my Henry and climbed up a little knoll to take the watch. It was a good vantage point, giving a view for several miles of the surrounding country. The moon was up good and it sure made a pretty sight the way the land stretched out with the moon shining on it and the big old barrel cactus throwing down shadows and the white rocks gleaming here and there. Off to the right I could see the horses wandering around and grazing off the sparse grass. We'd brought along feed and they'd been grained before we turned them out. They wouldn't wander far.

It was a quiet night with only the occasional call of a coyote to break the stillness and I kind of dozed off and on. I guess I plumb forgot the time, forgot to call Les, for I heard a step behind me and it was he coming up toward my station.

"Oh, Les," I said. He came up beside me and laid his rifle on the ledge I had mine propped over.

"Was you gonna keep it all night?"

"Not hardly. I just didn't take no notice of the time."

"Anything?"

"Coyotes and owls. Nothing else."

"Think I'll smoke," he said. He got out one of the little Mexican cigars that he prefers and lit up. "You want one?"

"Might as well," I said. "Before I turn in."

He give me one and we got lit up and sat there smoking a minute, hiding the glow in the palms of our hands. I could see from the moon that a good little spell had passed since I'd come up.

"Well, Les," I said. I'd figured our watches the way I had so I'd have a chance to talk to him. I felt bad about the thing that had passed between us. "Well, I was wrong this afternoon. Dead wrong."

He didn't say anything for a minute, just went on smoking and looking out over the country. Finally he said: "Yes you were. You sure as hell were wrong."

That made me laugh. I couldn't help myself. I clapped him on the shoulder. "You bastard, you sure make it easy on a man, don't you?"

He looked over at me and grinned. He was as relieved as I to have the bad occasion between us out and done with. "You don't make it none too easy on a man yourself."

It made me feel good, the best I'd felt in several days. A man only has so many real friends and I counted Les as just about my only one. The owl-hoot trail is lonesome and you don't get to stand in with a lot of folks.

We stood there, both watching the moon and listening to the coyotes for a while. Finally I said: "Les, I've got to tell you about something. Kind of explain, I guess."

"You ain't got to explain nothing to me, Will. I've been for you right along."

"I know that. And that's why I want to tell you this."

He looked over at me, puffing on his cigar. "Well, I figured something's been on your mind. Ever since that rancho, or that girl. Is that it? Have you fallen for that girl Linda?"

"Oh, goddam!" I said. "Don't play the calf. How in hell could I have fallen for that girl? I only saw her a minute or two."

"Then what is it?"

I studied a minute trying to think of the best way to put it. Finally I just said: "Les, I'm going to quit this game."

He took his cigar out of his mouth and stared at me. "What game? Bank robbing?"

"All of it. Every damn bit of it."

He was still staring at me. "Well, I'm damned. Do you mean it?"

"I mean it," I said.

"Hmmmph!" Les said.

"I mean this to be my last job. If Howland is right about that bank, that we can take thirty or forty thousand out of it, I mean to take my share and quit. But either way I'm going to quit."

"What'll you do, pard? You know, you've got a little too much reputation to get a job in the post office. What will there be for you to do?"

"I've thought about that," I said. "I'll either go to Canada or Mexico and set up. If we get that money I figure to buy myself a little place and raise my own beef. If we don't get it, then I'll work for the other man."

"You have studied over it, haven't you," Les said. "How long you been thinking on it?"

"Long enough to be sure," I said.

"Since that Rancho Fernando, I'd bet on it."

"Oh, don't come that on me again, Les. What makes you say a thing like that?"

"Because you ain't been yourself since then. I think it embarrassed you the way we looked upside that don and his niece. You tell me I'm wrong."

"You're wrong," I said.

"I don't believe it."

I didn't know. Hell, goddamit! I didn't know if he was right or wrong or what. I only knew I wasn't able to stand up and be myself around those folks. I only knew that girl had looked at me in a longing kind of way (and that was the truth because I'd seen it even if I had denied it to myself) but if she'd known who I really was and what I was she'd have looked at me with disgust instead. I knew that; I knew that for sure.

But then there was that other thing. There was that thing I'd done that had been the lowest I'd ever come to. "Les," I said, "you're the best friend I got." "Aw, hell," he said, but I held up my hand and cut him off. "I want to tell you about something. Will you listen and not say a word until I'm through?"

He said he would and I commenced telling him about

going to that whorehouse; about running off that young cowboy (out of just plain meanness) and then taking the girl upstairs, intending on staying all night, but not being able to do it on account of feeling bad about myself and not being able to find what I was looking for in the girl.

"Then," I said, "I come back downstairs and got in a little low-stakes poker game. There was another game going on, but I didn't have but three or four dollars, which wasn't enough to sit in."

I told him how they'd cleaned me out pretty quick and how I'd gone over to the bar and had a couple of drinks on my last four bits.

"Got to talking to a foreman from a ranch. A Texan. He had a pretty good roll of bills and was sporting them around, so I up and propositioned him about buying my spurs. I figured I could take the money and get in that big poker game and maybe win a little stake. So we went on outside and got my spurs and I asked him a hundred and he offered me eighty and we settled on eighty-five."

"I thought you said you never sold them spurs."

"Goddamit, Les!"

"All right. Go ahead."

"Well, I got that money and got in that game, but I couldn't do no good. Finally, I did get a little ahead, maybe had a hundred, and I got to thinking about them spurs." I drew on my cigar and felt it burn my finger, it was getting so short, and dropped it to the ground and scrubbed it out with my boot. "Les, I think a right smart about them spurs."

"I know you do."

"I wanted them back. I just kept sitting there and thinking about them spurs and I figured I had to have them back. Finally, I got up and went over to that foreman. He had them spurs looped around his neck and it just got right through me seeing him with my spurs. People was standing around admiring them and he was making a to-do about it and I walked over and offered him ninety to let me take them back. He just laughed. Said he wouldn't sell. Said he knew a bargain when he'd got one."

"I offered him ninety-five and, when he wouldn't sell at

that price, went to a hundred. Finally I got out every penny I had—about a hundred and four dollars—and laid it out on the bar. Said that was all I had and would he take it."

"That was fair," Les said.

"Yes, it was, and I thought it was, but that foreman said he didn't need no hunnert and four dollars, but that he did need them spurs. Said he wouldn't take a hundred and fifty for them."

I guess Les could see where I was heading, for he got real quiet. I hated to tell him, but I felt like I had to. I wanted him to understand. "Well," I finally went on, "I went over and sat back down at a table. After a good while that foreman finished drinking and went on out. He went out alone." I looked over at Les. "Les, I went out and took them spurs back. I went out and caught him in the dark and took them spurs off him. I done it. I bushwhacked him."

Les didn't say anything, just kind of shook his head from side to side.

"So there's your Mister Wilson Young. He's come to a common back-alley bushwhacker. I've come pretty low, Les."

"Yes, you have," Les said. He didn't have to lie to me or try to jolly what I'd done. We both knew.

"So I've got to quit. A man that can sink that low, there's no telling where he'll stop."

"Is that why you didn't say anything to Tod about that horse he stole?"

"That's right."

"I wondered," Les said.

"Well, that's the reason. And that's the reason I've got to quit. I've got to get out of this else I won't be able to shave no more."

"You want another cigar?"

"No. Reckon I'll turn in." I was feeling pretty low in mind and spirit. I started to turn away but Les put out his hand and stopped me.

"Will, I wouldn't feel too bad about that if I was you. I know that ain't your style. You was drunk and not thinking."

"No, it ain't my style. But a man ain't supposed to have to think about that, is he? It's supposed to come natural, ain't it?"

Les didn't have no answer for that, so I started away again. But I turned back after a step or two. "Do you think the less of me over this?"

He shook his head. "No, I don't. I know that ain't you. I just think you ain't been yourself here lately."

"Les, how about throwing in with me? How about me and you taking off for Canada or Mexico after this job? We'll pool our money and get us a place and set up as patrons on our own. Run cattle or maybe good horses."

"It won't work, Will."

"It's got to work," I said.

He'd got out another cigar and lit it and he drew on it a second before he answered. "I made me many a mistake a good ways back and went wrong. But now that I've done it they ain't no way to change. No, Will, I'm what I am. Ain't no use me joshing myself. I just figure to live with it and do the best I can."

I shrugged. "Suit yourself. But you're wrong."

"Maybe so," he said.

"No maybe about it. I'm going to sack out. Call Howland next."

"All right," he said, and I turned around and walked on down the little rise and got in my blankets. It'd turned off a little cool.

CHAPTER 7

Uvalde

We made it to Uvalde midways of the third day. The land had turned hilly and rolling and we come up a rise and there the town was. It wasn't much to see, one main street with a collection of buildings in the middle and dwelling houses scattered along at either end. One or two streets led off the main thoroughfare, but the rest was just alleys. We were still a good mile, mile and a half from the town, but Howland raised up in his stirrups and pointed.

"See that building looks newly whitewashed? That there's the bank."

"The one about midways on that corner there?"

"That's the one. Cattleman's National."

I looked a minute longer and then reined my horse around. "Let's go."

The others turned to follow me, but Tod just sat there. "What! Ain't we going in?"

I shook my head, "No, we ain't going in. C'mon."

"Aw, Will!" he said. "Hell, we been out three days now. Let's at least go in and get us a drink. Just one drink."

"Don't be a donkey," Les said. "We can't go in that town, not this close to Carrizo Springs. Somebody would recognize us sure."

We'd rode off a few yards and pulled up. He was still sitting there watching us.

"We could get just one drink. That wouldn't hurt nothing."

"Goddamit, Tod, I believe you get to be a bigger baby every day," I said. "You and that red hair, you reckon they wouldn't recognize you? Howland and Chico will go in this evening. They'll bring a couple of bottles back."

"Ah hell!" he said. "That ain't the same." But he grudgingly put his mount into a trot and came up to us.

Howland knew the country pretty good, having spent considerable time in the area, and on the way I'd talked to him about a good place to hole up until we were ready to make the strike. He knew of a canyon a few miles out of town that had a little stream in it and we made for there.

The canyon was good. There was a little natural box at the end full of mesquite and prairie grass and we run the horses in there and strung a couple of ropes across to hold them. Where we was we wanted them close at hand in case we had to make sudden tracks. Tod and Chico unloaded the gear and slung it up under an outcropping off the canyon wall and Howland and I made a little fire out of mesquite, which doesn't smoke much, and boiled some coffee. It would be a good place to wait out the two days until Saturday.

We'd settled on Saturday morning because that would be the time the bank would have money out of the vault for the ranch owners who would be coming in to pick up the wages for their hands they'd be paying off that night. Also, Howland said there was a big MKT track-laying crew in the area and the paymaster might have his money in the bank. If that was so we might really make a haul.

"How much you figure, Howland?" Tod asked. "Tell me again."

We'd put the fire near out and were all sitting around it drinking coffee. There'd been a little rum left and we'd had a drop or two left for each cup. It was relaxing after the long ride we'd made.

"Forty thousand at least," Howland said. "Maybe more. Maybe sixty or seventy."

"Hot damn!" Tod said.

"I mean it's going to be a real gold mine, ain't it, Chico?"

"Sure," the little Mexican said. "Clearly."

"How you know?" Les asked him.

"Hell, common sense and then some talk I've heard. This is the only bank for fifty miles and this is mighty rich country. I was here myself when J. B. Calhoun—that's one of the bigger ranchers around here—deposited twenty thousand in species just himself."

"That's a power of money," Tod said reverently.

I spit on the ground. "We got to get it first."

"Easy," Howland said. "Easiest thing in the world. They's just that old sheriff. He's so old he can't hardly sit a horse anymore and he ain't got but two deputies and one of them is his nephew that he appointed 'cause his sister made him. It's a cracker box, ain't it, Chico?"

"How about the Cattleman's Protective Association?" I asked. "If this is such big cattle country they'll have a pretty strong association."

"They've got a few agents," Howland admitted, "but they don't generally stay to town. Hell, Will, this town ain't never been hit before. Other than a little rustling here and there ain't nothing ever happened around here. Hell, they've got so used to it they're asleep."

"Maybe so," I said. "I hope you're right."

A little after dark Howland and Chico rode into town. They'd go in separately and have a look around and kind of get the town layout straight in their minds. Friday, I intended to send Howland in and let him go in the bank and get a good picture of that. For the time being, however, they was just gonna get the straight of the streets and see who all was around and like that. Tod made a little commotion about going in with them, but I came down firmly on him and he shut up. It looked like he'd have sense enough on his own to understand the situation but, with Tod, you could never be sure. He didn't think with his brain, he thought with his mouth and his gut and his balls. All he was looking for was to satisfy any of those three. But I guess the money we were playing for had finally got through to him, for he didn't take on overmuch.

After Howland and Chico rode out we sat around the

remains of our supper fire not saying anything but just
enjoying the rest. Tod was fidgeting around, but me and
Les had pulled our saddles up next to the fire and was
just laying back agin them like we was country squires.
Howland had promised they'd bring us a bottle back, but
I didn't look to see them. They'd get into town and get
drinking and forget all about us. I figured they wouldn't
be back until the saloons all closed up. We'd brewed up
another pot of coffee and had it sitting on the coals staying
warm and every once in a while we'd reach over and help
our cup out a little. It was mighty pleasant. Looking up, the
canyon walls had carved out a nice private piece of sky for
me and I laid back and looked up at that, not really thinking
about much, but just kind of taking it in.

Well, it's funny how the mind works, the way it'll lead
you up one street and then down another and then around
this corner and so on until you're at a place in your thoughts
you hadn't meant to get to when you started out. I was laying
there looking at that sky, noting how blue it was, kind of
like a real pretty blue velvet dress a girl might wear, and
then I got to wondering just how big a piece of land that
chunk of sky covered that I was looking at. Next I got
to wondering if people in, say, Piedras Negras was looking
at the same sky I was, and then I kind of wandered back
the way we'd come from Villa Guerro and took that in
and then moved on out to the Fernando ranch. Next thing
I knew I was thinking about that girl Linda, which was a
thing I hadn't meant to do and in fact had been careful
not to.

But there I was, thinking about her.

Yet what in the name of Dick's cat did I have to think
about a girl I'd only seen for a moment or two and exchanged
scarce more than a look and a word? I knew her name, had
a fair guess on her age, knew where she was from, knew
her uncle and that was all. All, except for the look of her;
the way she'd looked in them clothes she was wearing, the
way that white mantilla kind of hung down in the back and
framed her Spanish face, the way her dress kind of rustled
when she'd come rushing into the room, the startled look

she'd got on her face when she'd realized her uncle had company. That and the look she'd give me, that and her face that I couldn't get out of my mind. I seen it, laying there, clear as the sky above me. The way it had little tones in it and highlights, the way it kind of heated up and blushed when she looked at me and our eyes kind of locked up for a moment, kind of locked up a little longer than was necessary. For a second I seen the way her breasts was trying to bust out of the cloth that had them and the way her hips just exploded out of that narrow waist of hers.

I tell you I didn't have any right seeing all that, nor business either, but I couldn't help myself. I couldn't get her out of my mind and it seemed it had been that way forever.

Across the fire, Les raised up and poured himself a cup of coffee. The movement brought me back to myself. I thought he'd said something, but I wasn't sure.

"You say something, Les?"

"Yeah. I asked you if you figured them boys would make it in before daylight."

"I doubt it," I said. "They'll get in there and get liquored up and forget all about bringing us back a bottle."

"What's that?" It was Tod's voice from back in the shadows. Whilst I'd been dreaming he'd slipped off from the fire and got in his blankets. "What's that you say, Will?"

"Aw, nothing," I said. "I was just speculating."

"You don't think Howland and Chico will be back in soon with something to drink and a little news?"

"I wouldn't wait up for 'em," I said.

"But you said they would."

"Oh, hush, Tod," Les said. "Will can't be sure of everything."

"Well, hell! Goddam, I'm getting mighty tired of laying out here on this prairie. I'd like to have gone in myself. Or at least had a drink."

"Will you stop playing the baby? What's the matter with you?"

"I'll tell you what's the matter with me—I'm getting tired of everything got to go your way, Mister Wilson Young.

I'm getting tired of you reading me out every little move I make. Hell, I'm a grown man!"

"Then act like one," I said.

Les's voice was gentler than mine. "It's plain sense, Tod, that you or I or Will can't go into town. If they spotted us it'd stir up a hornet's nest."

"Balls!" Tod said. "We've always moved around this country pretty freely."

"We've never had the rangers on us before, either," I said. "Nor a price on our heads."

"That's just Howland's talk. Besides, I ain't scairt of no rangers."

"Not even a whole company, huh?"

"Oh, balls!" Tod said, and I could hear him shifting around as he turned over in his blankets. After our talk stopped it suddenly made it seem so quiet you could hear your heart beating. Les reached over and poured the dregs out of his cup onto the fire. It made a hiss and a little cloud of blue smoke wafted up.

"You want more coffee?" Les asked me.

"I reckon not," I said.

"Ain't much left, reckon I'll just pour it out. I know Tod don't want no more. I can hear him snoring already."

"I would take one of them little cigars of yours if you can spare it."

"I got plenty."

He handed me one and we lit up and drew on 'em and spit in the fire.

"Let's see," Les said, "when'd we first get to knowing each other? Do you recollect?"

"School or church, I guess. I'm not real sure."

"Naw, I'll tell you when it was, it was in Tod's daddy's store. You and your paw had come in there and I was staying in town that week with Tod's folks and I was in there. You and him come in and Uncle Lester sent you out back to play with us while your daddy got his list up. I know real well 'cause me and Tod was back in the storeroom watching through the door. I remember we run and hid as soon as we seen you coming. You remember that?"

"By God, I do! Lord, that seems ever so long ago. I went out there in the back and didn't see nobody and ya'll was up in that chinaberry tree."

"Yeah, Tod commenced to chunking chinaberries at you when you started back in."

"Damn if it ain't so! I'd forgotten all about that!"

We had a laugh about that and then quieted down after a minute and went back to staring at the fire. It did seem ever so long ago. It didn't even seem like it was me it happened to.

"That's a lot of water under the bridge, ain't it?" I said.

"Yes, yes, it shorely is."

"That Tod, me and him had some scrapes back then."

"Oh Lord, I reckon!"

We got quiet again. I got to thinking about all the times we'd had together. It was funny that we'd ended up in such a rough business together, more funny because it seemed we hadn't really changed that much. Me and Tod had always been at each other's throats when we was kids and now it was still the same. The only difference was that, now, we were grown men and we didn't do our fighting with chinaberries, but with guns. Still, Tod had them early days to thank for his life several times. I'll put up with a hell of a lot more off him and Les than I would from anybody else. He's done things, lots of things, that I'd have killed another man for. Well, I've thrown down on him before, just like at the river, but throwing down is one thing, pulling the trigger is another. I ain't too sure I could do the last.

"Funny," Les said, "Tod used to whip you regular up until we got eleven or twelve or so and then one day you whipped him." He stopped and thought about it. "You whipped him good." He paused and then laughed a little. "Seems like it's been that way ever since."

"Well, Tod . . ." I said.

"I know," Les said. Across the fire I could see him look over in Tod's direction. "You reckon he's asleep?"

"Aw yeah," I said, "else he'd still be complaining about not getting to go into town."

"Yeah," Les said. "Well, Tod—well, he was always a little bit of the bully, I guess."

"He growed faster than you or I," I said.

"Yeah, but I'll tell you what, Will. I'll tell you something maybe you didn't know about old Tod."

"What's that?"

"Well, I kind of think Tod felt bad about being a town boy. Me and you was from the ranch and I think that kind of bothered him. I think it made him feel he was some kind of a sissy, being a town boy."

"Is that right?"

"Maybe that'd be why he kind of had to play the bully and was always showing out and everything."

"Well, he managed to spoil himself pretty good in the process."

"I don't deny that. His daddy always let him have just about anything he wanted. Him and his mother, both."

"Well, that's all done now," I said. A little cold chill had gone through me and I suddenly didn't want to talk about it any more. We'd been sitting there, resting, and having a nice talk about bygone days and I'd been feeling good and then the sudden thought had come into my mind that we were fixing to go in and rob a bank the next day but one. Generally, I don't get too fidgety about a job until I'm actually going in, but then the little thought had come flitting in and kind of grabbed me in the guts. It made me want to quit talking.

"I reckon I'll turn in," I said. "It's getting late."

"Yeah," Les said.

I got up and moved my blankets away from the fire and he did the same. It ain't much of a precaution, but it might buy you a second or two if somebody was to suddenly bushwhack the camp. I went over and laid my saddle against the canyon wall and spread my blankets out. I'd taken off my boots, but that was all, and then pounded me out a hip hole and laid down. The smell of the leather from my saddle come up strong and I laid there thinking about how many times I'd gone to sleep with that smell in my head. Well, I told myself, won't be many more times.

THE BANK ROBBER

After this job we're all through and after that we'll arrange to sleep in a bed once in a while. No more of this hoot-owl trail business.

Then the thought of the job stabbed me in the mind again and it kind of bothered me. I got to halfway wishing we wouldn't do it. But hell, that was silly. I was dead broke. If I didn't pull that job off I'd be in real trouble. There'd be no way I could go into Mexico and make a living on the straight without a little stake of some kind.

That made me kind of smile. Funny, before I'd been saying Canada or Mexico, but somewhere down the trail Canada had kind of lost out.

Then I thought, the hell with all this. I got to get some sleep. I sunk down deeper in my blankets and tried to put everything out of my mind. Sleep was what I needed. Finally I dozed off.

Sometime in the night I heard a little movement. I kind of half raised up, but I couldn't make out who it was, the moon being down. I figured it was Howland Thomas and Chico just getting back and I seen whoever it was settle down in their blankets, so I didn't think no more about it, just went on back to sleep.

CHAPTER 8

The Waterfall

Everybody else was already up the next morning before I finally threw off my blankets. They was all hunkered around the fire drinking coffee. Howland Thomas and Chico was off on one side, talking, while Les and Tod was on the other not saying a word. I went up to the fire and set down and took hold of the coffee can and burned my hand.

"Hot," Howland said.

"Damned if it ain't," I answered.

I got my hat off and used the brim of it for a guard and picked the can up and poured myself a cup. It was hot to the mouth; apparently they'd just made it.

"Well, ya'll didn't beat me up much," I said. "Judging from this coffee."

"Second pot," Howland said.

"Why didn't ya'll call me?"

He grinned at me. "Hell, you looked so peaceful laying there dreaming about them Mexican señoritas that I just didn't have the heart."

I give him a glance. "Yeah? What kept ya'll last night? I thought you was going to bring us back a bottle."

When I said it I was looking right at Howland and as soon as he heard the words he give a little glance over at Tod and Les and then kind of dropped his eyes.

"Well?" I asked. "What about it? Not that I'm too much surprised."

He didn't say anything.

"What's the matter with you, Howland?" He had me perplexed. I couldn't believe he was feeling bad about not bringing us back a little something to drink. "Cat got your tongue?"

He didn't say anything, just glanced over at Les and Tod again.

I looked around at them. Something was in the air, something I couldn't decipher.

"What the hell's going on?" I asked.

They just stared back at me.

"Les? Tod? Chico?"

Nobody said anything. I commenced to get angry. "Listen, what the hell is this? What the hell's going on?"

I looked from face to face, and finally Les turned to Tod. "You gonna tell him, Tod?"

Tod didn't say anything.

"Tell me what?" I prompted. "Somebody better tell me something and damn quick."

Howland laughed, suddenly, loudly, and I slewed around at him. "What the hell's going on, Howland? What the hell is all this?"

He looked over at Tod. "I ain't saying. Ain't none of my affairs."

"By God!" I said.

Les looked at Tod. "Well?"

"Aw . . ." Tod said. "It don't amount to that much. If it was anybody else than Mister Wilson Young."

"All right," Les said. He looked over at me. "Tod went into town last night."

"Tod done what?"

"Went into town. After we got asleep he slipped out and rode into town. Chico and Howland met up with him and made him come back."

"Well I'm a sonofabitch!" I said, marveling that the man could have been such an idiot. "Slipped into town?"

"And he was having himself quite a time when we come up on him," Howland said with a grin. "He had him a bottle in one hand and a dance-hall girl in the other and was helping out the piano player in his spare time. Now if that ain't a good start I don't know what is."

"Well, I'm a sonofabitch!" I said again.

"The hell with all of ya'll!" Tod said. "I wasn't gonna sit out on this prairie and—"

But he got no further, for I suddenly came off my haunches and leapt across the fire and slapped him backhand and forehand across the face. "You goddam fool!" I said and slapped him again. "You goddam blithering idiot!" I slapped him again. The first two had knocked him backward and he was supporting himself with his back-flung arms trying to get up while I was hitting him. "Don't you know you've ruined this job! Don't you know you've caused us to ride eighty miles for nothing!" And I kept hitting him. The slapping wasn't doing him much harm other than to humiliate him a little, but it sure as hell was hurting my hand. Finally I left off and stood over him, my chest heaving. He was down on one hip, up on one arm, with his other hand to his mouth, which was bleeding. Les hadn't said a word. Neither had Chico nor Howland. I stood over him, not quite knowing what to say.

"Slapping's the ticket," Howland said. "He ain't man enough to hit."

I stepped back from Tod and looked at him a second longer. Finally, I went back over to my side of the fire and picked up my cup. I'd set it down so violently when I'd jumped up that most of the coffee had spilled out. I poured myself a little more, my breath still short from either anger or the exertion.

A pause passed and then Howland said: "Yeah, me and Chico come up on him and knowed he oughtn't to be there. We brought him right on back in. On top of it, he didn't want to come." He laughed. I looked over at him, not saying anything until the laugh died.

Tod suddenly got up and walked back toward the box end of the canyon where the horses were. He never said a word, just got up and walked off. I guess he was bad ashamed about what had just happened to him and didn't want to face us no more.

Finally Les said: "Well, what do we do now?"

"Yeah," I said. "That's it, ain't it?"

"Now hold on," Howland said. He got up and walked around the fire and squatted down by me. "What do you mean, 'whata we do?' We go rob us a bank, don't we?" He looked from me to Les and back to me again. "Don't we?"

"I don't know, Howland," I said.

"Listen, didn't nobody recognize that boy. This don't change nothing."

"How you know they didn't? If they seen him they gonna know the rest of us around here somewhere and they gonna put two and two together."

"Oh goddam, Will!" Howland argued. "Ya'll ain't all that famous. You're seeing buggers under the bedstid, I tell you. Didn't nobody recognize Tod. Hell, he wasn't in there a good hour."

"How do you know that?"

"He said so."

"Sure. That's proof. Anyway, an hour's long enough."

We kept arguing. Howland doing most of the talking and me and Les not saying much. Chico didn't say anything either, but that was his natural way. Tod wandered back up and squatted down and listened to us carving up his carcass like he wasn't even there.

"Listen," Howland said, "we've rode a hell of a long ways and done a power of planning for this thing. I ain't to be done out of it, you hear me?"

"I hear you," I said. "Are you saying you'll go ahead without us? Just you and Chico?"

"Hell, you know that ain't no two-man job, Will. Are you saying it's all off?"

"I ain't said that yet," I admitted. "I'm thinking about it."

And indeed I was, though thinking wasn't the best handle for it. It was more like I was caught in two loops and being pulled first this way and then that. I tell you, my first reaction had been one of relief. I'd thought: well, we can't do it now. It's all off and I ain't got to go in there now and

96

take that risk which I've been having a bad feeling about.

But then, the other way, I was thinking that now I'd miss out on that stake and wouldn't be able to set up in Mexico and hunt down that girl (which, until that moment, I hadn't even let myself really believe I was considering) and that we'd have to ride out as broke as we come in. Maybe if I didn't get this job pulled and get a good stake I'd just never quit, but would just go on the way I'd been headed, getting more and more trashy and stooping to all kinds of low things.

"Well?" Howland asked me. "Are you thinking?"

"Not too well," I said, "with you jabbering in my ear."

"Leave off a minute, Howland," Les said, "and let Will put his mind to it."

"Well, balls!" Howland said in disgust and got up and walked away a few feet. "What is there to think about? I done told you they ain't nothing to this town. Anyway, didn't nobody recognize that boy. Hell!"

"Listen," I said, "this place ain't a hundred miles from Carrizo Springs, and wasn't it you that told us we was wanted for a killing and that there was a price on our heads and that they had the rangers after us? Wasn't you the very one that told us that?"

"Well, I wouldn't have told you if I'd thought it would spook you so bad." He walked away a few feet further and stood staring up at the canyon walls.

Les looked over at me. "What do you think, Will?"

But before I could answer, we heard a halloo from the top of the canyon. Looking up, we could see a rider sitting his horse and staring down at us.

"Hello, the fire," he yelled.

We all stood up, slowly, staring at him. Howland came backing toward us, his eyes riveted on the rider.

"Goddam," he said lowly to me, "that fool kid's brought a hornet's nest down on our ears."

"Everybody just take it easy," I said. "Just take it easy. Maybe it ain't nothing." I put my hands to my mouth and called to the rider. "Come on down. We got coffee." He seemed to hesitate for just a second, but then turned his pony and began to urge him down the steep decline to our camp.

"Just take it real easy," I said to everybody. "Don't nobody do nothing rash."

CHAPTER 9

Kid White

The rider came slowly down the canyon slide, guiding his horse expertly, until he'd reached the floor. I pointed toward the box. "Put your horse back there and come up to the fire for some coffee."

"Much obliged," he said as he rode by us, us watching him like hawks.

"Keep an eye skinned up top," I said, "in case he's got friends right behind him."

I watched the rider go down to our little corral, ride his horse inside and dismount. He loosened the cinch strap, but didn't remove the saddle. While I watched he stood there, one hand patting his own horse, and looked ours over. It seemed that he paid particular attention to the black that Tod had stole. The animal was standing in such a way that his hip brand wasn't evident. And the rider, instead of coming straight to the gate, walked out a little, so it seemed, as to bring the other side of Tod's animal into his view. He didn't linger after that, but came out of the corral and toward the fire.

"Take some coffee," I told him as he came up. "There's a cup there."

"Much obliged," he said. He squatted down and poured himself up a cup of the brew. "I seen your smoke about a mile away. Thought I'd ride over."

"Yeah?" I said. "You got good eyes." The fire wasn't smoking.

He looked up at me and grinned, exposing a row of blackened and broken teeth. "Yeah, got good eyes."

He was a short, stumpy little man with jet-black eyes and, from what I could see of it that stuck out from under his hat, jet-black hair as well. From the looks of his nose, which was broken and crooked, he'd either run into a lot of barn doors or done a lot of fighting. But what particularly took my eye was the gun rigging he had strapped to his right side. It wasn't the casual rigging of the cowboy that carries a gun for rattlesnakes and pot shooting, but the set-up of a man that figured to have to put it to use in a hurry. I took his gun to be a 34.40 on a .44 frame, which is a very popular model with many gunmen, it being heavy enough to give good balance in the hand, yet of a small enough caliber to give good accuracy while furnishing guaranteed stopping power. The holster and belt were both old, but well cared for and oiled. I judged the man to be in his middle forties, maybe less, maybe more. It was hard to tell, for his face was like old leather, browned and rough and lined.

We were all still standing there, staring down at him, and he finally looked up at us, grinned a crooked grin, and asked if we wouldn't have a chair.

"Much obliged," I said, mimicking him.

I squatted and helped myself to coffee. Les sat down too, but Howland and Chico walked off a few steps, Howland still watching the stranger narrowly. Tod had already sat, a little behind and to the right of the stranger. This seemed to bother him, for, after giving several quick glances back toward the redhead, he kind of sidled around until he'd come even with him. He apparently didn't want nobody behind him.

"Been coming far?" I asked, which is polite enough question since a man can answer it as vaguely as he wants to. He can say, "Not too," or "some," or "just a little piece," and that don't really give away none of his business.

But our guest give me the grin again, over the top of his coffee cup, and said: "Just from town."

"What town?" Les asked him.

"Uvalde. Didn't know they was any others around here."

"Wouldn't know," I said. "We're strangers. Just riding through."

He grinned at me again and didn't say anything. I looked at him, gauging him, trying to figure him out. A gunfighter does not squat to a fire like a cowboy. A cowboy squats on two legs, but a pistolero, depending if he's right-handed, only squats on his left leg. He keeps the other straight, bringing his knee straight down in the dust, so as to give him quick access to his weapon. Also, a pistolero does not use his right hand for much other than the business of guns. Our stranger was squatting one-legged and holding the coffee can with his left hand.

"Pretty good slug of ashes," he said, "for just one campfire. You did say you was just riding through, didn't you?"

"That's right," I said. "Maybe somebody else camped here just before."

We was both watching each other like a roadrunner and a rattlesnake. I'm sure he'd taken note of my rigging set-up and come to some conclusions of his own.

"Thoughtful of 'em, wasn't it, to haul up all these good cooking rocks?"

"Yeah," I said.

Howland took a step toward the fire, but I glanced over at him and give him a hard look. His bluster and temper might get us in a spot I wasn't ready for.

We were quiet for a moment and then the stranger said: "Whose horse is that out back? The black with the white stocking."

Well, he was pressing, but I didn't know for what. "Why, you want to buy him?"

He was still wearing that crooked, insulting grin. I felt like slapping it off his face. He said: "Well, no, but I bet a man could get a good price on him."

"Why's that?" I asked.

He looked at me for a second and then let his grin go bigger and ducked his head in his coffee cup.

"Why's that?" I asked him again. I knew what he was getting at.

"Oh, nothing," he said. " 'Cept that horse is carrying the same brand as mine. B bar B."

"Now looka here," Tod began, but I cut him off.

"Shut up, Tod!"

I looked back at the stranger. "Mister, what are you after? What's your game?"

Suddenly Howland stepped forward. "Yeah! Who the hell you think you are come riding in here asking questions like you was a schoolteacher? Listen, I'll tell you that—"

"Shut up!" I said to Howland. "Let this here man talk."

But he didn't, not right away, just sat there sipping at his coffee and watching us over the rim of his cup. Finally he took a long sip and set the cup down. "Mighty good coffee."

"Glad you like it," I said. "Now what about this horse? You work for B bar B?"

"Did," he said.

"When?"

"Spell back."

"What are you doing with one of their horses?"

"Took him for a month's wages, maybe. Maybe not. Maybe I stole him."

I stood up, slowly, watching my man carefully. "Tod," I said, "go out there and take a look at this man's horse. See if the brands match."

"Oh, they do right enough," he said cheerfully.

Tod was looking at me questioningly. "Go ahead," I said. I turned back to the stranger. "Now you better get your mouth to moving and I better like what you say. What business is it of yours about that black out there?"

"Why, none," he said. "Except I seen him in town last night and kind of followed them fellows out." He indicated Chico and Howland. "And that one you sent back there. That redheaded feller."

"Keep going," I said.

"Why, I don't mind telling you all about me," he said reasonably. "Considering I know all about you."

He let the last drop like a rock down a well. It took me

off-balance for a minute. Finally, I said: "Okay, who are you? What's your name?"

He grinned and stood up. "Billy Blanco."

"Billy Blanco?"

"I'm darned!" Howland said right behind me. "Kid White!"

"The same!" Bill Blanco said.

That brought it back to me. Kid White was an old-time desperado who'd done just about every lowdown thing there was to do. It was said that he was a fair hand with a gun, but had much rather get a man from behind. I'd never seen him before, but I'd heard about him off and on. How he'd run up on us was something I couldn't figure.

"Simple," he said. "Let me git me another cup of coffee and I'll tell you about it."

It seemed that he had been wandering around Uvalde the night before and he'd spotted Tod's horse. Having worked for B bar B up until a few days back, he'd been a little curious about the horse and its rider, especially in view of the fact that he'd made off with one of their animals himself. He'd waited around until he'd seen Tod and Chico and Howland come out and mount up and then had followed them back to our camp. At daylight he'd slipped up and give us all a good looking over and had recognized me. Seeing us had interested him powerfully because he'd been so down on his luck of late that he'd even had to take a job of ranch work, "just to tide me over, you unnerstan," and he'd seen us and pretty well figured we was up to something. He said he was wide open.

"I'm game for anything," he said.

I didn't like him. Didn't like him at all. "Well, Kid," I said, "I hate to disappoint you, but we ain't got a thing working. Like I said, we're just passing through. On our way up to north Texas."

He looked at me narrowly. "But you been laying over here two days."

"That's right," I said. "We was tired."

"Say, Wilson," Howland said, "let me speak with you a minute." He was backing away from the fire, crooking his finger for me to follow him. I knew what he wanted. I knew he'd recognized one of his own kind. But I followed him. I might as well let him have his say.

We got a little piece away from the fire and he began urging me to take Kid White in with us.

"No," I said. "I won't do it."

"Well, that's crazy. He's a good gun hand."

"The money's split up enough as it is. No more." Of course that wasn't the reason. I just didn't like the looks of the Kid.

Howland gave me a look. He was unshaved and his eyes was kind of red-rimmed from being up late and drinking the night before. "Well, what will you do with him then? He knows we're up to something and you can't just let him ride out of here. Even if he would." He added the last like it was a kind of threat.

But he had a point about what to do with the Kid. He knew me, had recognized us all, and had probably figured out what we was doing laying out in the boondocks.

"I'll worry about that," I said.

"Well, he's here now." He looked at me, letting the point he'd made hang.

"I know that," I said. "I ain't gone blind."

"Well, what are you gonna do? I think he'd be a help."

"Howland, you want to let me run this?" We sat there, facing each other. It was a face down. Finally he broke, not much, but he give in.

"You supposed to be running it," he said, a little lamely. He give in, grudgingly. I didn't like the way he was taking it. Somewhere along the line, since the Kid had rode in, it had become generally understood that we was going ahead and go through with the holdup. I hadn't remembered agreeing to any such thing, but suddenly it seemed like it had all been decided. I somehow felt it had been decided within myself. I somehow felt that I'd agreed within myself that I'd do it, that I'd do it for that girl. Somehow it had got to that in my mind. It didn't make a bit of sense. That girl would despise me for what I was about to do, but I somehow had to do it in order to get back to her. I had to get the stake to set up so I could come up to her like I was somebody myself. It began to seem like it was all lies and cheating. Everything seemed that way. I began to feel bad again.

We walked back over to where the Kid was squatting. Tod had come back and he looked up at me, a little frightened, and said that the brands were the same. "That's all right," I said. "I figured it."

"I told you," the Kid said.

I squatted down by him. "Look here, Kid, we ain't gonna pull nothing. It's like I told you, we're riding for north Texas in a little bit."

"I'll come along," he said.

I looked at him carefully. "Well, I didn't know that you'd been asked." I could see what he was. He was an old has-been, out of luck, that had lost all his pride and wanted in on just one more good job. He wanted that one last chance. I could see it was going to be a little harder than I'd figured. A man that has lost his pride is hard to deal with. I reached down and slapped a little dust off my breeches, waiting for him to answer.

He grinned that crooked grin of his. He didn't know he'd lost his pride. "Well, maybe I'm inviting myself in. What do you say to that?"

"I say it won't wash," I said. "We don't have a thing planned."

He give me that goddam grin again and I wanted to up and hit him. I was already a little mad. I felt angry about the corner the situation seemed to be putting me in. He kept giving me that goddam grin like he knew everything we were planning. The old bastard didn't know he was through. Looking at him, I could see what I'd missed at first glance, that there were gray hairs among the jet-black strands that were sticking out from under his hat. His unshaven beard gave him away, for a beard will show a man's age much quicker than his hair. Hell, he wasn't in his mid-forties, he was in his mid-fifties.

"You're after that bank in Uvalde," he said. He said it flatly, like he'd been reading our mail.

"Who told you that?" I could feel that icy chill settling over me.

"A man with one eye could see it."

"Well, maybe you're blind," I said carefully. "You've had coffee, now why don't you go ahead and cinch up and ride out." I said the last coldly and deliberately.

He was still drinking our coffee. He never even put the cup down, just kept sucking at it like a baby after a sugar tit. "I reckon not," he said.

Back when me and Tod and Les was kids there'd been an old dog that used to follow us along when we went fishing or swimming. I never knew whose dog it was, but he was some kind of retriever or something. When we went swimming we didn't mind that old dog along, but when we was fishing we'd try to run him off because he'd jump in the water and swim after the boat and scare the fish. We'd try to run him off by throwing rocks at him, but it wouldn't work. Somebody had taught that old dog to retrieve whatever was thrown and he'd just watch that rock that was sailing through the air, dodge it, and then chase it like we'd thrown it out for his pleasure. We used to wear our arms out throwing at that old dog until we learned better. Finally, one day, Tod shot him. All the rest of that summer we could see him rotting down there by the lake. Finally the ants and the sun finished him off and all we could see was his white bones gleaming in the sun. I always felt bad about that old dog. He wasn't a bad dog; he just didn't understand that he didn't fit in. I never much liked Tod shooting him. I reckon that old dog had been along on so many duck hunts and what not that he automatically figured he ought to come along any time the boat set out. Tod oughtn't to have shot him, but he did.

"You may reckon not, but I reckon." I was starting to get angry. I stood there staring down at him, still idly slapping the dust out of my breeches. The old man was starting to give me a bad feeling. The whole job had me a little spooked, what with it being my last and all, and I was beginning to get the feeling he might be bad luck. I don't generally think that way, but that was what was coming in my head. Besides, I'm damn careful about the men I ride with. Can't just anybody get in on a job I'm gonna pull.

He still hadn't give me an answer when I'd told him I'd reckoned he'd better move along. The way he was just sitting there, staring down at the ground with that crooked grin of his, was starting to give me the willies. First there'd been that business with Tod slipping into town and now this old clod shows up. I was really beginning to feel spooked about the job. I turned around and walked over to where Howland was and motioned him back a few more feet. "Go on into town," I said, "and see if everything looks all right. If it does you go into the bank and cipher me out a little drawing of just where everything in that bank sits. Can you do that?"

"Shore," Howland said. "But what are you gonna do about him?" He gave Kid White a little nod.

"I'll tend to him in a minute," I said. "First, I want to see if there looks to be anything stirring in that town. You look damn sharp, you hear me?"

Les walked over to me just as Howland made for the corral. He'd been listening all the while to the talk between the Kid and I without saying anything.

"Will, that old man didn't just come out here on account of that B bar B horse. He knowed something before he came."

"I know it," I said. "Or at least I figured it. Let's go talk to him some more." We walked back over to the Kid and I squatted down in front of him. He'd helped himself to another cup of coffee.

"Looka here," I said, "you said you come out here on account of that horse. That ain't so, is it?"

He give me that grin again and didn't say anything.

"You come out here because you knowed something was up. Now ain't that so?"

"It might be," he admitted.

"Well, how about telling me what made you think that?" I looked at him and waited. "Now listen," I said, "if you don't get that goddam grin off your face and quit sittin' there lookin' like a dawg sucking eggs, I'm gonna run you right off."

"I heard talk," he said. "Then I seen that feller." He half

turned and pointed toward Tod with his chin. "I recognized him and knew he rode with you. They's a dodger out on all of ya'll, you know, for that little job over in Carrizo."

"I'd heard," I said dryly.

"Fifteen hundred on you," he said. "Five hundred on these Richter boys, apiece."

"Well, what'd you mean talk? Just general talk? Or did somebody else recognize Tod, that redheaded boy over there?"

"Oh, the talk I heard was from them two. That one that rode out and that Mex out there." Chico had walked back to the corral and was tending to the horses. That was probably the reason the Kid hadn't wanted to talk before in front of Howland and Chico. I was dumbfounded.

"What were they saying? Were they saying we was gonna pull something in Uvalde?"

"Not straight out like that," the Kid said. "They was in the saloon and I was sittin' pretty near to them and the little Mex kept complaining about why they hadn't done a job in Mexico, and this other'n, that one that rode out, went to laughing and saying it was because you wanted to be nice down there. Said you had something for some little señorita and didn't want to upset her. Said she'd made you promise you'd allus come to the States to do your dirt."

I looked over at Les. "Did they call me by name?"

"Called you Mister Young. But then that redheaded one come in and I put two and two together. Wadn't hard."

"I reckon not," I said slowly. Well, things had come to a hell of a pass. A man would be a fool now to go in and try to rob that bank. I looked back to the Kid. "Reckon anybody else recognized Tod?"

He shook his head. "They didn't let on if they did," he said.

I stood up. "Well, much obliged. We'll be eating in a little. Whyn't you stick around and take a meal with us?"

"I'd appreciate that," he said.

I walked away, then, to the shady side of the canyon and sat down to think. Les came along and sat down with me. He didn't say a word, but handed me a cigar and got out a match for us. We lit up and I sat there thinking. It was going to be a hell of a job to figure out.

A little before evening Howland came riding back in. He passed Les and me where we were still sitting, giving us a grin and a little salute, and went on back to the corral and turned his horse in with the others. When he came back to us he sat down and took off his hat and got a little piece of paper out of the sweatband and handed it to me.

"There it is," he said. "As pretty a piece of handdrawing as you'll ever want to see. Got everything all laid out."

I just took it, didn't look at it, looked at him instead. "Yes," I said, "you've got everything laid out. Including us."

"What's that supposed to mean?"

"That means you got a big mouth and you done a lot of talking in town last night." I was mad and didn't care if he knew it.

"Now hold on there, Wilson," he said, his face flushing. "I don't take that kind of talk from nobody."

"Well," I said, "that'd be your choice, wouldn't it?" I eyed him steadily.

"Say, what is this? I just rode in here and all of a sudden you're jumping me. Mind telling me why?"

"Well," I said, "it's been relayed to me what you had to say in the saloon last night. About how come I didn't want to pull no job in Mexico. Said I had me a señorita wouldn't let me. Said I had to come to Texas to do my work." I was biting off each word and staring at him, hard.

"Never said no such thing!" he avowed. "And any man says I did is a liar!"

"Then you better take it up with the Kid." I stood up and called to Billy Blanco, who was still over by the fire finishing up a plate of beans.

"What's up?" he asked, walking toward us with a kind of rolling gait that made me think he was more sailor than horseman.

"Man says you're a liar," I told him. "Says he wasn't doing no talking in town last night."

The grin suddenly vanished from Billy's face. He kind

of scratched his chin for a second and then, almost unnoticeably, stepped back a pace or two. "I'd say any man that said that is more liar than me."

"What's that?" Howland asked sharply. "You calling me a liar?"

"If that's how it sounded," the Kid said. "You can take it for that." He was standing there so relaxed he looked almost sleepy. But that slumped, hunched-over stance didn't fool me any. I could see he knew his business. Maybe he was old, but he still knew his business.

Behind me, Les said: "Don't let this go too far, Will."

"It's done gone too far," Howland said, bristling up. He was getting mighty brave all of a sudden.

I turned at him. "You still deny you said that?"

"Damn right!" Howland said.

I looked at him a minute longer. I knew who was doing the lying and it wasn't the Kid. "I ought to let him kill you," I said, but then turned to Billy. "Cinch up," I told him. "It's all done. Ain't gonna be no shooting and ain't gonna be no bank robbery. You might as well ride out."

He looked at me. "This man called me a liar."

"He knows who done the lying," I said. "Let it slide and ride out."

"No," he said.

"Yeah, Billy, go on."

"I'm pulling that job with you."

"Goddamit! I told you there wasn't going to be any job."

"Listen"—and his voice sounded almost pleading—"I'm down on my luck. I need a break. Let me come along, I ain't asking for a regular share."

God, he was giving me the willies. The whole goddam job was giving me the willies. I wanted him gone. "They ain't gonna be no job. We're breaking up and I'm riding for Mexico. I've had it. Now cinch up."

"No," he said.

Well, we were back to throwing rocks at the old retriever again. He'd made so many hunts he didn't know when to quit. He'd just watch the rock, dodge it, and chase it, and then come back for more.

"I'm a damn good gun hand," he said. "A damn good one." He was pressing, pressing real hard. I could see the want on his face.

"Billy, cinch up. This is my last time to tell you."

"Let me fight this feller. I can still go. I'll prove it. I know I'm getting old, but I can still go."

"No," I said.

"Hell," Howland said viciously. "Let him. I'll kill him if he fools with me."

"No," I said.

Then I didn't know quite what happened or how. Suddenly the Kid was backing up and suddenly his hand was going down. It was instinct after that. I pulled and shot him before he ever got his piece all the way out of his holster. The bullet took him mid-chest and he kind of gasped and then flipped backward.

"Goddam!" Les yelled.

I stood there, stunned at what I'd done. I'd never thought, I'd never considered. I'd never had no idea the old fool was really going to draw. But he had and I'd killed him.

When we got to him he wasn't quite dead, but he was going fast. He kept making faces against the pain and trying to say something. He never got the words out. A little bubble of blood come up on his lips and he sighed and then just kind of relaxed.

"Well, you've killed him," Howland said matter-of-factly.

"Yeah," I said. I got up and walked away toward the end of the canyon. I was feeling real bad.

I sat down there by the far canyon wall a long, long time. Dusk came and dark and the boys gathered around the campfire and went to eating. Every once in a while they'd give a little look off in my direction, but nobody came near me. I could hear the sound of their voices, kind of murmuring and low. I couldn't make out any words, but then I wasn't trying. I was just sitting there feeling bad and trying to make out what ought to be done.

The moon got up good and went to crossing the sky and I still sat there. I had a little makings with me and I rolled first one cigarette and then another and smoked 'em. I'd put my gun back in the holster, but I could sure feel its weight at my side. I tell you I was feeling miserable. I wondered if old Kid White had had much fun in his life. I wondered if he'd got his hands on most of the things he'd wanted. But then, I guess a man never does. There'd been the Kid, still wanting, wanting to go with us. Hell, he should have known when to quit. He should have known he was through. Why in hell had he had to go on like some old dog that doesn't know he ain't wanted until some kid in the prow of a rowboat sticks his daddy's carbine out and shoots him?

A man ought to know when to quit. He ought to go to searching for a little something better before it's too late.

I kept sitting there, trying to sort out what it all meant. Finally I became aware I'd stuck Howland's drawing down in my belt. I got it out and smoothed it on my knee and took a look at it by the light of the moon. It looked like something a schoolchild might do, but it showed everything in the bank right enough. I kept staring down at it, trying to concentrate.

The old fool had gotten so slow he hadn't even had a chance. He'd drawn first and I still got him before his gun cleared leather. That's slow, even fast as I am, that's still real slow. Hell, even Tod could have killed him.

The old fool hadn't known when to quit. He'd stood there slouching like he knew his business and that was right enough; he just didn't have nothing left to go with the knowing. He'd got down so far that he'd had to come to begging to go along on a job. That was a sorry comedown for a man. Not that I'd really known much about the Kid. I'd heard of him a few times, but he was considerably older than me and past his prime while I was coming up. He'd been just a name I'd heard every once in a while, in this saloon or that. Cattle rustler, bank robber, the whole sly game, and now he'd come down to begging.

The funny thing was, I didn't know if he was funning, meaning to show me how fast he was, intent on killing Howland, meaning to kill me, or what. All I'd known was

I'd seen a man standing in front of me go for his gun and I'd pulled and killed him.

Across the way I could see the boys turning in and settling down. Les stood, looking my way, undecided about coming out. Finally he went on to bed himself. He knows me well enough and knows there's times I want to be alone.

Well, the old fool should have known when to quit. He brought it on himself. A man that's on this dodge has got to get his while he can and then get out with some of it. This kind of life ain't no good over a long stretch of time. A man needs a good woman and a place, a few roots.

I suddenly got up and walked over to the fire.

"Listen to me!" I said loudly. Heads raised out of blankets.

"We're going in, in the morning. We gonna hit that bank. Let's be up at first light and I'll lay it out for you."

"Now you're talking!" Howland said.

I looked over at the direction of his voice. "Shut up, Howland," I said. "You've done enough talking."

CHAPTER 10

The Cattleman's National Bank

The bank opened at eight o'clock and we were there a little bit before. I had us come in by ones and twos in order not to attract much attention. There was a little alley right behind the bank that opened out on the street and I made that our rendezvous. We would go in the front door, then duck out the side and down the alley where Les would be waiting with the horses.

"Let me go in the bank with you," Les had said.

"No. I want a good man holding those horses. We may have to leave in a hurry."

Me and Howland and Chico would go in the front door while Tod come in the side door just after we'd entered. Howland would see to getting the money while I stood by the front door, covering anybody in the bank with Chico just to my left and helping.

There didn't seem to be a soul on the streets. Up the block a storekeeper was sweeping the dust off his windows and a drunk was laying in front of the saloon, but that was all.

We eased into the alley, dismounted, and then Howland, Chico and I set off up the boardwalk with Tod just a step or two behind. Howland would go in first, then me, then Chico. Behind me I could hear a low word from Les. I looked back and he give me a little salute. He was mounted on his black gelding holding the rest of the horses well back in the alley where they couldn't be seen too easy.

We passed the side door and Tod dropped off. He'd lounge around until he seen us go in, then he'd slip in himself. He was supposed to help cover and make sure the side door didn't get jammed up.

It was about five minutes after eight and we figured to be the first customers. Saturday mornings most folks don't start showing up in town until a little later. I wasn't worried about it being quiet; we'd figured it that way.

I paused at the door and looked at Howland and Chico. "All set?"

"Sure," Howland said. "Let's get on with it. Me and Chico's okay."

I didn't know if I was okay myself or not. I felt odd, not at all the way I usually do. Usually I feel pretty tense, but right then I was feeling kind of dead inside. I wasn't nervous and excited inside the way I usually am.

"Well," I said, "let's go." Howland took hold of the door handle, opened the door and stepped inside. I took a deep breath and followed. Just as I stepped through the door it seemed that I thought of the girl.

The bank was exactly as Howland had drawn it. Straight ahead and to the left was a long L-shaped counter that run from the back wall and then cut over and connected to the side wall. It had two high, barred tellers' cages. Just behind that was a couple of offices and what I took to be the main safe. It was closed and locked.

Tod stepped through the side door just as me and Chico got spread out. We still hadn't drawn a gun.

There wasn't but one man that we could see behind the counter. He was, I reckoned, a teller, being in one of the cages. He was a young blond-headed feller, kind of tall and thin, wearing armbands. Howland walked up to him and leaned on the counter. I was roving my eyes over the back trying to spot any movement.

"I'd like to make a withdrawal," Howland said. He was kind of lounging on the counter, grinning. He seemed to be enjoying it.

The clerk looked nervous. "Wha-what name, sir?"

"Get on with it, Howland," I said sharply.

Howland grinned over at me, his face saying: "See, what'd I tell you? A real cracker box."

The clerk asked him again what name and Howland grinned and pulled his revolver.

"Colonel Colt," he said, "and I'll take it all."

I don't know what it was that bothered me, maybe the nervous way the clerk had of turning his head and kind of looking to the side and down. Whatever it was I got a yell out just before all hell broke loose.

"Let's git!" I yelled and went low and began to back for the front door.

Then it happened. I didn't get a straight count, but what looked to be five men suddenly came up from behind the counter and began blasting left and right. I snapped off a quick shot, felt something tear at my neck and then kicked out backward, knocked the door open, and scuttled through still shooting.

Poor Chico never had a chance. He was wrong placed. Just as I went through the door I got a little side glimpse out of my eye of a big ranger raised up behind the counter and letting Chico have it with both barrels of a double-barreled shotgun. The blast knocked him all the way to the wall.

Howland's luck was in that he was standing so close to the ambush that they couldn't get a clear shot of him right off. He dropped to the floor and scuttled across like a crab and went out the side door. He was coming out just as I came tearing around the corner running for the alley. Tod was running beside him, but I noticed the redhead had a big red splotch on the back of his shirt. As I dashed by the side door I snapped off a couple of quick shots to slow anybody up that might be coming. By then I was almost deafened by the boom of the gunfire inside the bank. I don't know how many shots were let off inside, but it had seemed like one continuous explosion.

Les had come out of the alley leading the horses. He'd heard the gunfire and knew something was wrong. Howland got to his animal first and mounted up and then began firing back toward the bank. Les had his rifle out and was shooting over Tod's and my head as we came running toward them. I heard gunfire behind me and saw one of the horses Les was holding suddenly scream and rear and then began pitching around. It was the black Tod had stole.

I came up on Tod just then and, as I started to pass him, he seemed to kind of stumble. He was blowing mighty hard for the little run we'd made. I put out an arm, steadied him, and then scrambled for my mare and swung in the saddle. Les threw my reins to me. My pistol was empty, but I carry a spare in my saddlebags and I jerked that out and began firing. A man was kneeling at the corner of the bank, firing at us, and I held my revolver in both hands, steadied against the movement of my little mare, and shot him in the knee. He let out a yell and fell backward. Out of the corner of my eye I could see Tod clutching at his saddle horn trying to mount up. He was trying to get on Chico's horse and the animal was cutting around and turning pretty bad. I seen him get a foot in the stirrup and I yelled: "Let's git! Ride!"

We wheeled and started thundering up the street. Howland was out in the lead, then Les, then me and Tod was somewhere behind. I shot a quick glance behind and seen something was wrong with him. He was slumped over in the saddle, one hand kind of hanging down, and the horse was running sideways, spooked and frightened by the noise and the blood. I wheeled my little mare back, firing toward the bank as I went, for men were starting to tumble out the doors, and came up alongside Tod. I tried to support him in the saddle and get hold of his reins at the same time, but I couldn't handle it. He was limp, like he was bad hit, and his horse was jumping around so bad I couldn't get hold of a lead. I jammed my revolver back in my holster, intending to make a grab for the horse's halter and then, suddenly, Les was there. He came up to the front of the horse, grabbed the reins and then turned on lead and spurred us up the road. I rode alongside, holding Tod in the saddle, and we went up the street, bent low and spurring, while the bullets just whistled around our ears. Howland was at the end of the street, rifle in hand, firing cover for us.

"Hit it!" I yelled at him as we come up to him.

We went down the road, Howland out in front and me and Les back with Tod, raising a cloud of dust you could see for a mile. After a little Howland cut off the road and started south across prairie. We swung right in behind him. I was still alongside Tod, supporting him as best I could, and quirting my little mare with my free hand. Les was strung out on that big black of his, leaning forward with one arm flung backward pulling that horse of Chico's along, making him run faster than he'd ever thought he could go. Les took a quick look back and hollered something.

"What?" I yelled at him.

He shot me back another quick yell. "Here they come!"

I looked back and sure enough I could see a little cloud of dust leaving town and coming at a kind of angle up on our right. I couldn't see how many men it was, but they couldn't have got too big a party together right away.

Well, we was in a fix and no mistake. With a wounded man slowing us down we just couldn't make the time we might of. And then we generally depend on a quick raid and then figure to get away in the confusion and build up a big lead before any posse can get organized.

But they'd been ready for us and, what was worse, they was even more ready for the chase. It was looking bad.

We tore along over the rolling land, mesquite and cactus and sagebrush tearing at our legs. Tod was acting worse, hardly giving me any help at all in keeping him in the saddle. I didn't know how bad he was hit. Hell, I got to thinking, he might be dead already. But just then he kind of moved his hand and took a clutch on the saddle horn. He was alive, but looked to be bad hurt.

Behind us, the chase party had seen they couldn't head us and they'd swung in and laid into our trail. They appeared to be a half mile or so back, but I knew that we couldn't keep up the pace. The country we were dashing through is terribly rough on a horse and we'd been running them hard for near four miles. Already I could hear my little mare beginning to struggle for breath. We had to do something and no mistake. Ahead and off to our left I could see a clump of trees with a little draw down in front. A few rocks scattered around might give us some cover. I yelled at Les and he looked back.

"We got to fort up!" I yelled. He nodded, understanding, and I waved my arm toward the trees. He looked, saw what I meant, and then began angling toward it. It was still a good three quarters of a mile away.

Howland was well out in front and I yelled at him as loud as I could, but he couldn't hear me. I hadn't expected him to. He'd see what we were up to. He'd have to swing back, but he could manage.

We pounded along, closing on the trees. I watched Howland and he finally looked back. I pointed and he understood. He had to sweep his horse around in a big arc, being nearly even with the trees himself. We closed on the cover, us coming in from one direction, Howland from another. Behind I heard a faint rifle report. Somebody was showing out because they wasn't going to hit anybody at the distance we had on them. I looked back and seen that the posse had made up a little ground on us. It was going to be a near thing, but I figured we'd have time enough to get in among the rocks and get cover before they came up to us.

Just then, Howland's horse stepped in a gopher hole. It was a bad fall, the horse going near into a somersault. Howland was thrown clear, but he landed hard on his chest and face. I yelled at Les and he pulled back and got hold of Tod. Chico's horse was running all right now, so there was really no need to rein-lead him. I looped the reins around the saddle horn so the horse wouldn't trip over them, then cut away and went to aid Howland. He was up on one knee by the time I got there. His face was all cut up and scratched and the shirt was nearly tore away from his chest, but I could see that he was generally all right. I skidded to a stop by him, flung myself off, pulling out my carbine as I did and got down behind his downed mount. The poor animal had broken two legs. He kept trying to rear up, not knowing in his dumbness that he'd never get up again. I put a quick bullet between his eyes.

Howland was standing straight up, a kind of dazed look

on his face. I grabbed him by the shoulder and shoved him for the trees. "Run!" I yelled at him. "Run!" He was near out on his feet, but he finally took off in a kind of stumbling lope. He only had a hundred yards, maybe a little better to go.

I turned my attention to the chase party. There appeared to be six of them and they didn't seem to be aware of me. They seen Howland making for the trees and they bore down on him, riding along off to my right. I got a lead on the first rider and squeezed off a shot. The big Henry slug knocked him out of the saddle like he'd been clotheslined. I made the shot at a distance of about three hundred yards, which is no mean feat at a moving target. I got off another shot, but missed the second rider and then they became aware of me. Two riders split off and came barreling directly at me, firing as they came. Well, they wasn't going to hit me, down behind Howland's horse as I was, but my little mare was standing, like the good horse she is, just behind me, and they might hit her. I hated to do it, but I put the sights on the breastplate of the lead rider's horse and dropped the animal. The bullet just cut the legs out from under the pony and sent the rider flipping over its head and tumbling through the sagebrush. Well, that give the second man pause, and he made to wheel around and light out, but I got him just as he came about. I didn't hit him solid. He went over the side of his saddle and then come clawing his way back up, riding slumped over and low. He took out the way he'd come, his horse running crazy like an animal will with a rider shifting and lurching around in the saddle.

Meanwhile Les was putting down a good fire on the other three riders and they were milling around trying to get off a shot about a hundred yards short of the trees. Just as I looked Howland made it to cover with little puffs of dust kicking up around his feet. It was time for me to make cover myself. I mounted up and laid a few shots into the group. It was a long distance and my little mare was jumping around so I wasn't too accurate, but one of the riders suddenly went down. I didn't know if it was me or Les who'd got him. I figured it was probably Les. Well, that was the chance I was waiting for. I put spurs to my mare and made a bee-line for the trees. I was riding low in the saddle. I'd emptied my Henry, so I'd stuck that in the boot and had my revolver in my hand. Suddenly I felt something strike me hard in the left thigh. For a second I thought it might be a mesquite branch whipping up, but just then I heard the report. Off to my left, sitting down with his leg stuck out in front of him and holding a revolver with both hands, was the rider whose horse I'd dropped. I'd forgotten all about him. As I looked I saw smoke puff from his gun, then heard the boom and then the lead sang over my head. My thigh was hurting like hell. I looked down. Blood was soaking through my breeches leg. The sonofabitch had shot me!

I wheeled my mare toward him, riding low in the saddle and aiming at his chest along my horse's neck. I saw the puff again, trying to get my sights lined on him. I was gonna kill the bastard. Then, he was standing up, awkwardly, one leg at a strange angle, and I figured he'd broke it in the fall. I came on. He was still holding the pistol pointed at me, but then he drew it back as if he'd throw it when I got in range. He was out of cartridges. I came on, waiting until I was at a sure range and then fired. I got him point-blank in the chest and he went over backward. I fired again and then almost rode over him, swerving my little mare at the last second.

Then I was riding for the trees. The remaining two men had had all they wanted and they was back a good ways. They tried a couple of shots at me, but they was too far to be effective and I raced into the little circle of rocks and jumped off my horse. My poor little mare was just about done in. She was sweated up and heaving bad. Before I ran for the rocks I loosed her cinch, which gave her some relief. Then I joined Les and Howland in laying down a fire on the remaining two men. They milled around a minute or two more, then turned and began riding for town. We knew what they were doing. They weren't quitting. They were just going for help.

We slumped back. I let out a breath. Howland said: "Goddam!"

"Yeah," I said. "Yeah, goddam!"

We were in a little kind of draw. The trees banked up to our back and on both sides and we had a scattering of rocks out in front of us. It wasn't a bad place to fort up, but we wasn't in no position to stand off anybody for very long even if we'd been in Fort Davis. We were laying up among the rocks with the horses standing around in the bottom of the draw, their heads hanging and their sides heaving. I saw where Les had laid Tod out in the shelter of a rock that had rolled down to the bottom. I could see his chest moving.

"How's Tod?" I asked Les.

"I don't know," Les said. "I didn't have a second to see."

"I reckon not," I said. We was all speaking in short sentences, being out of breath ourselves.

Les looked at me. "But, my God, Will, you're shot to pieces yourself! You've got blood all over you!"

"Yeah!" I said and looked at my thigh. It suddenly began hurting.

"No, I mean your neck. You got blood all over it."

"My neck?" Then I remembered the tug I'd felt while we were in the bank. I put my hand to my neck and found the wound. It was a groove along the left side that you could have hidden your finger in. It wasn't serious, but it had sure bled a lot. I'd been lucky. An inch the other way and I'd have been keeping Chico company.

"It ain't nothing," I said. "But my thigh is hurting like hell."

"I'll see to Tod, then," Les said. He got up and went over to his cousin. Howland was sitting, his revolver hanging loosely in his hand, staring at the ground and not saying anything. I got my pants down and seen I'd been lucky again. The bullet had gone in high on my leg, missing the bone and going all the way through. On the left side was a kind of pouched-in hole and, where the bullet had come out, the flesh was blown open and ragged around the edges. It wasn't too bad, but it was hurting like hell. Then I suddenly thought about the bullet going all the way through.

I jumped up, struggling to pull on my pants. If the bullet had gone all the way through it might have hit my little mare. I took off for my horse in a kind of stumbling run. My leg was beginning to stiffen up already. "If that sonofabitch . . ." I said aloud, but then remembered that I'd already killed him. I got to my little horse and looked at the saddle. A hole was in the outer leather and I lifted that and saw the bullet embedded in the saddle stock. "Goddam!" I said. I worked the cartridge head out. The lead was flattened and misshapen. It hadn't touched my horse. My leg and the saddle leather had stopped it. I was gladder about that than anything that had happened the whole bad day.

I put the flattened bullet in my pocket and limped over to where Les was squatted down by Tod. The cousin was down on his back breathing in little short gasps. I could see with one eye he was bad off. Les had his shirt ripped apart in a couple of places.

"Bad," I said.

"Damn bad," Les said. "He's caught one in the side here and one from the back." He half turned the redhead on his side. "See there. I think it nicked his lungs."

A bullet had entered from the back and had come out a little above the nipple on his right side. I figured Les was right about the lung because a little blood was coming out Tod's nose and mouth. He had his eyes closed.

"Is he conscious?"

I squatted down beside them. Les was trying to plug up the holes with some pieces he'd torn off his own shirt. Both bullets had gone all the way through, so we didn't have nothing to dig for. And we might could stop the blood from coming out, but there wasn't a thing we could do about the bleeding that was going on inside Tod's body.

"We're in a bad way," I said.

"You got that right." It was Howland. He'd come up and was standing over us, the revolver still hanging loosely from his hand. He stood there, glaring down at us.

"They'll be back," Les said.

"Damn right they'll be back," I said. "And pretty quick. Them was either rangers or Association men. None of your townspeople. They'll be back." I knew damn good and well they were professional gunmen. I was thinking about the man with the broken leg still trying to shoot me when he could have laid low and hid in the brush. A storekeeper might have hid, but not a gunman.

"They know we've got a wounded man and are short a horse," I added. "They figure they got us."

"Ain't they?" Howland asked.

I looked up at him. "Maybe they got you, but they ain't got me." Blood and dust was caked all over his face. "You got any of that rum left?"

"Sure," he said, biting off his words. "In my saddlebags." He jerked his head. "Out yonder."

"Well, how about getting it?" I said.

He sat down. "You get it."

I looked at him for a second, then heaved myself up. "All right," I said. "Can I take your horse, Les? He's had more rest. I'll just walk him."

"Sure," Les said, but he looked over at Howland. "You ought to go, Thomas. Will is hit. We got to get something into these wounds to keep off gangrene."

"Let him go," Howland said. He sat down. "I ain't."

Les stared at him. "I'm thinking," he said, "that if Will hadn't cut over to cover you that you'd be laying out there shot to pieces. They'd have rode you down like a dog."

Howland didn't say anything for a minute. Finally he got up. "All right," he said. "But it was Wilson Young that—"

I cut him off. "What? What's that you're saying?"

"Nothing!" He jerked on by me and went and mounted up and rode slowly out of the little draw.

Les was sitting on the other side of Tod, slumped, his chin on his chest. Things had come to a hell of a mess. If nobody was hurt and we had horses enough we could have been making tracks and been clear of the country before a posse could come. I could imagine them back in town rallying up support, telling everybody that it was duck-shooting time. They'd be saying they had them some outlaws pinned up and they couldn't move, that half of them was hurt and they were short horses. Oh, they'd get together quite a blood-thirsty bunch. Most men are willing to go in for a little killing if it's easy enough. What most men don't like is when they's a chance they'll get hurt themselves. Well, some of them might get surprised.

I looked over at Les. "That old Rio Grande's a long way off."

He nodded slowly. "I know it."

"Reckon old Tod can make it?"

"I don't know," he said, then looked up at me. "But I ain't leaving him."

I laughed as best I could. My thigh was hurting like hell. "I know it," I said. "And I ain't neither. You know me."

He ducked his head and kind of half smiled. "Yeah, I know you, Will. I ain't worried about you."

We sat there, quiet, in a kind of half stupor. The day was very hot but now and then a stray breeze would kick up little swirls of dust in the ravine floor. A few flies were buzzing around the blood caked up on Tod's shirt and Les flicked at them tiredly. I looked up at the sun and was surprised to see it nowhere near noon. It was still early even though it seemed like a whole week had passed since we'd rode into the bank that morning.

I don't know. Things had gotten so bad that I just didn't know what to think. I wondered, sitting there in the sun and dust, what the girl Linda was doing at that moment. Probably she was sitting in an upstairs room of that cool hacienda writing poetry or something. She'd be smelling of lilac water and clean and pure and not thinking anything at all about a wounded, bloody, dusty cowboy sitting in a draw just outside Uvalde, Texas, maybe fixing to get killed in the next little while.

And I wondered to myself if I hadn't got myself in this fix on account of her. I wondered if my decision to quit hadn't been on account of her. Or better, if my decision to quit with a little something in my poke hadn't been on account of her. I could have quit, sure, and gone north and went to punching cattle or something without the worry of having money enough to set up.

But would I? Hell, I didn't know.

But the girl was the most beautiful thing I'd ever seen and anything I'd done in her name hadn't been her fault. It had been my own doing.

Well, they'd been waiting for us and I didn't know who to blame. It could have been Tod's doing or Howland's talk or both of them. But in the end it was my own doing. I was the one said we're going in. It had been my mistake.

Howland came riding back through the rocks. He came slowly, his head down like he was thinking. He was carrying a bottle of rum in one hand and his carbine that he'd rescued out of his boot in the other. He came on and pulled up a few feet from me and Tod.

"Here," he said. He pitched the bottle of rum down to me. I caught it and passed it to Les. He took the cloth plugs out of Tod's wounds and then poured in the rum. The redhead stirred and jerked as the hot liquor burned into him, but he didn't open his eyes. Howland watched him, still sitting atop Les's horse with his rifle propped across the saddle.

Les finished with the wounds, doused the plugs with rum and replaced them and then passed the bottle across to me. I first slapped a handful against my neck, the burning almost raising me up, and then pulled down my breeches and went to work lacing my thigh wound. I had to turn sideways to pour it into the opening.

"Goddam," I swore.

Les grinned. "Hurts, don't it?"

"Like the hinges of hell!"

"He ain't gonna make it." This came from Howland. I looked up at him. He was gesturing down toward Tod. "Look at him. He ain't gonna pull through."

"He might," I said. "If we can get him to a doctor."

"How?" Howland said, sarcasm heavy in his voice. "Catch the train? Hell, Wilson, we're short a horse! We're in a tight! We ain't gonna make it if we don't leave Tod!"

"We ain't leaving nobody," I said evenly.

"But look here, man! We've got time to get a good start before anybody gets back. Hell, we could make ten miles and then let them try and track us!"

"No!" I said.

He stared back at me, the rifle still across the pommel of his saddle. "He's the one," he said, "got us in this mess. If it hadn't been for him we'd be riding out of here now with a sack full of gold. He caused it by going into town."

Beside me, Les said: "No need for that kind of talk, Howland."

"Anyway," I put in, "you might have done a little causing yourself. You and your big mouth."

He looked back at me, his face flushing and his neck swelling. I was conscious of the way he was holding the rifle. "I done told you that man lied."

"Yeah," I said. "Sure."

"Listen," Les said, "this won't get it, this kind of talk. We got ourselves into this, now we just got to get ourselves out."

Howland pointed at Tod with the rifle. "There's the way," he said. "Without Tod to hold us back we could be clean out of the country by the time they get a posse together."

"We ain't leaving Tod!" Les said, a little thread of anger in his voice.

"Les," Howland said, "I wouldn't have said it if he had a chance, but look at him. Man, he's hardly breathing now. Why, just loading him on a horse would bring his end. Look here," he added, making his voice friendly and reasonable, "is it right he should get us all done in when he hasn't got a chance? Now is it? If it was me laying there I'd say, 'Fine boys, take the horses and ride out. I ain't got a chance anyway.' That's what I'd say if it was me."

Me and Les just stared at him.

He looked back, waiting for us to give him some kind of answer. Between Les and I, Tod stirred a little. I looked over at him and thought for a second he was going to open his eyes. But his lids just kind of fluttered and then relaxed. I didn't know how he'd made it as far as he had. His shirt was just all over soaked with blood. I figured he must have lost a gallon. But he was a tough boy. Who could say whether he'd pull through or not?

"Les," Howland said again, "look at it this way. If we

try to drag that boy cross-country he just ain't gonna make it. You know it and so does Wilson. If you leave him here that posse'll find him and get him into a doctor. That way we'll all make it."

Les didn't say anything. I looked up at Howland. "Listen, Howland," I said easily, "whyn't you give that horse a rest and find a rock to sit on?"

He acted like he didn't even hear me, just went on looking at Les, waiting for him to say something. Les was busy with Tod.

"What do you say, Les? Time's running out. I'm for the boy, you know that. But this is his best chance."

I was starting to get a little angry. I didn't like the way Howland was staying on that horse with that rifle just kind of casually pointing toward us. "Say, Howland!" I said loudly. "How about getting off that horse!"

He finally looked over at me. "What's your rush?"

"No rush," I said. "Just do it."

"Well," he said, drawling a little. "After that mess you made of things this morning I wouldn't have reckoned you'd had the gall to still be giving orders. Mister Wilson Young."

I felt a little chill hit me in the pit of the stomach. Now I seen what he had in mind, had had from the very moment he'd rode back. I was surprised he hadn't just kept going and not bothered to bring us the rum. But running out on your partners is pretty serious business and I reckoned he hadn't had his mind fully made up. Or maybe he'd really thought he could talk us into leaving Tod. What he thought, however, didn't make any difference, for there he sat, the rifle balanced across the pommel and just kind of pointing in our direction.

"Get off the horse," I said steadily.

He looked right back at me. "No," he said.

Well, that was the way the dice were cast. I still hoped he'd come to his senses. "Howland, we got to have that horse. Get off him."

"No," he said.

"Well, then what are you planning on doing?"

"I'll tell you what I'm not planning on doing, Mister

Wilson Young, and that's staying here and catching a bullet for a job you and that redheaded fool messed up."

"You figure to ride out then?"

"That's right. I'm riding out."

"I wouldn't try it," I said. It had got very quiet in the little draw. Our voices seemed to just boom and echo. Looking past him, I could see little heat waves shimmering off the hard rock. "I sure wouldn't try nothing like that. I'd have to stop you."

He sneered at me. "Yeah? And how you figure to do that, you with your breeches down around your ankles. Hell, you couldn't even stand up without tripping."

He raised the rifle just a little and I saw his finger go inside the trigger guard. "I don't reckon you'll do anything."

From my left, Les suddenly said: "What about me, Howland?"

Howland cut his eyes sideways to take in Les and it was all I needed. My gun belt was laying on the ground beside me and I jerked my revolver clear and fanned off three shots. They went *boom, boom, boom,* in the little draw. Howland went flipping backward off the gelding and hit the ground hard. The noise had spooked the black and he ran off to stand with the others. I got up, pulled my breeches up, and walked over and looked at Howland. I'd hit him in the chest, the neck and the forehead. That's the way of it when you fan a gun. If you're not careful it will gradually bring your sights up. Fortunately I'd started low.

Howland lay on his back, his legs drawn up. Then he relaxed and his legs straightened.

"He's dead," Les said at my shoulder.

"Yeah," I said. I walked back over and sat down. "Well, now we ain't a horse short."

CHAPTER 11

Heading South for Mexico

Once Howland lay dead we got busy breaking camp. We caught the horses and loaded Tod on Les's black gelding. He was the strongest and the most rested and it was proper for the black to carry Tod.

Just as we got ready to go I rode up to the top of the little draw and looked back toward the town. I figured it had been about fifteen minutes since we'd run the posse off and they would just about be making it back to town. As to how long it would take them to round up fresh men I didn't have no idea. Getting up a posse is a hard thing to figure. Most townspeople don't want any part of going after desperados. They figure they've got this to do and that and, anyway, it ain't their job. Still, a town can get aroused and a catch party can be put together in the wink-of-an-eye. Of course there were the professional lawmen to consider, but we'd cut them up pretty bad that morning in the gunfight. They'd want to fill their ranks out a little because they wouldn't know we were down to just two. And they might not know how bad Tod was hurt. They might figure to be chasing four armed men and they'd be a little careful how they went about that.

I stared at the horizon, but couldn't see a thing. Finally I turned my horse and rode back to where Les was waiting. He was mounted on Chico's pony and had a lead rein on his black. We'd tied the redhead astraddle the gelding with his legs roped in position. He was slumped over the pommel and we'd passed a rope around the horse's belly and over his back to keep him straight. I didn't myself know how long he could make it. He'd probably die on the trip, but that was a hell of a lot better than being taken in and dying in some cell. We hoped we might find a doctor, but I doubted it. It had just been Tod's bad luck to catch a bullet at the wrong time.

I took one last look around. We'd taken Howland's firearms for ourselves and then drug him back in the rocks and done our best to hide his body. The draw would be the first place the posse would make for and we didn't want them to know we were short yet another man. He was hidden but not good and, if they looked hard, they'd find him.

"Let's move out," I said and turned my horse up the south bank of the draw and scrambled to the top. Les followed, spurring the pony he was on and tugging at the black's lead rein. Tod rocked and swayed in the saddle, but it couldn't be helped.

We trailed south, keeping the horses to a walk. It was early afternoon and hot as hell. All around I could see heat waves shimmering up from the sandy soil. The chapparal and cactus was thick and we had to wind around to make our way without getting scratched up. Les was riding alongside Tod, fanning at the flies that were swarming around the dried blood on his shirt. We'd done our best to clean him up with a little of the rum, but it hadn't done much good. I was feeling bad low in my mind. It had been a job that was jinxed from the start.

There'd been five of us and now two was dead and the third nearly so. More than that had been a stranger who'd rode in, wanting to cast in his lot. He, too, had died and by my hand.

I looked back at Les. "Do you feel bad about Howland?"

Without leaving off from his fly-fanning he shook his head. "No, he had it coming. He was going to run out on us and there just wasn't no choice. It was a thing had to be done."

"I never liked Howland," I said. "Never trusted him neither."

"Yeah," Les agreed. "He was always looking out for Howland."

I watched him. "You ain't really bothering them flies much, Les. They smell blood."

"I guess," he said. He put his hat back on his head. He looked tired and whipped down. "At least we didn't let him run out on Tod."

"True," I said.

As we'd been getting ready to take off, Les had said about Howland: "He's got money in his pockets. We can use it."

"Then you get it," I said. I was busy tying Tod in place. "I ain't robbing the dead."

Les had looked at me. "Fair enough," he'd said. "You killed him. I'll take his money." He'd gone and got it and put it in his pocket. It must have been over two hundred dollars.

We could use the money and I was feeling ashamed about the way I'd spoke. I looked back at him again. "You was right about the money. If we hadn't taken it some of that catch party would have—that is if they find him."

"No matter," Les said.

We slogged along, the sun burning down on our backs. The horses was still a little whipped down from the morning's run, but they were starting to come back. Both my filly and Les's gelding are roadwise and hard as iron from good graining and care. I looked back, but still couldn't see anything. The slow pace was making me impatient and I was praying for dark to come to hide our sign. I knew it was still several hours away. In the meantime all we could do was slog along, praying the townspeople of Uvalde was cowards.

I watched Tod, slumped over on the horse. It seemed I couldn't see him breathe, but then every once in a while he'd make a kind of racking sob and gasp a little.

"Les," I said, "that boy's lungs are filling up with blood."

Les turned and give him an anxious look and then just shook his head. "Ain't a damn thing we can do, Will. It's all inside him. What this boy needs is a doctor. And damn quick, too."

"I know it," I said.

We were making for Pearson, a little town about thirty miles south. It was the nearest place unless we went north and that direction would be the undoing of us all. "You reckon they's even a doctor in Pearson?"

"I don't know, Will. Last time I was there it wasn't much. Couple stores and a few saloons."

"They ain't gonna have no doctor, Les."

He didn't answer me. I knew he knew it as well as I did. But, still, you have to try and do something, or at least feel like you're doing something.

And back behind us somewhere was a posse. They might be two miles behind or ten, I just didn't have no idea. There'd been no sign of them when we pulled out and we'd come maybe six miles. If they didn't come on us before dark we might have a chance. But then maybe not. There'd be rangers and Association agents in that posse and they don't give up too easy. Also, there was a ranger company billeted at Del Rio, which was on the river about forty miles west of us. They might wire them and have a couple of rangers sent over to try and head us off. I just didn't know. It might depend on how many people we'd shot up that morning in the bank and how important they were. Lord knows we'd done a fair job of throwing lead. It was a cinch somebody had gone down.

Well, there was one thing I could face up to; after that business in Carrizo Springs and our work of the morning I was through in Texas, I could kiss it all goodbye, for my life would be forfeit if I ever stepped foot across the river again.

That is if we made it to the river.

We kept going with the sun just hot as hell. I was getting mighty tired, hungry too. As always I hadn't been able to eat any breakfast and we hadn't had time for a noon meal. We had a little of the rum left and I reached back, undid the flap, and rummaged in my saddlebags until I found the bottle. It was hot to the touch from the temperature inside the pouches. I uncorked it, the vapors that came forth nearly taking my head off, and had a drink. For a second I didn't know if I was going to hold it, but then it settled and I had another. I slackened my pace and dropped back to Les.

"Here," I said.

He took it without a word and had a good swallow.

"Have another," I said. "It's picking me up already."

He did, then corked the bottle and handed it back to me. I kept it out, holding it by the neck and letting it swing by my leg. We had a nip every now and then as we rode along. I kept looking back. I felt uneasy. The horizon was still clear, but I felt it was time we speeded up. I offered Les the last drink in the bottle. He refused, so I upended the bottle and finished it myself. I was on the point of casting it aside, but thought better of it and put it back in my saddlebag. There was no use giving them any more sign than what we were already leaving. I looked over at Tod. He was still sagged into the horse, both hands hanging down. His face was a kind of ashen gray color.

"We got to move along a little faster," I said to Les.

He hesitated and then nodded. "All right."

"We got to lope these horses," I said.

He looked at me.

"I know," I said. "But he'll be just as dead if they catch us. Besides, your gelding has got a sweet rack. He'll rock old Tod like a baby. Let's move!"

I put my filly into a canter and Les put spurs to the pony he was riding and came along, his black picking up the pace just as nice and easy as you'd want. We went fast through the brush, winding our way.

The fast canter or lope or rack as some call it is a pace my little mare can hold all day when she's fresh. Unfortunately she'd been put to kind of hard usage of late and it wasn't long until the sweat began to stand out on her neck and foam along the saddle. But she's a willing little beast and will try and run through a brick wall if I put her at it.

We held the pace for quite a while. It was hard on Tod. I could see him jouncing around in the saddle. Les called to me and motioned at Tod's shirt. There was a brightness

among the dried blood that told us he'd started bleeding
again. We pulled up and Les got down and did what he
could with the bandages.

"He's lost a lot of blood. If we don't get him to a doctor
he ain't gonna make it."

I didn't say anything. There wasn't anything I could say.
I was willing to walk the horses awhile, but Les remounted
and led out at a trot. I fell in by Tod, holding my hand on
his back and doing what I could to make the ride easier.

We tore along over the rough ground, eating up the miles
at a good rate. Ahead, I could see the pace beginning to tell
on the pony that had once belonged to Chico. His flanks
were heaving and his dappled coat was wet with sweat. My
little filly wasn't liking it any too well either, though she
was a better horse than the pony. That pony, I thought, has
been bad luck. First Chico had been killed, then Tod had
took him and had been shot; now Les was riding him.

I didn't figure the posse could be gaining much on us.
They'd be loping their horses too, but they wouldn't be
gaining much ground. I found myself wishing we didn't
have to go to Pearson. The border was only forty or fifty
miles on beyond and we could ride all night and come near
making it. But that wasn't no way to think. We had to do
what we could for Tod. I still had my hand on his back.
He was warm, but his breathing was mighty irregular and
every once in a while he'd kind of gag and make a whistling
sound in his throat. It was a sure sign he had blood in his
lungs. I'd heard it before and it's a bad sound.

Finally, the sun began dropping and dusk came upon us.
It was still light enough to read newsprint by, but it was
considerably cooler and that was a relief. Unfortunately,
dark wouldn't bring all the help I'd first thought it would.
There'd be a moon and it would be a bright moon. Still, it
might make tracking a little harder.

"How far you figure to Pearson?" I asked Les.

"Can't be far. We've stayed after it pretty good."

And indeed we had. Except for the few times we'd
stopped to rest for a minute or two we'd kept right on.
We were walking to rest the horses and my feet were sore

as hell and my thigh was bothering me bad.

"How's your leg?" Les asked me.

"It's all right," I said. "This walking will keep it from stiffening up. But you're going to have to switch breeches with me."

"Why?"

"Because these are all bloody and got a hole in 'em. When I go into Pearson to see about a doctor they might cause speculation."

"Hell, Will, I better go in."

"No," I said. "I've done got this thought out. We'll hide you and him out somewheres close and then I'll ride in. With this neck it'll be a natural for me to ask about a doctor. If anybody asks I can say I done it on a hay fork. Then if they got a doctor it'll be just pie for me to bring him back to where ya'll are."

"Well, you've got a head, Wilson. I never argued that. But I hate to see you take the risk."

We walked a little further and then pulled up a little wash that was lined with mesquite trees. We wanted to wait until dark before moving any further. Les wasn't exactly sure where the town was and, if we were close, we'd be able to see the lights after it got dark. We got down in the wash and hunkered down on our heels. There wasn't any profit in taking Tod off the horse because we'd be moving out again in less than an hour and the joustling around wouldn't do him any good.

CHAPTER 12

Light in the Dark

We stayed hid out in that little wash until it got good dark and then some. Me and Les was laying on the bank, looking over the edge for some sign of the town, some little glow in the dark that would give us a direction. Down in the wash Les's black would stamp his feet every once in a while, impatient and unaccustomed to standing around with a load. We'd been checking on Tod every little bit, but his condition hadn't changed any.

"Wonder why he don't open his eyes?" Les asked me.

"Loss of blood," I said. "Or maybe just being knocked unconscious from the power of them slugs he was hit with. I've seen men take on like that before."

We were speaking quietly though there wasn't much point in it. All around us the insects that light the night had come out and were making their sounds. Down off to our right I heard a bull frog croak.

"Must still be a little water in this cut," I said. "Hear that bull frog?"

But Les was thinking on Tod. "Still, I don't see why he don't come to. Looks like he'd either come out of it or just go ahead and expire."

"I've seen it before," I said. "Oncet in Montana I seen a cowboy, young kid, get no more than a little horn wound in the shoulder and he taken on like that. We was branding and the old cow broke out of the bunch and run over just as he was about to lay the iron on the calf. Hooked him in the shoulder. Didn't even look bad, but he just all of a sudden turned white and passed dead away. Laid on his bunk like that for three days." I started to go on and say the young puncher had died, but I caught myself in time. We'd even had a doctor for the boy by the second day, but it hadn't done any good. He'd never come out of it, had just laid there and died. I'd never understood it myself. My own theory had been that it had scared him to death seeing that old mama cow bearing down on him.

"What happened to him?" Les asked me.

"Oh," I said, "I never heard. I rode out not too long after that."

Les looked over at me, but didn't say anything. It was as dark as it would get that night, the sun being down and the moon not yet up, but we couldn't see a single light that would point us at Pearson. I was beginning to get a little case of the fantods. I didn't know where that posse was, but I knew I'd feel better if we were moving.

"Les?" I said, kind of urgingly.

He knew what I meant, I expect, but he said: "You know old Tod ain't seen his folks in near three years."

I didn't say anything.

"You know his daddy was a deacon in the church." He looked over at me. "Did you know that, Will?"

"Yeah," I said. "I knew it."

"His daddy never knew what we'd been up to these last years. He's a mighty old man now. His mother's dead, you know."

"So's mine," I said. It was making me a little sore him talking that way. Tod hadn't been the only one with folks. I wasn't too concerned what his folks thought. He'd made his own choice and I'd never seen him give a lot of thought to it.

"Tod's daddy was my daddy's older brother," Les said. He had his chin propped on his hand, staring out at the horizon. "My daddy had a lot of respect for him."

"How about your daddy?" I asked him.

"Well, I don't know. I just don't know. That wanted

notice out of Carrizo Springs would be the first on us, wouldn't it?"

"Not on me," I said. I was getting a little tired of his line of talk.

"Well, maybe not on you," he said.

"What the hell does that mean?"

"Nothing," he said. "Nothing. You and me know old Tod wasn't no prize, but I hate to think of him laying out here like this, dying, and his daddy not knowing a thing."

I pushed myself to my knees. "Listen, we got to get out of here. I know you feel bad about Tod and I do too. You're kin and I'm not, and that's all right, but he still rode with me and I want to do everything I can for him."

"Don't get sore, Will. I know what you mean."

"Then let's get on the scout," I said. "We've got to find that town and laying here ain't doing us a bit of good."

We mounted up and I led out. First we ranged to the southeast a mile or so and then turned back to the west. The moon was starting to come up and it was throwing light and shadows all over the prairie. We'd been trailing almost due west for near a mile when Les suddenly called up to me, "Will!"

I pulled up. "What?"

"Look yonder."

I glanced back at him to see which way he was pointing and then looked off toward the southwest. I didn't see anything.

"That's just a rise," I said. "A butte."

"Naw," he said. "Look at the face of it. See that kind of glow, like it was being reflected?"

I looked but still couldn't see anything. "Hell, let's try that way. It's as good as any and maybe you're right."

We set off over the rolling land at a lope and the closer we came to the rise the better I could seem to see a little glow shining on its face. It was very faint, but distinct. There was quartz rock in the country and it will pick up the glow of a campfire from a mile or better. We were riding up gently ascending terrain and, when we got to the top of a little knoll, Les pulled up and swept his arm down to the left. "Look there!" he said.

Sure enough I could see the faint outlines of buildings down in a little flat valley off to our left. Out of maybe ten or twenty structures, it being hard to tell at night, only about five were lit up.

"Pearson," I said. "Has to be."

"Ain't nothing else around."

We turned our horses down the slope and began riding toward the lights. We wanted to get close, but not too close, and then find a place for Les to hide out with Tod while I went on in. After a little, as we got near to the floor of the valley, we struck a little narrow limestone creek meandering along. Willows lined both sides of its course and they give us a start for a moment, suddenly rearing up in the dark as they did.

"Let's follow this," I said. "I imagine it'll wind around toward town."

We did, riding alongside the line of trees. We could see it was leading toward town. It was probably their water supply. Finally the little creek made a sharp turn where the water had thrown up a little beach protected by a bluff.

"Let's head down in there," I said.

The sand was soft under our horses' hoofs, but we made it down and dismounted. The line of trees shut off the lights from Pearson. I stood in the soft sand looking around. The little bluff was two or three feet high and lined on both sides by a heavy growth of willow trees. Through their leaning branches we could see the moon, hanging full and yellow in the blue sky. I figured Pearson was maybe a mile away.

"Let's get Tod down and make him comfortable," I said.

We untied him and carried him, as gently as we could, up to the base of the bluff and laid him down. Les was going to take the saddle off his black and put it under Tod's head, but I cautioned him not to. "Unsaddle Chico's horse," I said. "And cover Tod up with the saddle blanket."

"But it's hot," Les said, looking at me.

"I know it," I said. "But that's what that sawbones told us to do with that cowpuncher in north Texas."

He got it done and then we switched breeches. Me and Les are nearly of a size and they were a good fit. He stood, looking at me, in his undershorts, my breeches in his hand.

"You better put them on," I said jestingly. "I'm liable to be coming back through here in a terrible hurry and we won't have time for you to dress."

"Maybe I better go in, Will." He looked worried.

"Oh, hell!" I said. "Les, ain't nobody coming back here with me unless he's a doctor. Anybody else tries it will be carrying about three pounds of lead. Now don't worry about this."

"Well," he said. "Well—"

"It's all right," I said. "Take a rest." I walked over and got on my mare. "I better not dally," I said.

"Be careful, Will," he said.

I touched my hat to him in a little salute. "Don't you worry," I said. "Ain't nobody gonna fool with me, you just set easy and I'll be back with a doctor for Tod before you can shake a stick at a polecat. We'll pull him out of this."

He gave me a salute and I turned my pony and worked her up the bluff and then struck off for Pearson. The prairie was rolling and smooth. It was cattle country and the rough places had been worked down smooth. I put my little filly into a high lope. I didn't want to waste too much time.

The dim lights got closer and closer. Finally I turned off the prairie and struck the little dirt road that ran down between the row of buildings that made up the main part of town. I passed a blacksmith shop, then a general mercantile store and pulled up in front of the first saloon I came to. There were other lights down the street but I figured one saloon would do as well as another. I dismounted and loose-tied my filly. The town didn't boast boardwalks. I paused just outside the door of the saloon and scratched at my neck until I made it bleed. The wound didn't look deep and could easily pass for the ragged mark of a hay fork. I wiped my bloody fingers on Les's breeches and went on in.

The place wasn't much. They had a fair mahogany bar and a number of rickety tables, but there wasn't much business in the place to speak of. A few men in tattered clothes that I took to be sheepherders were drinking at a back table and there were several cowboys standing to the bar. The bartender was a fat man with a heavy mustache and beard. He was leaning back against the wall with his arms crossed. Except for the sheepherders everyone looked up when I came in. I went up to the bar and ordered whiskey.

The bartender pushed himself off the wall and set me up a glass. He got a bottle out from under the bar and poured me up a drink without a word.

I took about half of it down with him watching me. It was raw stuff, cheap corn whiskey.

"Two bits," he said.

I dug for change and flung a coin on the bar. The price was high for the quality of the drink. I stuck my finger down into what whiskey was left in the glass and daubed it on my neck. It burned like fire, but I didn't let on to wince. I figured the move would call attention to my wound and get somebody to asking questions so I could ask about a doctor, but nobody paid me the least attention.

"Gimme another whiskey," I said. The cowboy nearest me, standing to the bar like a hip-sprung horse, give me a casual look and then went back to his drink. I watched him out of the corner of my eye and saw him say something to the other one standing beside him. I couldn't hear what was said, but the far cowboy leaned back and give me a look over the head of his friend. I could see they were talking about me.

"Say," I called down to them, "wonder if there's a doctor around here?"

For a second they didn't either one look at me, just went on drinking. They were both pretty hard case-looking lots, travel-stained and grimy. I figured they were both off a nearby ranch and just in town after Saturday chores. Finally the nearest one, still without looking at me, asked what I wanted a doctor for.

It was a rude question, but I just touched my neck and said I wanted to get something done about a cut.

"That little thing?" It was the bartender. He laughed.

"What the hell you want a doctor for that for? That ain't nothing."

I come around on him and give him a look. "Infection," I said.

He laughed again, his belly shaking under his white apron. "Put some more of that pop skull on it."

I didn't say anything else to him, but looked back down to the two cowboys. "No doctor?" I asked again. "Sure?"

The one lounged around and looked at me. He seemed to take an awful long time looking me over. "Reckon we'd know if we had a doctor." He paused. "One in Uvalde."

"I reckon they is," I said.

"You not heading that way?"

"Could be. What's it to you?"

"Nothing to me. You're the one asking all the questions."

Then his friend spoke up. I couldn't see much of him except the brim of his hat. He said: "They's a ranch about twelve miles east of here run by two brothers. I think one of 'em studied dentistry back east for a time. He's generally pretty good about them kind of things. Barbed-wire cuts and what not."

"Well thanks," I said. I was suddenly not liking the looks of the set-up too much. For a Saturday night the place seemed awfully quiet, like maybe a telegram had come advertising a reward for some wanted men that might be headed that way and all the able-bodied men had gone out to have a look and try their luck. Motioned for the bartender to give me another drink. I was wondering mightily if there was a telegraph line into the town. I couldn't figure out any good way to ask.

"How'd you say you got that little scratch?" the cowboy nearest me asked.

"I don't remember saying," I said. He was making me mighty uneasy. I took the drink the bartender poured and drank it off. After I got the drink down I looked at the cowboy. "If I had of said, I'd of said I done it with a hay fork."

He just kind of nodded his head like he understood and motioned for the bartender to give him another. I studied him closely, wondering just how fresh the dust was on his clothes. It could be fresh from just riding into town or it could be fresh from riding around the boondocks looking for several bank robbers. I decided it was time to go on back to where I'd left Les. I paid the bartender and stood away from the bar. "Well, I'm much obliged for your help." I turned to leave, but the near cowboy called to me.

"Don't be in such a rush. Stay and have another drink."

"Don't believe," I said. "I got to get kicking."

"Hell, I'm buying," he said. "Belly up."

"Reckon not." I was near the door and he'd turned on the bar, leaning against it, to watch me.

"Man can't stay for a free drink must be in a hell of a hurry," he said. "Must be in a powerful hurry."

"No, I just don't want any more."

"Say," the poke on the other side asked, "haven't I seen you before?"

"That'd be up to you," I said. I put my hand on the door, pushed it open, and half stepped out into the night. "I just couldn't answer that for you."

"Seems like I have," he said. He rubbed one hand crossgrain against his whiskers and stared at me. "Not here, though."

"I got to go," I said. I stepped through the door, let it swing back and then grabbed up my little mare and took out of the town. As I rode I watched to see if they'd come out after me, but the door stayed closed. At the outskirts of town I pulled up and looked around. I wanted to see if I could find a line of telegraph poles leading into the town. It was still good moonlight, but I couldn't make out a thing. Pearson wasn't a railroad town as far as I knew, but still, they might have a telegraph. I wasn't sure. I just looked a minute, then put my filly into a lope and headed for the little creek where Tod and Les were. Every little bit I looked back, but couldn't see anything. As I rode, I noticed clouds coming up from the south. They were big black thunderstorm clouds and they were drifting right for the moon. Every once in a while one of the little outriders from the main pack would drift across and cut off a little of the light. If it would come a real gully washer it would be a big help, not only in washing out our tracks but in covering up the moon. I wished for it to get as dark as the inside of a cow.

I pulled up near to the line of willows and let out a little whistle. For a second I didn't hear anything, so I whistled again. Finally I heard Les come back at me and I rode on into the tree line and went down the bluff. My partner was sitting by the bank with his back up against a tree. Tod was laid out flat a few yards away. I pulled my mare up and got down.

"Les," I said, "I'm sorry. They ain't a doctor. They told me there's some kind of dentist about ten miles west of here."

"Never mind," he said. He had his head kind of down and was playing with a handful of sand. "Tod's done passed on."

I squatted down beside him. "Tod's dead?"

"Yeah," Les said. He was still playing with the little handful of sand, picking it up and letting it run through his fingers. I could see he was feeling pretty bad about it. Tod had never been the kind you felt real good about, just being around him, but once he was gone you realized how long you'd rode with him and how much you'd been through together. I started feeling bad about it myself.

"Nearly 'bout right after you rode out," Les said. "I had him laying over there about where he is now and I'd gone down to the creek to wet a rag and try to clean some of the blood off him. I got down there and I heard him say something, couldn't make out what it was, and I looked around and he was trying to stand up."

"Was he awake?"

"Will, I don't know. I couldn't tell in the dark. Before I could get back to him he kind of keeled over and then tried to crawl a little ways. When I got to him he was drawed up in a knot with blood coming out his mouth and nose. He was saying something, but I couldn't make it out. I tried to straighten him out, but he flang around for a minute, waving his arms and yanking his head and then I reckon he just died."

"I've seen it like that," I said. "I think they see it coming."

"See what? You mean like they teach in church—the archangel or the death angel?"

"Well, I don't know," I said. It made me uncomfortable to talk about it. "Something makes 'em thrash around. I don't know as I could give it a name."

He shook his head, slowly, from side to side. "He really took on. Made me feel pretty bad."

"Well . . ." I said. "Well . . ."

We were both quiet for a moment. I looked over at Tod, but couldn't see him too well. The clouds were gaining on the moon and the night was getting darker and darker. "I hate it, Les," I said. "I feel real bad about it."

"I do too," he said. "I'm damned if I know what I'll tell his daddy. He'll blame me, I imagine. He never thought Tod could do wrong for one minute."

"Don't worry about it," I said. "It damn sure wasn't your fault. Tod's string just ran out, that's all."

"It's funny, ain't it, Will?"

"What?"

"Aw, how me and you and Tod grew up together, was boys together."

"That was a long time ago, Les."

"That's what I mean," he said. "I mean, it went on so long you just figured—I mean . . . Well, it's just funny, queer funny, about one of us getting killed."

I could see Les was taking it hard. He's not generally much of a hand for long speeches. I didn't say anything, just let him sit and think about it by himself. They'd been kin, so it was more his affair than mine.

Finally, I had to say: "Les, it's coming on to rain. Don't you reckon it's time we buried Tod, if we are, and then got out of here?"

He nodded slowly, then stood up slowly and dusted the sand off his hands. "I reckon," he said. "We can scoop out a little hole in the sand."

Above us the thunderstorm was starting to get itself together. Away off little flashes of lightning were darting through the sky and we could hear the rumble of the thunder. It wasn't going to be long before it was on us. We got down on our knees in the soft sand, scooping out a little shallow trench to lay Tod in. It would wash him out. We both knew it, but we went ahead anyway. It ain't a question of what's done for a body, it's the attempt that's made. It wasn't the little hole we was making that was so important, it was the time we were wasting in doing it that counted. If it'd been just me I'm not too sure I'd of taken the time, but I knew Les wasn't about to ride off and leave Tod without doing something for him.

The wind was getting up and beginning to whip the willows about. It was going to be a real storm. I figured the rain was about five minutes off. We got the trough finished and then started for Tod. Just as I took a step I heard a sound. I grabbed Les and pulled him down. We squatted in the sand staring at the line of trees for some movement, but it had gotten too dark and we couldn't see a thing. The sound I'd heard had been that of horse's hoof on rock. It's the only thing that sounds that way and it couldn't have been one of our horses, for they were standing in the sand. I leaned my mouth close to Les's ear.

"Mount up," I whispered. "We've got to run."

He looked at me and then nodded.

"We'll go south down the creek," I said slowly.

We couldn't ride up the bank, for I didn't know from which side the sound had come. If there were men laying for us they might be on both sides and we'd be riding right into their guns. Besides, the sand was too soft for good footing for our horses.

Our mounts were just a few yards from us. I crouched and then suddenly burst for my filly, running low and having trouble in the sand. I frightened her a little, coming at her so wildly, and she shied, but I grabbed the pommel and swung myself into the saddle. Les was right behind me. Just as he got astride his black all hell seemed to break loose. Guns were exploding from both sides of the creek going *boom, boom, boom, boom!* We never made a move to fire back, just clapped on spurs and hit the water running, heading down the creek. All around me I could hear lead whistling, but there wasn't nothing to do but ride and I crouched low over my filly's neck and really laid into her with my spurs. Over the sound of the gunfire I could hear Les coming right behind me. The noise had frightened Chico's pony and he'd torn loose and was running with us. There must have been a power of men out in the darkness, for the gunshots just kept blasting. I thanked our lucky stars for the rain clouds. If it hadn't been for that and the little noise the horseshoe had made on the rock we'd have been laying right alongside of Tod. As it was it was still chancy going. The creek bottom was pretty smooth, but still rough riding. Chico's pony had jumped past Les and had come up alongside of me. I grabbed his rein, holding him in tight for protection of that side. Suddenly I heard an awful thunk and felt him jerk and then veer off to the right. I let him go and he went down before I even got good past him. If he hadn't have been there it would have been my little mare going down with me atop her. That Chico pony had been in bad luck all the way.

Suddenly there was a little bend in the creek and we swept around that and then jumped up on solid ground and took off cross prairie. Behind us I could still hear guns going off, their muzzle blasts looking like big fireflies, but the men behind them were just shooting in the dark. They couldn't see a thing. Les pulled up beside me and we laid into it, forcing our horses to give us some breathing distance.

"Townspeople!" I yelled at Les. He nodded without looking at me. He'd known. Nobody but fools would have lined up on both sides of that creek and then fired across. I imagined they'd been a few of them hit by their own bullets.

We kept going, eating up the distance. I made my little mare run longer than she likes to and then gradually pulled her down into a hard gallop. I didn't know how many posses might be in the neighborhood and our only real safety lay in reaching the Rio Grande. Beside me, Les was leaned over his black's neck, pushing him up. We kept the pace, whipping along through the chaparral. Overhead the thunder was booming louder and louder. Suddenly, big wet drops began to strike me in the face. In an instant the drops had turned into a deluge and the rain was coming down in sheets. It was raining so hard that the water hadn't time to be absorbed into the dry ground. I felt my little filly beginning to lose her footing on the slick ground and I slowed her, motioning at Les. We got the horses down into a trot and kept going, going right into the driving rainstorm. I'd got my wish; it'd got near about as dark as the inside of a cow and while that was helping us by making our track harder to follow it was also making it hard going in the rough country we were riding through. I could feel the chaparral and cactus tearing at my legs and I figured it was doing a fine job of scratching up my mare's shoulders. But there was no help for it; this was where she had to earn her keep.

Les rode close and said something. The wind and the thunder were making so much noise I couldn't hear a word he'd said. I yelled, "What?"

He leaned in toward me and yelled, "Reckon they're coming?"

"I don't know," I yelled back. "I doubt it. I don't believe they were a posse from Uvalde. I believe they were ranch hands out from Pearson. I think they telegraphed for us."

He didn't get the last. "What?"

"Telegraphed!" I yelled back. "From Uvalde, about us heading this way. I think they followed me out from town." Rain was running down my face so hard that every time I opened my mouth I'd get a mouthful. In the flashes of lightning, which were right over us by now, I could see Les. Rain was pouring off the brim of his hat and his clothes were soaked. His shirt was sticking to him like it'd been painted on. I reckoned I looked the same. We were still going at a fast trot, the footing insecure, but that nothing we could do about. We had to keep the horses moving. Occasionally my mare or Les's black would start to slip and then catch themselves. Limestone rock and sand is mighty tricky going in wet weather. It gets like riding on lye soap.

"Reckon it'll rain?" I yelled at him.

He still wasn't feeling much like a joke. He just give me

a weak grin and kind of shook his head.

"We better hit it up," I said. He nodded and we put the horses back into a lope. It was a good way to break a horse's leg, but it just couldn't be helped. We had to get some distance under our belt.

When the storm finally passed the moon came back out, but it was lower in the sky and nowhere near as bright. We had the horses in a walk. They were just about whipped. For one day's riding we'd covered a power of miles. We plodded along. After the rain the air smelled nice and fresh. Rain won't do that by itself, but rain and lightning will. It made me think of when I was a boy and the way it would smell. It's funny how a smell can suddenly come back on you like that, like a memory. There'll suddenly be a smell you haven't thought of in a long time and it'll hit you and take you right back to where you was when you first smelled it or last smelled it—whatever.

Me and Les were as wet as drowned kittens. I don't reckon we could have transported another single drop of water. We were full up, as the cowboys say, full up and running over. We both had slickers in our bed rolls, but it was a little late for that.

"How far you reckon?" I asked Les, meaning how far to the river. From the moon I judged it to be after midnight. That would have meant we'd been riding hard for at least three hours.

"Can't be far," Les said. "Fifteen miles, maybe."

"We better rest these horses," I said. "Else they gonna crater on us."

We rode until we came to a particular piece of high ground and then dismounted and loosened cinches. There wasn't any cover to speak of, but the ground was high enough to afford us a good view in all directions.

Les sat down on the ground and leaned back, hooking his hands behind his head. "I'm about whipped," he said. "Been a long day."

"Close your eyes a minute," I said. "I'll be watching."

"Naw," he said.

"Sure, go ahead. We'll be riding out in just a minute and

I ain't a bit sleepy. I had several drinks in town and I'm pretty well fixed up."

"Well, I won't sleep," he said.

But I could see he went to sleep almost the minute he closed his eyes. I figured old Les had had a pretty hard day. He deserved a minute or two of shut-eye. Things hit him a lot harder than he lets on and I knew he was still feeling pretty bad about old Tod. I guess when you grow up with somebody and visit back and forth and sleep over as he and his cousin had done that it takes you up kind of short to see him catch one. But yet, in our line of work, you've got to figure that it'll happen. You can just bet, once you start into robbing banks, that somebody is going to be shooting at you. It just works out that way.

But I'm out of it, I suddenly thought. It made me feel good all of an instant. It was the best I'd felt in some time. It seemed as if I'd forgot all about it and then, when it came back over me and I remembered it, it was like found money.

I hunkered down on one heel and looked up at the sky as I'd done at the camp we'd made outside of Uvalde. It was a clear sky, the direction I was looking, all the clouds being to the north, and I stared at it, noting the stars, and again wondered if it was the same sky over the girl. Being that much closer to the border I figured it probably was. It made me feel good thinking about that.

Then a little bad thought came in and hit me. Would the fact that I'd give up bank robbing really change me? Wouldn't I still be the same Wilson Young? Would I really be that much different where I could go about consorting with grandees and their nieces?

The thought made me angry and, to shake it, I suddenly got up and walked off a few feet. I told myself I wasn't quitting bank robbing because I wanted the company of such people, but simply because it was time to quit. I told myself the girl had absolutely nothing to do with it because I wasn't such a fool as to think that girl would care for me whether I was a bank robber or a bank president. Men don't think that way, I told myself, and I certainly wasn't.

But I knew, even as I was talking to myself, that it was about half lie. I hadn't been myself since the moment I'd seen that girl and, sure as hell, once across the border I'd find me some way to make it back to that ranch.

All the thinking was making me angry with myself. I said aloud: "Aw, go to hell!" It startled me to hear my words in the quiet night and I whipped around to see if Les had heard and what he'd think. He was sound asleep. It made me smile seeing him sleeping and remembering how he'd said he wouldn't. Well, I'd give him a little more time. I hunkered down and reached for my tobacco sack. It was wringing wet and I threw it on the ground. The cigarette papers had made a soggy ball in my pocket and I got them out and threw them on the ground too. After a minute I began wishing for a drink but I knew there wasn't any, so I finally just sat back and stared out at the country. If anybody was coming I'd be able to see them for a long ways off.

I let Les sleep until the false dawn was beginning to streak the sky. He and the horses both needed a rest. Finally I went over and roused him. We still had some miles to go. I shook him.

"Time to go," I said. "We got a river to cross."

CHAPTER 13

Mexico

The sun was well up by the time we got to the river. We'd taken it easy the last ten miles or so, there being no sign of pursuit and the horses being fairly fagged. After the storm the weather had turned off pretty, a high sky, a gentle little breeze and the sun feeling good on our backs. We'd dried out finally, but our saddles were still wet and they creaked as we rode along. We pulled up at the edge of the river and looked at it. By chance we'd come straight to a good crossing. We could see bottom most of the way across and we knew we'd have no trouble.

"Well?" Les asked. He looked at me.

I turned in my saddle and took a long look behind me. I wanted Les to think I was checking to see if any pursuit was at hand, but I was really taking a good look at Texas from Texas soil. It might be a long time before I could do it again.

"Let's go to Mexico," I said, giving spur to my mare and riding her into the river.

We pulled up on the other side. Neither of us had said a word about stopping, we just reined in at the same time. For a while we didn't speak, just sat our horses. I looked at the land that lay ahead thinking it didn't really look much different from that on the other side of the river. Men may make boundaries and create nations, but the land don't care: the land stays the same.

"Well . . ." Les said after a little. He reached in his pocket and got one of his little cigars. It was still a little wet, but he broke it in two and handed me half. "My last," he said.

I put it in my mouth and chewed on it. After being soaked with rain water it tasted pretty rank. "I ain't got no dry matches," I said, "have you?"

"In my oilskin." He turned in the saddle and undid his bedroll and reached inside and came out with a little packet of phosphors. After a few tries we got one going and lit up. It was pleasant sitting there, knowing our hard run was over, and smoking.

"Bad job," I said after a little while.

Les nodded slowly, the cigar clenched in his front teeth. "Bad job."

"Three men," I said. "We never lost three men before."

"Four, if you count Kid White."

"Four, then."

We fell silent again.

"You mean it?" Les asked.

"About quitting?"

"Yes."

"Yeah, I mean it."

"What'll you do? We didn't get no stake out of that bank, so you can't buy a ranch."

"I know it," I said.

He nodded in that slow way he has.

"We better ride on in a ways," I said, "and rest ourselves and these horses for a while." I got my mare moving and he followed.

After an hour or so we found a little patch of grass and some trees and unsaddled the horses and went and sat in the shade. My filly let out a long sigh when I finally got the saddle off her. I expect she was almighty tired of it. Both she and the black went right to work grazing. They hadn't been eating too regularly the last day or two.

After the horses were seen to, me and Les got comfortable, put our hats over our faces and went to sleep. I hadn't realized how tired I was until I got stretched out good and kinda unwound.

It was good afternoon by the time we woke up. I came awake with the feeling somebody was watching me. It scared me for a second, not being sure if that posse might not actually have come on after us and followed into Mexico. If they had, my judgment had been bad wrong. I eased my head around, acting like I was still asleep, until I could just see out from under my hat brim. There, about ten yards away, was a Mexican peon sitting his little burro and staring at us. He was an ordinary-looking country Mexican—big straw sombrero, serape, and them white pants they tie at the ankles. I sat up and pushed my hat back.

"Buenos días," I said. My sudden movement had kind of startled him and he made as if to rein his burro around. "Pardon me," I said. *"Está bueno."* I looked out past him to see if the horses were all right. They were and he didn't seem to have any company. He'd just come riding along, seen a couple of gringos and decided he'd take the opportunity to give them a good looking over.

He sat there, staring at us, his burro switching flies, not saying a word. I poked Les. "We got company," I said.

He sat up suddenly, making the little Mexican flinch again. "Don't scare him off," I said. "I want to find out where we are." Running in the storm the night before, I'd kind of lost my bearings and I wanted to get a line on exactly where we'd crossed.

"Buenas tardes," Les said.

"Ask him if he's got anything to eat," I said. "I'm about starved."

"Tiene comedo?"

The little peon shook his head, still staring at us. He had a rope bridle looped around the under jaw of his burro. It was a rig an Indian might use.

"Tell him we'll pay," I said. "Maybe he thinks we're bandits."

"Nosotros pagar," Les said.

The peon shook his head again.

"Well, my God!" I said. "Then see if he at least knows where we are. Damn!"

Les talked to him in Spanish, not getting much response.

Finally the little peon put out his arm, without taking his eyes off us, and pointed to the northwest. "Villa Union," he said.

"*Quánto?*" Les asked him.

The peon shrugged. "*Quién sabe. Quién puede decir.*"

"What'd he say?" I asked Les.

But Les was still working on the peon. "*Próximo,*" he asked him.

"*Medio días,*" the peon said. "*Todas días.*"

Les looked around at me. "Says it's a half day's ride, maybe a whole day's ride to Villa Union. Probably about five miles yonder. These peons travel pretty slow."

"Here," I said. I got up and walked over and handed him a peso. He looked at the money for a minute without taking it and then suddenly rummaged in a sack he had over his burro's neck and came out with a fistful of tortillas. We swapped bread for coin and I laughed. "He didn't really believe we'd pay," I told Les. "We must really look like bandits."

Les didn't say anything and I looked around at him. "Did you hear what I said?"

"I heard you," he said.

"Well?"

"Well, ain't we?"

I thanked the peon as well as I could and walked over and sat back down by Les. I handed him half the tortillas and we sat there eating. The peon was still watching us, except he'd taken out a tortilla and was eating along as we did. The cornbread tasted mighty good as hungry as I was. I waited until I'd finished before I said anything.

"You figure I'm wrong?" I asked.

"I just can't see how you'll make it," Les said. "Why don't you wait until you get you a stake of some kind?"

I studied the ground. The peon was still sitting his burro. We were talking like he was the bark on the tree. "Les, I've been trying for better than ten years to get me a stake. I went into this with the idea of just getting a stake together and all I've got after all that time is that horse yonder and this

158

saddle and them silver spurs. I could turn gray waiting to get me a stake."

"Well . . ." he said.

"I don't know what I'm gonna do either, but I'm full up. You know I've never taken much to Howland, but he used to have a saying that kind of describes the way I feel. He used to say he was like the house cat humping the skunk—he hadn't had all he wanted, just all he could stand. That's it, Les. I can't stand no more."

He looked off at the sky. "Do you know where you're headed?"

It kind of hit me right then. Me and Les and Tod had rode together a mighty long time. Now Tod was dead and it looked like me and Les were about to split up. I guess I'd known it was coming, but I hadn't really thought about it. I shook my head at his question. "Not right out," I said. "I've got an idea I'd like to head down to Monterey maybe, but I'm not sure." I pretty well knew, in the back of my mind, what I was going to do, but I didn't want to talk about it. We'd made our crossing about where I'd had an idea we would. We were south of Villa Union and therefore south of Villa Guerro. Rancho Fernando lay right on the way.

Les finished his tortillas. "Wish I had a smoke," he said.

"All my tobacco was wet," I said. "I throwed it away last night."

"Hey, Señor!" he called to the peon. *"Tiene fume?"*

"Si," the peon said. He got down off his animal and rummaged around in one of the sacks he had slung all over the jackass.

"Well," I said, "I'm glad to see him get off that mule for a minute anyway. Goddam, I thought he was glued to him."

The Mexican came over and handed Les a handful of tobacco leaves and Les give him another peso. I expect he figured he'd found him a good thing, for he squatted down, crossing his arms over his knees, and stared at us. Les handed me a bit of the tobacco. I rolled it between my hands to break it into cigarette makings. It was still green and didn't crumble too easily. "I ain't got no paper," I said.

Les didn't say anything for a minute. Finally he reached in his hip pocket and come out with a little soft-bound book. It was maybe three inches by five. I leaned closer to get a look. It was a Bible.

"Where'd you get that?" I asked him.

"It was Tod's," he said. "His daddy give it to him a while back." He opened it and tore out a page.

"Here!" I said. "What are you about? I ain't rolling no cigarettes outa Bible paper."

"Tod did," he said. And then I could see that many of the pages had been tore out. I figured Les must have gotten it off him after he'd died.

"Tod tore them pages out?"

"You never noticed him doing it?"

I shook my head.

"He done it. He used to always give me a wink when he done it."

"That's bad luck," I said. "Mighty bad luck."

Les shrugged. "Tod made his own luck." He took the paper he'd offered me and began to roll himself a cigarette. It was flimsy, being well suited to cigarette rolling. It made me uneasy seeing him do it.

"That's bad luck," I said again.

He didn't say anything, just licked the paper and finished the cigarette, shaping it and putting it in his mouth. He got out a match and lit it and got it going pretty good. I watched him smoking, me and the peon.

"Here," I said. "Give me a page out of there." I held out my hand and he tore out a sheet and I rolled myself a cigarette. It wasn't too good a smoke. The paper burned too fast and the tobacco was green and not cured properly.

"I've done some bad things," Les said. "Lots worse than burning a piece of Bible paper."

"Still," I said, "it's bad luck."

He shrugged. "Hey!" he said to the peon. "You want a smoke?" He repeated it in Spanish and the peon made a kind of half-about smile and nodded his head. But he wouldn't take any of our tobacco. He got a leaf of his own and rolled it into a kind of cigar. Les offered him a match and he took it gravely and lit up, holding the match after his smoke was going and staring at it. Finally it burned down to his fingers and he shook it out and put it on the ground.

"See, even that Mexican was scairt of it," I said.

Les spit on the ground and didn't say anything. He was not acting a lot like himself and I knew he was feeling bad about both Tod dying and me and him splitting up. Les is not a loner kind of hombre. He needs himself a friend. He makes a good friend, too.

I said: "Reckon whyn't you ride along with me. We'll find something good going on somewhere." I said it easily, hoping he might just say what I wasn't expecting him to.

But he didn't. He shook his head. "No, Will. I don't want to go inland. I want to stay on the border. I'll need to go back and tell Tod's daddy what happened."

I shook my head. "It'll be a while before you can go back to Texas, Les. South Texas, anyway. They'll be looking for us pretty good."

"I know," he said. "I'll bide my time. But I want to stay on the border."

My cigarette was about gone. I jammed it out in the dust. The paper kind of unfolded as I did and I could see a little printing on the pages. It made me uneasy. Les would have never done nothing like that before, burning Bible paper. I guess he somehow figured he was doing it for Tod.

"Les, they's a price on our head. You know as well as I do that that little river ain't gonna stop a ranger from coming across bounty hunting. You better come on south with me."

"No," he said.

I nodded. Les is a man that, once he gets his mind made up, is hard to change. What I was telling him was true. Texas rangers and other lawmen didn't think no more of violating the border than they did of skinning a cat. If they heard about a wanted man in one of the border towns they'd come on across, singly or in pairs, and bring him back one way or another, either dead or alive. There were a lot of ways to get a man across without taking the bridge.

"Les," I said, "you better listen to me."

161

"I'm not as well-known as you are, Will. Nobody will be looking for me."

There wasn't anything else to say. I shrugged.

Les turned to the little peon. *"Tiene agua?"*

"Si," the peon said. He was ready to do some more business.

Late in the afternoon we got the horses in and saddled up. We didn't say anything through the chore, but, when we were finished, we stood looking at each other.

"Oh!" Les said. He went into his pockets and came out with the wad of money he'd taken off Howland. "We've got to divvy this."

"Aw hell!" I said.

"No, half of it's yours." He counted it and then handed me my half, near a hundred and ten dollars. I still had some of the money left I'd taken off the ranch foreman and the two lots together gave me about a hundred and fifty dollars.

I held up my mare's reins and looked at Les. "I'm heading up for Villa Union," I said.

"I thought you were going south for Monterey."

"I am, pretty soon," I said. "Got a little business first. You?"

"Nuevo Laredo," he said. It was in the opposite direction.

"Why don't you come on up with me, Les, and then we'll ride back down together?"

"I reckon not," he said. He looked at me, a little smile on his face like he knew what I was up to. "I reckon not," he said. He lifted himself into the saddle. I did likewise.

"Well . . ." He held out his hand and I took it. "Will, when you get located, get a telegram to me at the Del Prado Hotel in Nuevo Laredo. I'll probably be around there for some time."

"All right," I said. We finished shaking hands. He give me a little grin and then reined around and headed south. I watched him for a minute and then turned my own pony and rode off. The peon was still sitting in the dirt watching us. I guess he'd never seen anything like us before.

I spent the rest of the evening getting into Villa Union,

THE BANK ROBBER

arriving there a little after dark. It wasn't much different from a hundred other little towns and I hunted up a dray station that did double duty as a livery barn and left my filly. I gave instructions to see she was rubbed down and given a double bait of corn. After that I shouldered my saddle and walked up the street to the cantina. They had a room or two to let and I took one for three pesos and settled in. It was Sunday, but there was still a good little bit of traffic in the bar. I could hear them warming up, but I never paid no mind. I was feeling a little low in spirit and the main thing I wanted was a bath and a little supper. The supper was easy to arrange, but the bath took some doing. Finally they rigged me a tub out in the back and I paid a kid a little coin to fetch me in water from the well. I took it cold, not caring whether it was hot or not. The lye soap I was using would have worked just as well in a frozen pond.

My clothes were tolerably clean from the rain, but I made a deal with a woman that worked in the cantina to take them and give 'em a good scrubbing. While she was at it I stayed in my room eating some cabaritto and beans and tortillas and drinking rum. When I'd taken off the pants to give 'em to the woman I'd remembered they were Les's. We'd forgotten to swap back, or rather I'd forgotten and he hadn't said a word about it. After I finished eating I took a survey of my wounds. My neck wasn't nothing and I didn't pay it no mind. The hole in my thigh seemed to be coming along all right. It had been a clean wound and didn't seem to be going bad at all. It was still a little sore, but I pulled it open and poured a little rum in it just to be on the safe side. It burned like hell, which I've heard is a good sign. There was a little angry flesh around where the bullet had gone in and I scuffed that up pretty good and made it bleed and gave it another drink of rum. All in all I figured I'd gotten out mighty light.

It was getting on pretty late when I finally got my clothes back, but I went ahead and dressed and wandered into the bar. I wanted to get a good line on where Villa Guerro was before I went to sleep. I planned to make an early start and might not be anybody much around to ask. I'd figured

163

Fernando Rancho was right on a line between the two towns and I'd just make for Guerro and ask as I went along.

The bar was near empty and the bartender was putting up his stock and getting ready to close. I stepped up and ordered rum and asked about the direction to Guerro. He didn't speak any English and my Spanish is not of the best, but, after about three drinks, I was able to understand that the town was about forty miles away in a straight northwesterly direction. That'd been about what I'd figured and it'd put the ranch at about thirty miles distance. I should be able to make it with an early start by about midafternoon. I paid for my drinks and went back to the little room I'd rented and went to sleep.

It was a long, lonesome ride. I guess I'd been riding with partners so long I'd forgotten what it is to make a long trail by yourself. Les was always good to ride with. He never said too much, but what he did say was generally worth listening to. Tod was either one of two ways—not saying a word because he was sulled up about something, or talking a blue streak and not saying anything. Of the two I always preferred the sull.

About early afternoon I figured I was getting close and I began looking for a little piece of water. After a little riding I found what I was looking for and pulled up and dismounted. It was a little limestone crick, not much wider than a horse's back, but the water was clean and cool. Lot of artesian springs in the area and they're some of the best water in the world. I had a clean shirt in my saddlebags I'd been saving and I got that out and then stripped off my old one and stuck it in its place. First I washed as much of the trail dust off myself as I could and then I got my razor out and made a job of shaving. My beard was tough and, not having any lather soap, I had to make do with a bar of the lye variety I'd brought along from Villa Union. Getting rid of the three-day growth hurt worse than my thigh ever did, but I kept after it until my face felt clean and smooth. Next I done what I could about combing my hair, having just my fingers to work with, and then I put on my clean shirt. It was near new. I'd bought it a number of weeks back but had only worn it several times. Still I didn't feel as well dressed as I wanted and it made me kind of low in mind again. It got me thinking about the kind of gall I had to be riding up to that rancho with any idea of getting to see that girl.

And of course that wasn't just any rancho I was going to be riding up to, but one which I'd left under some disgrace. There was a hell of a good chance the old don wouldn't even receive me and, if he did, he might be downright unfriendly. I could feel my nerve slipping and I began to curse myself, calling myself every kind of fool for coming on such a hare-brained errand. A man seems many things to other men, but down inside him he knows what he is. I was known far and wide as a man you didn't fool with, as a man you didn't give no trouble, but here I was acting as something less than a man—acting more like a damn fool kid.

Finally I made myself mad. I was still Wilson Young and that was goddam good enough for me whether it was for anyone else or not. I determined I would ride onto that ranch like I owned the place and anybody that didn't like it could go to hell.

My outfit wanted one last touch and I got my silver spurs out of my saddlebags and put them on. They felt strange, heavier and more awkward than my regular pair. I looked down at them, admiring the way they shone and glistened and dressed up my old, scuffed boots. Then I sat down and took them off. If I wasn't good enough to see that girl without silver spurs, then I wasn't good enough with them. I don't like to make a show and that was what I was setting out to do. I put my spurs back in my saddlebags, caught up the reins and mounted and rode out. I didn't have an exact idea of where the ranch headquarters were, but I knew they lay somewhere due north of a line of little mountains I'd noted on my first visit. I could see the mountains far off in the background and I quartered in toward them expecting to strike some kind of sign before long. Home-range cattle were beginning to show up and I knew I couldn't be far.

After about an hour's ride the tops of the house and outbuildings of the ranch suddenly rose up out of the prairie.

The sun was in the lower quarter of the sky and I figured it to be around four o'clock. It was just about the time I'd been aiming at. I'd figured if I could arrive early, but not too early, I might get invited to dinner and that would give me a chance to see the girl.

A little further on and the ranch came into plain view. I put my mare into a smart gallop and swept in under the main gate and made for the front of the house. A peon run out as I pulled up and took my reins. I got down, not quite knowing what to do, and stood a minute knocking the dust off my breeches. The peon that was holding my horse looked at me, awaiting instructions as to whether to take my mare to the barn or not. I ignored him and went up on the veranda steps. A house servant came out. He inquired politely what my business was and who I desired to see.

"Tell Señor Fernando that Wilson Young is back in the neighborhood and would like to visit with him a minute."

He turned and went into the house and beckoned me into the hall. It was cool and quiet and just a little dark. The peon asked me to wait and said he'd tell the señor I was come. The hall I was standing in was the main breezeway between the two parts of the house. A water stand was against the wall and I poured out a little water in the bowl and had another go at my face. As I finished up putting a little more water on my hair the servant came back and said the patron would see me. "Pray walk this way, Señor," he said, motioning me toward the big sitting room off to the right.

CHAPTER 14

Mexico

The old patron received me very stiffly. He was sitting in a big, highback leather chair and he made no move to get up as I entered. A cutglass decanter of cognac was sitting on a table by his chair and he had a glass in his hand.

"Well, Señor Young," he said, "what is your business here today?"

I stood in the center of the room, my hat in my hand. I tapped it idly against my leg. I wondered if he was going to ask me to sit down or offer me a drink. "I have no business, Señor," I said in Spanish. "I'm only traveling and chanced to pass your rancho."

"That is our good fortune," he said formally. He didn't mean it, it's just something the Spanish say.

"I hope I don't come at an inopportune time," I said. I was still standing.

"Not at all," he said. He fell silent, waiting for me to say something.

I was feeling uncomfortable. "Señor," I said, "I would apologize for my behavior on my last visit. We had just had some very bad luck and I'm afraid I allowed it to affect my manners. We repaid your hospitality very poorly. That is the purpose of my visit today, to apologize for my bad manners. I have ridden many miles to deliver this apology and I hope you will accept it." I figured if I was going to have to eat crow I might as well make a good job of it.

It softened the old don. He looked at me a minute then nodded. "No apology is necessary," he said. "I was not aware of any bad manners on your part." He motioned toward a chair just to his left. "Will you take a seat and I'll send for another glass. I'm sure a little liquor would be welcome after such a long ride."

"With many thanks," I said. I sat down in the chair and crossed my legs and put my hat on my knee. I'd made a little progress, but I still had to make the don believe I was a good, upright citizen. While the servant was fetching the glass I told him I'd decided to leave the cattle-buying business. "We were only small operators," I said. "And fortune didn't smile on us. We were traveling with cash— gold—and we lost it all along with a good horse in the river. Over four thousand dollars, Señor."

"*Mala suerte!*" he said. "Yes, the river was at flood stage at that time. Upcountry rains, I believe."

"So there we were, all our funds gone and a horse short. Being such small buyers, we had no letter of credit from a bank, only the gold. It ruined us in the cattle business."

"I can see how it would cloud your mind." He'd got out a cigar and lit it and was nodding and agreeing with my story. "I believe you smoke cigars, do you not?"

I nodded.

"There are some excellent ones in the drawer of the desk. Please help yourself. I have a bad hip that has been bothering me of late."

I got up and got a cigar and lit it. I almost struck the match on my boot heel, but I caught myself in time and flicked it with my thumbnail. All the stiff talking we were making was bothering me. It made my mouth uncomfortable.

"Where is your friend?" the patron asked me. "The quiet one."

"Oh, him," I said. "He's gone back to Texas. He has decided to continue in the cattle-buying business. He's gone back for some more money."

"What will you do then?"

"Señor, I plan to become a resident of Mexico. I've always liked the country and I believe I'll just settle down here."

"Indeed," he said. It pleased him. I expect he'd been sitting in that chair with a bad leg just wishing somebody would come along he could visit with.

The servant came with my glass and the old patron poured me a generous drink and we made a toast to our mutual luck and health. I kept looking around waiting for the girl to show up. I just about had the patron won over and I was starting to get a little impatient to see the girl. We talked on, discussing this and that, and I told the old man that I intended to settle around Monterey and raise horses. "I've had experience with good horse flesh," I said. "I think they could be raised cheaply here and sold for a good profit in the United States."

"Ahh," he said. It was a subject he liked and we discussed the horse market to some extent. Fortunately I knew a pretty good bit about it and I continued to make a good impression on my host.

Finally he invited me to stay for dinner. I told him I really should be getting on, but he urged me to stay and I finally accepted. After a little more talk I asked after his niece.

"Ah, Linda! She is well."

"I'm glad to hear that," I said. I stopped, waiting for him to tell me more about her, but he didn't, just sat there puffing on his cigar and looking at me. Finally I cleared my throat. "Uh, does she enjoy it here?"

"Ah, yes!" he said. "It seemed very agreeable to her."

Well, damn him! Why didn't he tell me something. I got bold. "She'll be dining with us?"

"Oh no," he said. "Unfortunately not."

I looked at him. "Why not?" I asked.

"Why, she is not here, Señor. She has gone back to her home. The bandit trouble ended at her father's place and she left yesterday to return."

I sat there, not knowing what to say. It was the worst kind of luck. "Well," I said, "that is a surprise."

"What?" he asked. "A surprise?"

"Well," I said, "a surprise in that the bandit trouble was overcome so easily. Usually it takes longer."

"Ah . . ." he said again.

169

I never felt such a letdown in my whole life. Until the moment he told me she was gone I hadn't really realized how anxious I was to see the girl, how much I'd been pining for her. I asked, as casually as I could, if she'd gone by rail.

"Partly," the patron said. "I've sent her in my coach to Rodriguez and from there she will take the railroad to Sabinas Hidalgo."

"Rodriguez?"

"Si," he said. "It's a matter of a little more than a day. They stayed last night at a rancho near Progresso. A kinsman of mine."

"Yeah," I said. I knew where Rodriguez was. It was a railhead town about sixty miles south of where we were. I might could make it in a day, but the girl would surely be gone by then. I became impatient to go. I tried to think of some way to get out of the supper.

"Don Fernando," I said, "I really believe it won't be possible for me to eat with you. I'm anxious to get to Monterey. I have business there."

But he wouldn't hear of it. He insisted that my horse was tired and that I'd feel much better after a good dinner and a night's rest. "It's late now. It's no time to be traveling."

I tried to tell him I couldn't possibly stay overnight, but he argued me down. He said he'd already sent a servant to prepare a room for me. I gave in. There wasn't much else I could do. I'd never catch up with the girl and my horse was tired. I'd ridden her forty miles already and she wasn't in shape to go another sixty. I slumped back in the chair. What a hell of a piece of luck. I was aching inside to see Linda and being in the place where she'd been just made it worse.

We went in to supper after a little and it was good, but I wasn't in a mood to enjoy it. Now that I was in pretty good with the old patron he near talked my ear off. After supper nothing would do but that we sit up and talk for a while. I was plumb out of things to talk about and only wanted to go to bed and make an early start the next morning. I didn't know what I was going to do, but I knew which direction

I was going. Finally, I got away and went to bed. I set my mind to wake up before good light. I'd thanked the don for his hospitality and told him I'd be riding out early. He said he'd see that my horse was ready and something was made up for me in the kitchen to take along. He was a polite old man, but I was certainly glad to get away from him and get to bed.

I was on the road before daylight. My little mare had been well cared for, grained and rubbed down, and I had a sack of food in my saddlebags. If the girl had been there I believe I would have stayed on until I was run off. And I'm not too sure the old don would have ever done that. He'd taken a big liking to me and several times had hinted he'd considered hiring an American foreman who knew the horse and cattle business. By then, though, I wasn't looking for a job in that part of the country, so I never gave him any encouragement to come out with a firm offer.

The last stars were still in the sky and I picked me out one for my compass and set off for Rodriguez. Mexican trains are undependable and it's nothing for one to be a day or two late making a schedule. There was a chance that the girl might still be there. I didn't know what I'd do if she was, what I'd say to her, how I'd even get to talk to her, but I planned to worry about that once I caught up to her.

I patted my little filly's neck as we went along. One side of my saddlebags was filled with oats for her, but she was going to have to show me some miles before she got to put on the feed bag.

The country was big and empty. Occasionally I'd see a campesino herding a few goats or one cow, but mostly it was just mesquite and cactus and sand and rocks. I rode hard for about six hours and then pulled up by a little stream and gave myself and my filly a little rest. I shook her out some oats on a clean flat rock and made a meal for myself out of beef and cornbread and beans. The don must have told the cook I was a big eater, for he'd laid me in a lunch it would take three men to eat. I was grateful. There was no telling how long my money would last and it was much better eating gratis than having to pay for it.

After I ate I had a drink of water and then lay back in the sun and shut my eyes. I was on a fool's errand, but I didn't care. I'm the kind of a man gets something fixed in his mind and can't shake it. I had that girl in my mind and I wasn't going to rest until I came up to her. My daddy had once told me I was stubborn enough to be a lawyer. I don't know where he got the idea lawyers were stubborn. I guess it came from all his legal troubles. He'd determined I'd get an education. When they were taking his land he used to rage around and swear that he was the last Young would ever be beat because they were too ignorant to know their own rights. He'd sworn I was to have an education, and not just grade school either, but better. And I'd gone. I'd gone steady until I was fourteen or fifteen—I couldn't remember which. Les and Tod had both dropped out but I'd kept on, going to the secondary school in Corpus and living with my old aunt. It come back to me about them long hours in that schoolroom studying mathematics and Latin and all that other stuff. I hadn't liked it a bit and I'd finally wore my daddy down until he'd said he didn't give a damn what I did. Said it looked as if I was determined to be no account and there was nothing he could do about it.

I reckoned I'd been a disappointment to him. Fortunately he'd died before he found out just what a disappointment I'd turned out to be. Still I'd had more schooling than most. It hadn't done me a damn bit of good.

I allowed myself about an hour's rest and then mounted back up and lit out. The day had got awful hot and my little filly was sweating up pretty bad. Every once in a while I'd take off my hat and wipe the sweatband out, but it didn't do much good. It was just hot and a man will naturally sweat when it's hot.

I wasn't too worried about finding Rodriguez. It's a fair-sized town and there would be plenty ranchos and haciendas in the area I could get exact directions at. I figured to make it by late afternoon.

The only thing I'd inherited from my daddy had been his gold watch. Of late I'd been carrying it in my saddlebags because I'd let it run down, but I'd got the correct time off the patron the night before and I had it in my pocket. After I began to see some signs of a settlement approaching I got it out and made the time to be near four o'clock. If Rodriguez was close I'd made pretty good time. I spotted a little adobe with a rickety corral out back, but judged the people might not know much, so I passed them by and kept on to the southwest. After a little more time I saw a rider at a water hole. He was a Mexican cowboy wearing a big hat and a serape and leather chaps. I pulled in beside him and asked directions. He said Rodriguez was just a little further on and that I was headed in the right direction. I thanked him and offered tobacco, but he said he had plenty and wouldn't take it. I thanked him again and headed out. I looked back after a little and could see him watching me. I guess he wondered what the hell I was doing out in that country. I kind of wondered myself.

It was just a little after five when I rode into Rodriguez. I made straight for the railroad office and tied my filly in front, loosening her cinch before I went in. She'd done good work for the day. I patted her and told her she'd have a nice rest now. Then I went into the big adobe building.

It was cool inside after the afternoon sun. Except for the clerk there was no one else in the office. He was a little sparrow of a man, got up in a suit as befits a man of his position. I went up and asked him if the train for Sabinas Hidalgo had left yet.

"Of course not," he said in Spanish. "It doesn't go for three days."

For just a second I thought it might have been delayed uncommonly long, but then I asked if that was the only train for the week. The clerk looked insulted.

"Clearly you're a stranger," he said. "The train goes south twice weekly. Twice weekly it goes north."

"When'd the last one leave?" I asked him.

He studied me as if trying to figure out what I wanted with that information. Obviously, if the train had already left I had missed it, so why should I want to know when it had left? Plainly, I was, to him, a man who didn't mind wasting his time. "Yesterday," he said. "In the morning."

It made me feel better. Even if I'd ridden all night I'd never have made it in time. I got out some currency. "I want a ticket on the next one," I said. "And I want to ship my horse with me."

"To where, please?" he inquired.

"Sabinas Hidalgo," I said.

He had his rate book open. "How was I to know that? This office is a busy one and there are many details. I can't know the destination of each passenger before they tell me."

"We were just speaking of it," I said.

"No, Señor," he said. "You were speaking of it. It was not I said a word about Sabinas Hidalgo."

"All right," I said.

"That will be forty-five pesos. Thirty for yourself and fifteen for your horse. The train will go in three days at approximately ten o'clock in the morning."

I paid him and got my ticket voucher and then asked where the telegraph office was.

"It's contained in this office," he said. "Where else would a telegraph office be?"

"All right. I want to send a wire to Nuevo Laredo."

"That's impossible," he said.

"Why? Ain't there no wires to Nuevo Laredo?"

"Certainly there are wires to Nuevo Laredo. The wires go everywhere the railroad tracks go and the railroad tracks certainly go to Nuevo Laredo."

"Then why is it impossible?"

"Because the operator is not here, Señor." He looked around and then back at me as if I were an idiot. "That is plain to see, clearly."

I was hot and tired from the ride and tired of listening to all his talk. I reached across the table and got me a handful of his vest and drug him out of his chair. "Now," I said, "you tell me and damn quick where the operator is. I want to send a wire. Is that clear?"

In a way it was funny. His eyes got big as saucers in his little sparrow face and he went so white I thought he was going to pass out.

"He's at his meal, Sẽnor," he said. He was scared to death.

"Then you go get him," I said.

"But that's not possible. I can't leave the office."

"When will he be back, then?"

"Soon, Sẽnor. Very soon."

I let go of him and he sank back in his chair, raising both hands and smoothing his vest. Once he was set back down he got to looking official again. I told him I was going to see to my horse and that the operator had better be back when I returned.

"We can hope, Sẽnor," he said.

"You better do more than that," I said. "If he ain't back you better start praying." I went out and got my filly and led her down the street looking for a livery stable. The little clerk had been funny and it had lightened my mood. I imagine I wasn't the first had drug him out of his chair. He was about the most trying man I'd ever seen.

I found a livery stable and made arrangements for my filly to be kept until the train left. I told the proprietor I wanted her rubbed down right away and given grain and oats twice a day. She'd earned a little good times herself.

After that I shouldered my saddle and walked up the street until I found a cantina that had rooms to let. I left my gear behind the bar and settled down at a table to have a drink or two. I figured to give the operator plenty of time to get back. If he wasn't there when I walked back in the office it might scare the little clerk to death. I had a couple of drinks of rum and then ordered up a bowl of chili. They had beer, there being a brewery at Monterey, and I had several glasses with the chili. It was good, cool and fresh. You can't get much beer down in Mexico unless you're near a brewery. It spoils so damn fast in the heat. But Rodriguez was on the rail line to Monterey and they could get it shipped up pretty quick.

I wondered what old Les was doing. He couldn't be living too high, not on just the little money he had because it was going to have to last him a while. It would be sometime before things would quieten down enough for him to slip back across the border and go into Corpus. The rangers are pretty smart men and they'd have our hometown staked out either by themselves or with the help of the local law. With the three-day layover, I figured to wire him and see what his plans were. Nuevo Laredo was the head of the line for the railroad that went through Sabinas and he might be willing to ride down for a while.

I could have ridden to Sabinas faster than waiting on the train, but I wasn't in any special hurry now that I had the girl placed and I thought it would be a change for me and my horse. The idea of laying around and not doing anything for several days kind of appealed to me. I'd been on the go so much lately that I was just a little fagged out.

I finished my meal and then went back to the railroad office. The operator was there and he and the clerk both started looking uneasy when I came in. The clerk got clear on the other side of the room, acting like he was doing something else, while I talked to the operator.

I wired Les in care of the Del Prado Hotel. I told him where I was, how long I expected to be there and that I wanted to hear from him. I signed it John Wilson. It was an alias I'd used before and one he'd recognize. I told the operator where I'd be staying and to send over as soon as a reply came in. He assured me he would and I paid him and went back to the cantina. It had got dark and I had a few more drinks and then turned in and went to sleep.

CHAPTER 15

Laying Around

Next day I got up early and just kind of lay around the town. Even though I'd left instructions where I'd be I still checked by the telegraph office several times. There was no return wire from Les. That didn't bother me too much. I figured he'd be out and around during the day and wouldn't get my wire until he went to his hotel for the night. I figured I'd get word next day for sure. Les had said he'd be in Nuevo Laredo at the Del Prado and you could be damn sure that's where he'd be.

In preparation for meeting the girl I bought a new pair of breeches and had my boots blacked and oiled. I really needed new boots, but I hated to lay out the money for a good pair and I wasn't about to buy some that were no good. My thigh was still bothering me a little, so I went by and seen a Mexican doctor. He said it was coming along all right, but he went ahead and reopened the wound and doctored it up proper fashion. I'd been mighty lucky with that wound. If the bullet had hit a quarter inch more to center it'd have broken the bone. That would nearly have amounted to the same thing as getting shot dead. I wouldn't have been able to travel and I reckon I'd have just laid there in that little draw until the posse finished me off.

That got me to wondering what Les would have done if both me and Tod had been shot up bad. Probably he'd have stayed right there with us. Howland would have run out, but Les would have stayed and we'd probably all three be dead as fence posts. Well, it's funny what a difference a little thing like a quarter of an inch can make.

I took supper that night in the cantina and then had a few drinks with some Mexican charros off a neighboring ranch. They didn't have much money, so I stood several rounds, the drinks being plenty cheap. One of the cowboys, a boy named Manuel Aquilla, had grown up around Sabinas Hidalgo. I'd gotten the straight of Linda's name from the old don and I asked Manual if he knew of the family.

"Ah, yes, the De Cavas, to be sure. Very rich. And a large family too. There are several girls—three, I believe."

We were all in a pretty good mood, me from the drinks and them from the fact that I was paying. "Are they all pretty?"

"Most are very fair," Manuel said. "But you understand I come from a poor family and there were not many opportunities for me to see them."

"What about the one they call Linda? You know much about her?" It wasn't good manners for me to be talking about a lady in a saloon, but I was eager to know all I could about the girl. I'd found out from her uncle that she wasn't betrothed though there was considerable interest on the part of the young bucks that lived around her daddy's place.

"Linda?" he said. "Ah yes! She and I are nearly of the same age and she went to the government school for a time. I didn't attend, but I saw her there. A very beautiful señorita. *Sabarosa!*"

"Here, give us another round," I said to the bartender. We were drinking tequila and it wasn't but a peso for a large shot. Manuel asked politely how I came to know the girl and what my interest was.

I told him I'd met her at her uncle's place, but the last part stumped me. I wasn't sure myself what my interest was. All I wanted, all that was clear, was that I wanted to see her again, get up next to her and talk and see what she thought about me. Where it'd go from there I hadn't the slightest idea.

One of the other charros give me a wink and made a circle out of his fingers. *"Pinche*, eh, maybe?"

He was just trying to be friendly, just joking. He didn't know the girl and didn't know she was quality. But it didn't make any difference. I set my glass down and then wheeled around and back-handed him across the face. I done it so sudden and so hard that it caught everybody off-balance. The charro kind of staggered backward, his head knocked over to the side. He was wearing an old navy revolver and his hand made a pass downward as if he meant to draw. I pulled my own gun and stuck it in his ribs before he could even get his hand around the butt of his piece.

"Tien cuidado," I said quietly. "Have care."

The cowboys had fallen back away from us, their eyes white in their faces. The charro I had my gun on looked down and then swallowed and slowly raised his hands.

"I'll have an apology," I said in Spanish. "That girl is a lady."

"Si," he said. *"Seguro."*

"Well?"

"Perdóneme! Madre de Dios, perdóneme!"

"All right," I said. He was standing staring down at the big gun in his belly, fear in his face. I slowly pulled it back and looked around at the cowboys.

"Finis?" I asked them. I let the gun travel the half-circle. *"Finis?"*

It took them a second to understand I was asking if it was all over, but as soon as they got it they began nodding and jabbering away in Spanish.

"All right," I said. I put my gun back in the holster, still watching them. Nobody said anything for a second. They stood as if they'd taken root, staring at me. Finally Manuel shook his head slowly and said, *"Muy rápido!!* Sonofabitch!"

It broke the tension. "Yeah," I said, "I'm fast all right." I motioned to the bartender. "Give that man a drink." I nodded toward the cowboy I'd slapped. He still had his hands in the air. "Come on," I said. "Have a drink. It's all over. You didn't know."

It was my fault in the first place. I shouldn't have been talking about the girl. That was me all over; I wanted to consort with a lady, but I didn't have enough breeding to keep my mouth shut about her in a damn saloon. I got just what I should have expected. The cowboys, except for Manuel, didn't know the girl and they'd just naturally think she was a cheap trick.

The good spirit was over. They stayed around drinking but that was just because the drinks were free. I knocked off my last one, paid my bill, and headed for bed. Manuel called out something as I walked off, but I just give him a backward wave and kept walking.

There was still no word from Les by afternoon of the next day and I walked over to the telegraph office and asked the operator to wire down and see if the message had been delivered. While he done it I walked over to the livery stable to see about my filly. They had her in a straw-lined stall and she looked pretty contented. I went in and rubbed her a little with a piece of tow sack and she looked around at me, pricking up her ears.

"Not yet," I said. "You just take it easy. We're going train riding and you're gonna like it. Beats the hell out of walking."

The owner of the stable was watching me, but he couldn't understand what I was saying. I come out of the stall and told him he was doing a good job.

"That's a fine horse," he said in Spanish.

"Yes," I agreed. "She is."

"Perhaps the señor would like to sell her? She would bring a good price."

I laughed. "Not likely," I said. I started out, but then turned around and looked at him. I give him a long, thoughtful look. "You know," I said, "if I was you I'd be damn sure nothing happened to that horse. There are many horse thieves in Mexico and my mare is a fine horse."

"Oh, no," he assured me. "We have guards at night."

"Good," I said, "because I'd feed you your own liver if something happened to that pony. I reckon you understand me."

He swallowed hard. *"Si,"* he said. *"Mi sabe."*

"Good." I turned away and walked on over to the telegraph office. The operator said he'd heard from Nuevo Laredo and that my message had been delivered to the hotel, but it hadn't been picked up. I wondered just where in hell Les could be. It was kind of starting to worry me. I hoped he wouldn't be damn fool enough to have already left for Texas. It was way too early to be making any such visit, no matter how bad he was feeling about Tod.

I lolled around the cantina the rest of the evening, having an occasional drink. Manuel and his friends come in about nine o'clock and we had a drink or two together. It seemed to me they got into town an awful lot for working cowboys. They were polite and agreeable enough, but they seemed to watch me mighty close. I figured I'd scared them with my quick temper and they just wanted to be on guard in case it happened again. I'd told Manuel I was going out on the train the next morning and he wanted to know if I was shipping my horse along. It was a kind of a strange question.

"Well, I don't know," I said. "Why?"

He shrugged. *"Nada,"* he said. "It is just expensive to ship a horse."

"How you know I even got a horse?" I asked him. I don't like people getting curious about my animal.

"Oh, I didn't!" he said. "I just assumed."

"Oh," I said. We were sitting at a table. "Tell me," I asked him. "I've heard there were bandits south of here. Are they still active?"

He shrugged. "Who can say. Of late they have not been too active."

One of the others laughed and said something in Spanish that I didn't catch.

"What?"

"He didn't say anything."

"Yes he did. What'd he say?" I looked around at them. There were five, including one who had not been there the previous evening. They were a poor-looking lot, but they were all carrying revolvers. I hadn't really taken note of it before and it kind of surprised me. A hand gun is a pretty expensive luxury for a working cowboy. I asked Manuel again what the cowboy had said.

He shrugged. "Oh, just something about how broke the bandits must be getting. It's a Spanish joke about not having any work."

"Yeah," I said.

After a little while I got up and went to my room. I lay down on the bed for a minute, but then got up and got my saddle and bed roll and went out the back and walked down to the livery stable. There was a sleepy old man on duty and he asked if I wanted my horse. "No," I said. "I don't." I went back in the dark of the stable and opened my mare's stall door. She looked around at me and made a little whinny. "All right," I told her. "Just take it easy. I'm gonna bunk with you." I fixed my bed roll in the straw in front of the stall door and lay down. The drinks had me good and relaxed and I didn't have any trouble going to sleep.

Sometime later, a little before dawn, I heard a sound and it brought me full awake. I lay still, but got my hand in under my blankets and got hold of my revolver. Somebody was fooling with the latch of the stall gate. I waited until they got the lock off and swung the door open and then I suddenly sat up and cocked my revolver. It was very dark and all I could see was a very dim form. The sound of the revolver cocking made a loud *click-click* in the quiet and whoever it was suddenly yelled, "Yiiii" and seemed to fall backward. I expect it was kind of startling. I could hear the sound of somebody running and I crawled through the stall door, my pistol in my hand, and I looked to the right and left. I couldn't see a thing. After a little I went up to the front of the barn to ask the watchman if he'd seen anything. He was sound asleep in a chair by the door. I kicked at the legs and the chair overturned and spilled him to the floor. It near scared him to death. "Goddam you," I said, "stay awake!"

I went back to the stall and lay back down. But my nerves were tensed up and I had trouble getting to sleep. I dozed off and on until dawn and then got up and went looking for breakfast. I would have give a pretty to have known who my visitor had been, but I didn't expect I was going to find out. My train would be leaving in about four hours.

About nine I saddled my mare, leaving her cinch loose, and led her over to the train station. A big crowd of Mexicans had gathered around, some with traveling gear, but some just come down to see the train. I'd been on 'em plenty of times before, so it wasn't no novelty. The clerk said the train had got away from Nuevo Laredo on time, so it ought to be pretty near on schedule.

There was still no word from Les. I figured he must have changed his plans.

I sat in front of the station watching the crowd. A good number of the passengers seemed to be quitting the country for good, for they had furniture and bed rolls and chickens in coops and one or two was leading goats. They'll get right into the chair cars with that kind of gear too. I've ridden Mexican trains before and it ain't no treat, unless you like to be sat on and shoved around and smell chickens and garlic and listen to a lot of noise.

It got to be ten o'clock and then a little past and the train still hadn't come. I went into the station and asked the clerk where the hell it was. He shrugged and said that was something he could not know. "Perhaps it has broken down, Señor. Perhaps bandits, perhaps it has simply stopped to rest the passengers. Who can say?"

I checked with the operator, but there was still no wire from Les.

Outside I settled back down. Finally, from a way off, there came a little whistle sound and the crowd began to get excited and gather themselves up. After a time you could see the train clearly. It looked to be about six coaches with several flat cars for the livestock. It came around a bend and then straightened up for the run into the station. I went down by my mare and petted her and tried to keep her easy. All the livestock was getting tense and fidgety. They could hear the noise of the train a lot better than we could and it was making them nervous. I soothed my mare, but she still jumped around pretty good when the train pulled into the station. It come in huffing and puffing and throwing cinders every which way and the operator was sitting down on his whistle to try to get the crowd off the tracks. They'd surged out off the platform and it was a miracle some of 'em didn't get run down. As it was, the train driver had to take it easy and inch his locomotive in little by little until he could get lined up with the platform. The crowd made a run for the chair cars, but I led my mare down to one of the flatbeds. A trainman came back and let down a little loading trestle and I led my mare up it and tied her in place. There were several other horses on the car, which was rigged up like a corral with posts stuck down along the sides and then stringers running along crosswise. I figured she'd be pretty jittery about the ride and I had no interest in trying to find a chair among that mob that had loaded in, so I figured to just ride along on the livestock car and look after my animal.

It took us a while to get under way, but I took me a seat up against one of the corner posts and got out one of the little cigars I'd bought a good supply of and settled down for the wait. Finally they got the crowd stuffed into the cars and then the locomotive commenced to get up steam. The horses were plenty nervous. I got up and patted my mare and done what I could for the others, but they was still mighty worried. After a bit the locomotive wheels began to turn. They had a trainman up in front of the engine pouring sand under the wheels to help them take hold and get up speed.

Then we were off. My mare didn't like it at first, but we went along so smoothly that she finally settled down and I went back and sat down. After a while we got up speed and then we were really flying along. I figured we must have been making near thirty miles an hour. A horse can run thirty miles an hour, but not for very long. Cinders were blowing back, but the wind was generally taking them out to the side. Occasionally one would blow in on us and hit one of the horses and make him snort and rear around, but it didn't happen often. I got to feeling pretty good. I was still a little worried about not hearing from Les, but I was comfortable and we were whizzing along toward Sabinas and I figured to get a chance to see the girl. I didn't know how I was going to arrange it once I got there, but I figured I'd think of something.

The prairie just flew by. It was starting to get a little hilly, but it was still northern Mexico land, cactus and rocks and sand. It's poor country and the people who live on it are poor. Some of them have nearly about all they can do just to scratch out enough to eat. The land just about won't support cattle. On the big ranchos, the ones that have more acres than you can ride over in a week, they raise hay and some grasses because they've got land enough to put to it and their cattle do all right. But the little man don't really have much chance. He's lucky if he can find enough for just one cow to eat and that's what he does every year, raises him just one cow and then butchers it along toward the end of the year.

About a half hour or a little better out of the station I felt the train begin to slow. I got up and went to the side and leaned over the rail and looked down the track. Way in the distance I could see a water tower rearing up. The train kept on slowing until we were barely creeping along. We were coming to the edge of a little bunch of hills. They weren't much, just some sandy mounds, but they were pretty thick with mesquite and cactus. I figured there was water under the ground on account of the water tower and the thick brush. We finally pulled in and stopped and then the engineer went to backing and filling until he'd got himself positioned under the spigot. I leaned against the railing, watching a train hand climb up the tower and swing the spigot through over the engine and release the water. A steam locomotive takes a power of water and they were some time at it. Finally they got full up and the train man got back aboard and the engine commenced jerking the cars forward. I could see the same man up front with a bag of sand helping the locomotive's wheels. We got going, still creeping along, though, and he run back to the locomotive and swung into the cab. It was a marvel to me all the things they had to keep tended. The engine huffing and puffing, but we weren't making much speed, maybe ten miles an hour. There was a good load aboard and it'd take a while to get all the rolling stock going. I leaned against the railing, smoking and watching the country going by. We were starting to get into the little line of hills. I finished my cigarette and flicked it into the air, watching it curving in the wind. Just before it hit the ground I caught sight of a band of men suddenly coming out of the hills. There must have been twenty of them and they were riding low, waving rifles and yelling and shooting. I quick run over to the other side and there was a bunch of about equal numbers coming from the other side. They were heading for the front of the train, but, as slow as we were going, they'd have no trouble coming up to us. They come on, yelling and firing off their rifles. I could feel the train jerk and shudder as the engineer crowded on steam trying to get up speed. I was a sitting duck as open as the flat car was. I run back to my mare and jerked out my Henry and lay down flat by one of the posts. The bandits had come alongside the train. They were mostly crowded around the front, shooting into the cab of the engine, but some had strung out alongside the cars. They were still a good fifty yards up from me, but the train was gathering speed and some of them couldn't keep up and they were beginning to drop back. I could see that most of them were so poorly mounted that they wouldn't last long if the train got to going any at all. I held my fire, hoping they wouldn't see me. If they began firing at me they'd be sure to hit my mare, as many shots as they were letting off. The ones that were dropping back were firing into the chair cars. Some shots were coming back at them and I seen one bandit go down but the cars were mostly filled with old people, women and children and what not. Hell, them damn bandits didn't care. They just rode along firing at they didn't give a damn what.

The train kept going, but I didn't think it would for long. I could see up to the front of the train and there was quite a bunch around the locomotive. They were shooting point-blank into the cab.

Then I heard a yell and swerved around to look the other way. A bandit had dropped nearly even with my car and he was pointing at the livestock car and yelling something at the riders ahead of him. I finally made out he was yelling, *"Caballos!"* which is "horses" in Spanish. As poorly mounted as they were, the good horses on the car would be a real find. The rider still hadn't seen me, so I eased around until I could get good aim on him and I let him have one right in the chest with my Henry. He never knew what hit him. One minute he was in the saddle, the next he was flipping off backward. Another rider came into view, coming backward because the train was going faster than he was, and I shot him too. Then another. But he saw me and got off a shot before I could hit him. It was easy shooting but I knew it couldn't last. My rifle only held five shots and there wouldn't be time to reload.

Then I became aware there were riders falling back on the side I was on. I swerved around, guns going off everywhere, and cut down on one. Just before I shot him he looked back and I seen it was one of the men that had been with Manuel. I didn't have time to speculate about that, for others were coming back and I seen one of them was Manuel himself. He seen me about the time I recognized him and swerved in his saddle and aimed over his shoulder at me. He was not quite back to my car. I seen the smoke from his revolver and ducked. He cut out away from the train and I followed him with my sights and shot him out of the saddle just as he wheeled for another shot. Ahead of him I recognized the charro I'd slapped. There wasn't much question what they'd do to me if they could. They hadn't forgotten what I'd done to the one I'd pulled the gun on. I remembered how they'd sat there the night before watching me. I reckoned they were just biding their time, knowing they'd get a chance at me.

Just then I felt the engine begin slowing. No doubt they'd killed the engineer and his fireman. I took a quick look toward the front and seen one jump from his horse and swing into the cab. The train was commencing to really slow. In another second it would be stopped. My rifle was empty and I left it laying right where it was and crabbed across the car and kicked open the little gate they had fixed up. Then I jumped up and run back to my mare and undid

her reins. She was jumping and trembling from all the gunfire. I tightened her cinch as quickly as I could and then
started to mount. I heard something thud into the back of
the car, right by my head, and I jerked around and seen
a bandit riding alongside shooting at me. He was cocking
his pistol for another shot when I got my own piece out
and thumbed off two shots. The second one got him and
he went sideways out of the saddle. I had it all over them,
shooting from the train, while they had to aim from a running horse.

The train was near stopped and I vaulted on my mare
and urged her toward where the gate was swinging open at
the side of the car. The boards under her feet felt strange
and she picked her way across the bed of the car. A bandit
come riding back just as we got to the gate. I snapped off
a shot, but missed him and he shied away to the front.
Then the train was stopped and I laid spurs to my horse
and jumped her off the train. It was pretty good height
and she nearly went to her knees when she landed, but
we made it all right. She scrambled around in the sand and
rocks for a second, then got her feet, and I laid the spurs
to her and took off for the north. A few of the bandits seen
me and let off a shot or two, but they weren't concerned
with me; they were more interested in looting the train. I
rode low, looking back every now and then, but no pursuit
developed. It wouldn't have mattered if it had anyway. Their
horses were so fagged from chasing the train they'd have
never been able to catch me on a fresh animal. After a
little I pulled my mare down to a lope and looked back.
The bandits were ganged around the train like flies on a
piece of fresh meat. The train was stock-still, a little thread
of steam rising from her smokestack. Occasionally a shot
would ring out, but they seemed to have pretty well taken
charge. I rode alongside the railroad tracks. I figured to head
back for Rodriguez. It couldn't be more than twenty miles
and it was near a hundred to Sabinas with the bandits in the
way. I figured to go back to town, get provisioned, and set
out horseback.

CHAPTER 16

Sabinas Hidalgo

When I finally got back into Rodriguez I headed straight for the railroad office and told the little clerk his train had been robbed. He'd already heard. The bandits hadn't killed all the trainmen and one of them had got the train into a little way station and they'd wired back. I asked the little clerk how many had been killed, but he didn't know, didn't seem to much care either. I expect he's pretty used to train robberies and, so long as they don't happen in his office, he don't get too excited.

I asked him when the next train would be going south and he shrugged.

"Who can say, Señor. You can understand an event of this nature would disrupt even one of the great railroads of the northern United States."

"But at any rate it will be a few days?"

"Oh, indeed. Yes, indeed. But then, perhaps not. Perhaps they will dispatch another train from Nuevo Laredo. If that occurs service will be much improved."

I got out a cigar and lit it. "Well, do you think that will happen?"

He give me that look again, like I was an idiot. "Señor, clearly that is not for this office to know. Surely you can understand that—"

"All right," I said. "Okay." I turned around and started for the door. Just as I got there the telegraph operator came in wiping his mouth. He'd been eating again. He saw me and put up his hand and said, "Ah!"

"Yeah? Ah, what?"

"Ah, I have the telegram for you, Señor."

I had completely given up on hearing from Les and it was a nice surprise to hear he'd wired me back. The operator went around his little fence and got himself settled at his desk and began going through some papers.

"It is right here, Señor. Ah yes, here it is!"

He handed me a handwritten copy of the wire he'd taken down.

"It's in Spanish, Señor. Would you like my assistance? There is only a small charge."

"That's all right," I said. "I can make it out." I walked over in the corner and sat down and went to working out what Les had to say. It was addressed to me as John Wilson and he'd signed it with his straight name except he only used Les. It said the reason he'd been late in answering my wire was that he'd had to lay out in the country, town being so hot of late. Then it said: BEST YOU STAY INLAND AS THE BORDER IS NO PLACE FOR A WHITE MAN RIGHT NOW.

It was easy enough to figure out. There was some kind of Texas law scouting around and he'd been laying low. He was letting me know that they were looking for me and that I ought not to come anywhere near the border. I wondered how he'd been able to pick up my telegram. Probably some friend of his had brought it to him. It was likely he'd know quite a few people in Nuevo Laredo, as we'd spent considerable time around there.

I went back over and told the operator to take a return telegram. In it I told Les I was heading down to Sabinas Hidalgo and that I wanted him to come down and join me. I said he could take the train and be there in one day. I asked for a return wire care of me at the telegraph office in Sabinas.

"Is that all, Señor?"

"That's all."

"Twelve pesos. That includes the translation, you understand."

"All right," I said. I paid him and went out and mounted and rode back to the cantina I'd been staying at. I figured to spend the night and then head for Sabinas the next morning on horseback. I was going to be real curious to see if any of Manuel's bunch would come into the cantina that night. Manuel sure as hell wouldn't—that is, unless he could navigate with a big hole in his chest.

But they never showed. I reckoned they'd make themselves scarce in the area, as the federals would be after them. I wished they'd catch them too, for all the trouble they'd caused me. First they'd eased off just long enough for Linda to get sent back home, causing me to miss her in Villa Guerro, then they'd started back up just in time to keep me from getting down to Sabinas Hidalgo. At supper I reflected that, if it hadn't been for the bandits, I'd be sitting in Sabinas at the very moment. It was going to be a long ride, a little over a hundred miles, and I intended on taking it easy. I made arrangements with the cantina cook to have two days' provisions put up for me. She said she'd lay me in some dried beef and cheese and beans and bread and have it ready for me the next morning. I figured to pull out early. I could make it in two days, but I wasn't going to try. Three days would be soon enough.

Sabinas Hidalgo was one of the prettiest towns I'd ever seen. After the long ride I pulled up on a little hill and looked at it down in the valley. All the buildings were whitewashed and the streets were straight and clear of the goats and chickens you see in most Mexican towns. It appeared to be a little bigger than Rodriguez. I let my mare go down the incline and then rode into the town. It was late afternoon and I stopped and inquired of a muchacho where a hotel was.

"Mirador, Señor," he said. "First-class."

I figured I might as well go first-class for a change. Besides, I wanted to put on a good appearance. I found the hotel and went in and took a room. The lobby was big and well appointed with a lot of chairs and tables sitting around. It was a first-class place all right. I asked about a bath and the clerk said it could be arranged. I booked one for the next morning. I also intended on getting my hair cut.

The hotel had a dining room and I took supper with them. There was a crop of Mexican gentlemen in the place, well dressed in suits and good boots. The whole town had a very prosperous air about it and I reflected, if I was still in the bank-robbing business, the bank of Sabinas might just deserve some attention. But, of course, I was all done with that.

After supper I sat out in the lobby until I was able to strike up a casual conversation with the clerk. I told him I was looking for a Señor De Cava, who, I understood, had a ranch in the area.

"Ah yes, Señor De Cava! Perhaps you are interested in buying some of his fine horses."

"I might be," I said. "If I can find the place."

"*Seguro*. It's very easy. The rancho of Don De Cava lies to the west of town some four miles. It is the easiest thing to find."

I questioned him some more, getting exact directions, and finding out all I could about the family. I hadn't as yet figured out what my dodge was going to be, but I knew I'd think of something.

I was turning away when he said, "However, you might find the family on the town square a little later. They have several daughters of eligible age and it has been their habit to escort them in for the promenade. I am not sure the don himself will be there, however."

"Yeah," I said. I'd forgotten it was Sunday. "Yeah, thanks," I said.

In Mexico, eligible young ladies of good families aren't allowed to mix and circulate like they do in the States. They're kept at home and watched pretty closely by their duenna or their parents. But on Sundays, in good weather, they all get dressed up in their finest and come into town and promenade around the square looking the young bucks over and giving the young bucks a chance to look them over. The whole thing is handled on pretty strict tradition. The girls go one way, walking with their chaperone, and the boys come the other, walking on the outside of the square. It's all right for the boys to give the girls a round staring at, but the girls are supposed to keep their eyes down and look neither to the right nor the left. Of course that's not the way it works out. If a girl spots a young blood she particularly favors she'll get a look at him and he'll come up and formally present himself to the girl's chaperone and then they'll all go sit on one of the benches that are in the center of the square.

It was still a little early for the affair to start, so I went to my room and washed as best I could, even though I didn't plan to speak to Señor De Cava or Linda, even if they were there. I was still pretty dusty and travel-worn and I figured to get myself fixed up before making a formal call.

I left the hotel and went over to the telegraph office to see if I'd had a wire. Nothing had come. It didn't worry me too much since I figured Les would have to step around kind of lightly for a time. But I did wish to hear from him and see if he was coming down. It kind of bothered me him being up around all that law. I knew he felt I was the one that was well-known and that they wouldn't recognize him, but I didn't exactly agree. We were all pretty well-known in Nuevo Laredo and, if there was law around, somebody was almost certain to slip up to one of them and tip them that Les had been riding with me. I doubted he'd come through. He had it fixed in his mind that he had to get into Texas and tell Tod's daddy what had happened and, until he got that done, he wouldn't come inland. It was just the way he was.

I told the telegraph operator where I was staying and asked him to send a boy over if anything came for me. I give him a couple of pesos and he assured me he would.

I wandered down toward the middle of town. It was just coming evening and the sun was low enough to cool things off a bit. I found it very pleasant. I stopped in at a little open-front café and had a beer. It was very fresh and cool and I sat at a table where I could see the street and watched the people pass. Some were headed for six-o'clock mass, but most were just out sporting around, taking the evening air. Now and then a carriage would pass with a young lady all done up in a white dress sitting by an elderly lady that was her chaperone. The chaperone would nearly always be holding a black umbrella and looking straight ahead, but the young girls, you could see, could hardly hold themselves down. Naturally they'd been told to behave, but you could see they was already starting to get excited about the promenade. It made me smile a little.

I had another beer and then went off toward the square. The promenade was already in full procession and I got me a station near one corner and leaned back up against a building to watch. I was only about twelve or fifteen feet away and I could see good. The young ladies, near all of them in a white dress, walked along very proudly, their heads thrown back and their busts thrown forward. Some of them had borrowed umbrellas from their duennas so they'd have something to do with their hands and they carried them closed, leaning them over their shoulders like a soldier carries a rifle. They made a pretty sight. I reckoned their ages to run all the way from thirteen or fourteen to up in the early twenties. The young bucks had gotten themselves up in their best also. They come along, walking in twos and threes, with their hands behind their backs. I reckoned they figured it made them look older and more dignified. And did they stare! It wasn't nothing for one to stop and just stand dead, staring right at a girl as she came on and not moving until she was past.

But I still hadn't seen Linda. I got out a little cigar and lit it, looking across the square to where I'd seen a carriage pull up. There appeared to be five females in it, three young ones in white and two elderly ladies. They got out and then one of the elderly señoras went and sat in the center of the square while the other four fell into the procession. They walked two by two, the elderly one back with one of the young girls. They walked down the opposite of the square and then turned the corner and come right at me. I was across the street, but I could see them clearly. Linda was in the first row nearest me. The girl to her right was younger and nowhere near as pretty and the one back with the chaperone was just a kid, maybe fifteen years old. They got nearer and nearer until they were right opposite me and the sight of Linda was almost more than I could bear. She was every bit as pretty as I'd remembered her. She was wearing a kind of rose-colored dress and she had a long, lacy mantilla falling from the comb in her hair. She walked proudly, staring straight ahead, not doing like her sisters, who were giggling and cutting looks at the boys. I just yearned to touch her, to put my hands on her tiny waist and then run them down her swelling hips. The bodice of her dress was cut down a little and you could see where her breasts started. I would have give a hundred dollars to run across the street and grab her and kiss her right where those soft breasts came rising out of her dress.

But naturally I just stayed pinned back against the wall I was leaning against. As far as I could tell there hadn't been a man in the carriage except for the driver, who didn't look like any patron. I figured her daddy must not have come in or else he'd gotten out somewhere else and gone to drink and talk business with his friends.

It made me feel queer, standing there hid out so to speak, and watching the girl I'd been dreaming about ever since I'd seen her for that brief moment. It was such a different thing for me to be doing. I've had women all my life, but never paid particular attention to them. And they weren't all saloon girls either. Some of them were right pretty town girls who I'd met and some of them came from good families. But it hadn't mattered. Once I was through with them and ready to pull out, I'd ridden away without another thought. But then had come this girl and I couldn't figure it. I didn't know if it was just her, or because I was getting old, or because I wanted to become respectable or just what. All I knew was that she hadn't been out of my mind for fifteen minutes ever since I'd seen her. I didn't know what that amounted to, whether there was a name for it or not, but I did know it was hurting me in a funny kind of way to stand over in the shadows and watch her walk past.

I smoked another cigar and watched her go around a number of times. She never give the young bucks so much as a glance even though she was about the main attraction in the whole parade. Every time she'd pass a bunch all the boys would sweep off their hats and give her a low bow.

But she never paid them the slightest bit of notice, just walked on by like they weren't even there. She had class all right, class enough and some to spare.

Finally I couldn't stand it any longer. I put out my cigar and went back to my hotel. It was still early, but I was tired from the ride in. I bought a bottle of rum in the hotel saloon and then went up to my room. For a good while I sat on the side of my bed and drank the rum straight out of the bottle. I wasn't thinking about anything particular, just staring at the wall and reflecting. On the ride down from Rodriguez it had come to me that I was going to be twenty-nine in a few days. That's near half a man's life. I didn't think too much about it, but I did contemplate what a mess I'd made out of things. Rum is like that. It's a fiery drink that will hit you quick, but you drink enough and it'll make you go to reflecting on things you generally don't think about. After a while I put the bottle on the bedside table and turned in. The rum was better than half gone.

First thing next morning I went out and bought the best pair of breeches I could find. Had to give near six dollars for them. After that I had my boots blacked. I'd had it done in Rodriguez, but I just decided to do it again. I was due back at the hotel to take my bath at ten, but I went to the barber first and had a shave and a haircut. The barber was a good one and he trimmed me up real nice and then put some kind of sweet-smelling tonic on my hair.

They had my bath ready for me when I got back to the hotel. They'd brought a hell of a big tub into my room and I got in it and then they run in a regular bucket brigade of boys carrying hot water. It was mighty pleasant to just lay back and soak in that hot, soapy water. It was the best bath I'd had in many a year. Cost me seventy-five cents, but I figured it was worth it.

I didn't want to go to De Cava ranch until afternoon, so I had lunch and then went down to see about my filly. She was doing all right, but I told the stableman that I wanted her brushed and curried and I wanted my saddle and rigging cleaned up and oiled.

I hung around the hotel for a while and then went over

to the telegraph office and checked to see if anything had come in. I'd told them where to find me, but you can't really trust some of them Mexicans too much. Nothing had come from Les. I went back over to the hotel and sat around the lobby for a while longer. Finally I couldn't stall any longer and I knew I was going to have to go if I ever was. I had good directions from the clerk and I went over and got my filly and rode out.

It was only four miles, but it seemed like two. Before I knew it I was at the ranch and going through the gate portico and riding up to the house. I got down and helloed and a peon come out and took my bridle and asked after my business. I'd give considerable thought to it and decided I'd try to hit somewhere near the truth. I told him I was just come from Villa Guerro and that I brought greetings from the patron's brother, the Don Fernando.

While the peon was inside I had a look around at things. The De Cava house, if anything, was grander than Don Fernando's. It was white adobe with a red tile roof and seemed as big as a church. There was one main breezeway right through the center of the house, but I could see others opening along the sides. The grounds were well-kept and there was some twenty or thirty outbuildings. A piece to the west of the house I could see a big bunch of corrals with a lot of horses in them. From what I'd gathered from the room clerk and the patron of the Fernando ranch the Don De Cava was in the horse-breeding business in a bigger way than his brother.

After a good wait the peon came out and said the don would receive me. He led me down a hall and then into a big sitting room that was whitewashed and had a hell of a big chandelier hanging from a beamed ceiling. They were all set up to receive me. Either I'd made a bigger impression on the peon than I'd expected or they thought I was bringing money, for the entire family was ranged out in a semicircle of chairs when I came in. It took me back for just a second, but I got my hat off just as the don got up to greet me. He was a number of years younger than his brother and he came forward and we shook hands.

"*Con mucho gusto,* Señor Young. You do honor to our house."

"It is my honor," I said. "I've just come from staying overnight with your brother, the patron of the Fernando ranch, and he commended me to your hospitality and asked that I bear his greetings."

I was speaking better Spanish than I thought I knew. It's amazing what a man can do when he has to.

"My brother was well when you left him?"

"Very well," I said. "He had a slight malady in the hip, but he expected it to go away shortly."

"Ah yes, his hip," Señor De Cava said. "An old injury from a fall."

Señor De Cava was a tall, slimly built man with a big mustache and glossy, slicked-back hair. He was wearing good clothes—linen pants and a leather jerkin coat with a brocaded vest underneath. You could see he'd been raised to quality. After we finished our greeting he led me down the line of his family, introducing me to each one. Besides his wife there was three girls and two boys. The first girl in line after the mother was Linda. I had been conscious of her all the time I was talking to the don. She was sitting in a low-backed chair covered with some kind of blue velvet material. As I was greeting the patroness I could feel her looking at me from the side. When I swung around, as the don directed me down the line, she was staring full at me. There was a look in her eyes that told me she knew me and that, perhaps, I might occasionally have passed her mind since we'd met last.

"My daughter," the patron said. "Linda Marquezza de la Piña De Cava."

I bowed low. "Your daughter and I have already met," I said. "I had the privilege at an earlier visit at your brother's house."

"Ah!" the don said. "You and my brother have been thick together."

I shrugged, still looking at Linda. "We are both lovers of good horse flesh," I said.

His eyes lit up. "Ah! You are a horse breeder?"

"Not really," I said. "I've been in the cattle business for a time, but now I'm thinking of locating in Mexico."

"Ah!" he said. I could see he wanted to talk more about it, but I turned my full attention to Linda. She hadn't taken her eyes off me.

"Your uncle says he misses you," I said. "He asks that you come back soon, for his house seems very empty without you."

I was saying the words, but they were just something to keep me in front of her as long as I could. I wanted, even in front of her family, to touch her.

"Thank you," she said. "You must have come just after I left."

"Yes. I missed you one day."

"Ah . . ." she said.

But the don was pulling me down the line and I had to leave. He introduced me to the rest of his daughters, who giggled and carried on something awful. I could still feel Linda just to my right. His sons were twelve and sixteen years old. The oldest couldn't keep his eyes off my gun. I expected he imagined himself a pistolero.

After we got sat down the don had me served up some brandy and a cigar. The children and the patroness stayed in the same line, but the don and I pulled our chairs out so that we were facing them. He had sherry brought in for his wife and Linda and his oldest boy. We made small talk for a while and then I told him about the bandit attack on the train.

"Yes," he said. "They've been very active. As you know, I sent Linda to my brother, where you visited, and Medina, my next oldest girl, to a kinsman in the south." He shrugged and smiled. "It wasn't really necessary, but they had been hoping for a visit somewhere."

For a time we sat in the living room and made talk. Then the patron took me outside, in the company of his eldest son, to look over the ranch. The don had sent for horses and he had the courtesy to have one of his own sent over for me. If you're wealthy and have a great deal of stock you don't insult a man by asking him to ride his own horse to look over your property. Especially if his horse has been taken to the barn and cooled out. But you do put the man's saddle on your stock. A man prefers his own saddle. I was pleased to see they'd done just that. They'd given me a big bay stallion. I suspected he was one of the top horses on the place and that the patron had given him to me just to show out. He had a tough mouth and wanted a bit of managing with the reins, but he trotted along like he knew he was the cock of the walk. As we rode along I told the patron I expected the stallion I was riding had sired a good deal of fine stock. It pleased him for me to recognize the quality of the horse.

"Ah!" he said. "Yes. Yes, indeed. The horse has been standing at stud for some time. You're the first to ride him in many months."

Of course that wasn't hard to tell. The way he fidgeted around you could pretty well figure he'd been standing in a stud lot for a good while.

It was hard to ride around the ranch and look at what the patron was showing me, knowing all the time that Linda was sitting just a short distance away. But it had been even harder while we were sitting in the parlor, for the patron had completely taken over the conversation and I hadn't been able to say a word to Linda. She'd sat across from me, so pretty in her blue chair, looking at me, looking at me so hard, and I hadn't been able to say a word.

But I was going to have to be patient. You just don't run into the house of a quality family and sweep their daughter out the door. It takes a good while, even, before you dare let them know you're interested at all. What I had to do first was make the patron believe I was a gentleman of equal standing with him. We rode around for a time, like quality, me and the patron with a cigar stuck in our mouths and the son trailing along a little behind as is proper. Behind us we had his head charro and two or three others just to make a decent escort. We looked at everything, spending most of our time at his remuda corrals, where we examined damn near every horse and made talk about each one's fine points and breeding lines. I was impressing the patron and I could see it. If there is one thing I'm comfortable talking about it's good horses. I've always had them around and always respected them for what they are. My daddy had had as fine a remuda of blooded Morgans as could be found on a small ranch in the Southwest. During the Civil War he told me that some of them had brought as much as two hundred dollars apiece in lots of tens.

We finally went back in the house. The patron had invited me to stay for supper and I'd naturally accepted. We took it in a room near as big as the sitting room. It had a big, long dining table that could have seated twenty even though there were just seven of us. There was me and the patron and his wife and eldest son and Linda. He'd invited in his head overseers and his head charro, but they sat down at the end and didn't mix in the conversation. Linda had been the last to come in and, for a while, I thought she wasn't going to make it. I hadn't dared ask, but I was hoping awfully hard.

The patron sat at the head of the table with his wife on his left and me the first chair to the right. Linda was on my side and down two chairs. It made it almost impossible to talk with her. I ate, being conscious all the time of her presence so close to me. We had beef and wine and some other stuff. The patron did it up fine, having a servant for damn near every course. It was a strange feeling for me, a bank robber wanted all over Texas, to be sitting there and being treated like quality.

After the dinner was over we got up to got back in the sitting room. The patron said the ladies would pay their respects and then go to their rooms. He led the way, but I could see Linda hanging back, so I did likewise. We had to go down a long hall to the sitting room and the patron went first followed by his wife and his eldest son. The two men that worked for him had vanished. I went into the hall just behind Linda, watching her walk. Suddenly she turned around and looked at me. Ahead I could hear the patron talking as if I were right behind him, but all I could see was Linda. She looked me right in the face.

"I saw you on the square yesterday. At the promenade."

"Linda," I said. I put out my hand and just touched her

arm. It was the first time I'd ever touched her. "Linda," I said.

But the patron was calling from the sitting room. "Señor Young! Are you lost? Señor Young?"

She turned and went away from me, walking quickly up the hall and into the parlor. After a second I followed.

"Ah, Señor Young!" the patron said when I entered the room. "I thought we had lost you." He laughed with good nature.

"No," I said. "Your fine dinner slowed me, Señor. It was more cargo than I'm used to freighting."

"Yes," he said. He laughed and drew on his cigar. "I'm afraid the ladies must leave us now. They'll bid you good night, Señor."

I said good night to the patroness and gave her a bow. When I came to Linda I wanted badly to take her hand, but I dared not. I gave her a bow also and she dropped me a curtsy, all the time giving me that look, that look that had haunted me those many nights on the trail.

"*Buenas noches*," I said.

"*Buenas noches*, Señor Young," she said. "*Adios.*"

And then she was gone. I watched her walk out of the room until she was through the door and I could see her no more.

"Well, Señor," the patron said, "let us sit and have a cigar and a glass of good brandy. And perhaps you'll be kind enough to tell me your plans for living in Mexico."

We sat and made a lot of talk. Once Linda was gone I was impatient to go, but I knew I'd have to stand in with the patron to have a chance for the girl, so I put on my best. The patron liked me, I could see that. I don't know why, but I've always been able to make people like me. His son sat over in the corner but didn't say anything and I told the patron of my plan to bring a string of blooded Texas horses into the country and set up a horse ranch.

Naturally I didn't have no string of horses nor no plans for setting up a horse ranch. My only intent was to impress the don so I could become a welcome guest at his ranch.

He was excited by my talk. "Perhaps," he said, "I have

stock that could be mated with what you will bring in. It might be a fine idea."

"Perhaps," I said.

We talked on until about ten o'clock and then I insisted I had to leave. He sent a peon to bring up my filly and then walked me to the door with his hand on my shoulder.

"You've made a pleasant evening for us, Señor Young. We don't often see such interesting strangers."

"Your hospitality was famous," I told him. I had my hat in my hand and I put it on as we got to the door. It was a clear night outside, moonlit and cool.

"You're a welcome guest," he said. "I insist you come often so long as you're in Sabinas Hidalgo."

"I will," I said. We shook hands and then I mounted my filly and rode away from his ranch. I rode away knowing that I'd done a good night's work with the patron and that the look Linda had given me the first day had not been my imagination. She'd remembered me all right and she'd thought on me. I rode away with my heart singing in my chest. Things were working out very well. They were working out mighty well for a reformed bank robber. I didn't know how long I could keep up the pretense of starting a horse ranch, but I wasn't going to worry about it for a spell.

Sabinas was pretty well shut down by the time I got back to town, but I could see a light on in the railroad station as I rode by and I thought I'd go in and see if a message might have come. I doubted it, but I was feeling so good I didn't want to go to bed.

I tied my filly and went into the office. Both the clerk and the telegraph operator were asleep in their chairs. I stomped a boot on the floor and made them jump.

"Hey!" I said. "No sleeping!"

I was feeling damn good.

They come awake, neither one of them looking guilty. The telegraph operator was a fat fellow with such big hands I wondered how he was able to operate the little telegraph key.

"You got any messages for me?" I asked him.

"Ah, Señor," he said. "Señor Wilson. We had a wire for you and I sent it over to the hotel with a boy. Unfortunately you weren't there."

"I know," I said. "I've been out. That's why I stopped by."

"I have it here," he said. "Somewhere in this desk." He rummaged around for a moment and then finally handed me a piece of paper with some Spanish words on it. I was leaning up against the railing smoking a cigar and I took it and looked at it.

I stood there, staring at the paper, trying to handle what the words were saying. After a minute I dropped my cigar and handed him the paper back. "Put that in English," I said. My throat was so tight I damn near couldn't get the words out.

"Oh no, Señor," he said. "That's not possible. Neither I nor the man of the railroad speak nor write English. You'll have to wait until morning."

I couldn't talk. There wasn't much breath left in me enough to speak. I pulled out my revolver and simply pointed it at him. "Get it in English," I said.

He understood. For a second his eyes got round and he began to open his mouth, but I gestured toward the door. "Go," I said. "Get it in English." The railroad clerk had come full awake and was watching us with fear on his face.

"Right now," I said.

"*Seguro,*" the telegraph operator said. He grabbed up the message and came scurrying around his little fence and vanished out the door. I didn't know where he was going or who was going to help him. What's more I didn't care. I went over to the wall and sat down. I hadn't put my pistol up and I kept cocking it and then letting the hammer back down with my thumb. It was making the clerk awfully nervous, but I didn't care. I didn't really need the telegram translated. I knew what it said. I just didn't want to believe it.

The clerk was gone a long time. When he came back he paused in the door as if afraid to enter.

"I have it, Señor," he said. "The clerk at your hotel . . ."

"All right," I said. "Bring it here." I put my revolver up.

It was addressed to me as John Wilson and it was signed by Jack Basset. Onyx Jack Basset was his straight name, but we'd always called him Black Jack. Me and Les and Tod had known him for many years. He'd been a good friend of ours.

CHAPTER 17

Catch the Morning Train

The wire said:

> LES LAYING NEAR DYING IN THE NUEVO LAREDO
> INFIRMARY, CONTACT ME AT THE DEL PRADO
> HOTEL BUT BE CAREFUL.

I read it again and again. It wasn't hard to figure out what
had happened. I wheeled around on the railroad clerk and
asked him what time the next train north left.

"*Mañana*, Señor," he said. He and the telegraph operator
both was still a little frightened of me. "At eight of the
morning."

"Give me a ticket," I said. I went to my pocket and
began spilling out money. I wanted to go, wanted to leave
right then, but it wouldn't do any good. The train was my
fastest way.

I got my ticket and then took my filly to the livery stable and made arrangements to leave her for a time. They
promised they'd look after her carefully.

After that I went to the hotel and got ready to leave the
next morning. I had my two revolvers and I cleaned them
and oiled them and checked their action. They were both
in good shape.

I turned in after a time, but I couldn't sleep. Finally I got
up and finished the bottle of rum I had left over from the

207

night before. It wasn't enough and I went downstairs and woke up the room clerk and made him rout me out another bottle. He didn't give me any lip. I expect the way I was looking was enough to put anybody off.

I took the bottle back upstairs with me and drank all of it, but it was still a good while before I could get to sleep. Me and Les had rode many a mile together.

It took twelve long hours for the train to get to Nuevo Laredo. It had to stop about every fifty miles to take on water and, when it wasn't for that, it was stopping to let some campesino and his wife and livestock off out in the big middle of nowhere. I often wondered where those Indians came from and where they went. Riding across country, you'd suddenly come up on one just standing out in the middle of the prairie without a sign of civilization in any direction. That was the way it was on the train. It would suddenly stop and you could look out the window and see this family getting off, the mother carrying a baby, maybe, or a big roll of clothes and the father shouldering a chicken coop or leading a goat. Away off you could see the mountains, but between them and the railroad tracks there'd be nothing but flat, sun-baked Mexican plain. That family would start off walking and, after the train pulled out, you could stick your head out the window and look back and they'd still be trudging along. You had to figure they were heading for the mountains because there didn't seem to be anything else, but you couldn't believe they figured to walk all that way. I rode in the chair car and I wouldn't have minded it except for worrying about Les and being in a hurry. The train wasn't as crowded as the southbound one had been and it wouldn't have been too bad a trip. But what with Les and all I was pretty damn impatient by the time we finally pulled in.

The train station at Nuevo Laredo is close to the International Bridge and I could see across the river and into Texas when I got off the train. I didn't hang around looking, however, as I had business and I didn't want to be bumping into anybody before I got it tended to.

It was just about good dark, but I went quickly down

into the low part of town and went into a saloon to have a drink and let it get a little later. I didn't know how much law was around or whether they'd recognize me on sight, but I didn't plan to take any chances. I'd need to find Jack Basset first and after that I'd see what needed doing.

At nine o'clock I walked nearly to the town square and stopped about two blocks short of the Del Prado Hotel. A bunch of muchachos were skylarking around on the street corner and I picked me out a likely looking boy of about twelve and called him over.

"You want to make a peso?" I asked him.

"*Si!*" he said. "*Si, Señor!*" It was a lot of money to a poor kid.

"All right, you know where the Del Prado Hotel is, don't you?" He said he did and I told him I wanted him to go there and find a man named Jack Basset.

"Can you say that? Jack Basset?"

"Jack Basset," he said. He was a bright-looking kid.

"All right. I want you to go and tell him an old friend of his is in town and wants to see him. You bring him back to that saloon right across the street there. You got that?"

"*Si*, Señor. *Seguro.*"

"Now here's one peso for right now. If you bring the man back I'll give you another."

"Two pesos?"

"That's right, two. But you be careful and you don't tell anybody else about me, you hear?"

He scooted off and I walked over to the saloon and went just inside the door and looked around. It was all right. The place was pretty dim and there weren't but a few customers. There were some tables in the back and just beyond them I could see a door that led to the alley. The proprietor called to me to come in and be served, but I just waved and went across the street and got in the shadows and settled down to wait. I wanted to be damn sure it was Jack that come and that he was by himself.

About fifteen minutes later I seen the kid come tearing around the corner and then stop and motion to someone behind him. After a little a man came around the corner, coming slow and seeming to take it very carefully. I could hear the kid talking to the man. He was telling him it was just across the street and they were almost there. The kid was awfully anxious to get his job done and get him another peso. The street was dark and I couldn't tell if it was Jack or not. It seemed to be, but I wasn't going to let on until I knew.

They got to the saloon and the kid went to gesturing for the man to go inside, but he wouldn't, not right away. He got the kid by the arm and kind of peeked inside, not showing himself, but just kind of looking around the corner of the door. They were just across the street and, in the light that was coming out the door, I could see it was Jack Basset. I walked across toward them. As I got near I could hear Jack telling the kid that the man looking for him had better be who he thought it was or the kid was in trouble.

"I promise, Señor," the kid was saying. "He is a friend of yours."

"Hello, Jack," I said.

He whirled around, but then recognized me and relaxed. He let go of the kid and put out his hand and we shook.

"Here, boy," I said. I give the kid his other peso. "But you forget all about this. *Seguro*!"

"*Si*, Señor," he said. He went skipping up the street, his money clutched in his hand, just tickled near to death. I watched him, envying him and wishing that two pesos was all it took to make me that happy.

"Let's go inside," I said. "I've looked the place over."

"All right," Jack said. We went in and took a table at the back and the bartender came over and we both ordered whiskey.

Jack Basset is a little slight man about thirty-five or -six. He'd been around Corpus when we were all growing up and he'd always done right by me and Les and Tod. I think he'd worked for Les's daddy for a spell, but I wasn't sure. I remembered him best from when I was about twelve years old, him showing me how to rig a drag rope on a horse I was trying to break that had a bad habit of kicking. I knew that he'd been in and out of trouble. Nothing big, just stuff that'll come to you if you're a little wild and don't mind a little easy money. As far as I knew he hadn't been up to anything for a while. The last I'd heard of him he was buying Mexican gold and then smuggling it back into the States, where he could get a better price and make a little profit. It wasn't much of a business, but them as didn't need much were said to be content with it.

"Well, Jack," I said.

He raised his glass and I did likewise. "Here's luck," he said.

We knocked our drinks off and then set the glasses down. "I didn't know for sure it was you," Jack said. "I figured it was, but I didn't want to take no chances."

"I didn't want to give the kid my name. I didn't know who he might talk to and I figured you'd be looking for me anyway."

"Yeah," he said. "I was expecting you."

I signaled for the barman and he came over and gave us another drink. I waited until he'd gone and then looked at Jack.

"I appreciated the telegram."

He shrugged. "Aw hell, Will. That's nothing. I've always been friendly with you boys, you and Tod and Les."

I'd taken about half of my second drink, but I finished it and set my glass down. "Les?" I said. I looked at Jack. "Is he alive, Jack?"

"He was this morning, that's all I can tell you. But, Will, he's shot up bad. They hit him four times. Two in the chest and one in the neck. The one in the neck ain't bad and then he caught one in the leg, but one of them ones in his chest is dead center. I don't know how he's hung on this long."

"I see," I said. I could feel a feeling rising in me. I called to the bartender again and told him to leave the bottle. I didn't want to say anything for a second or two, so I spent the time pouring us out another drink.

Finally, I asked: "Who done it?"

"They was two of them, Will. One of them I don't know too much about except what I've found out since they went for Les. His name is Morton. The other one you know."

"Who?"

He was looking at me. "Bob Bird," he said.

"Bird. Bob Bird."

"The same."

I took another sip of my drink, thinking on what Jack had told me. "Hell, Jack, they're not law. They're goddam bounty hunters."

"Bird ain't," he said, "and we both know that. But this Morton is. I understand he's with the Cattleman's Association and he's supposed to be some kind of federal marshal. He's let it out that he's been about one jump behind ya'll ever since you hit a bank over in Uvalde. He tracked Les to here."

"Well," I said, "I can't take them on two at a time, but I'm willing to try them in singles."

"Why don't you think on it?" Jack said. He got the bottle and poured himself another glass of whiskey. "Don't go rushing into anything, Will. I'd help you if I could, but both these boys is pretty tough customers."

"I don't want no help," I said. "Les was my partner. Besides, Jack, you've done enough."

Jack was right about them being rough customers. I didn't know Morton, of course, but if he was running with Bob Bird it was a good bet he'd qualify. Bird had been a deputy sheriff up in El Paso for a time and then he'd got in the rangers. He had a hell of a reputation for quick and the word was that he was a damn good shot in the bargain. Some said he was about half outlaw, but I didn't know. He hadn't stayed with the rangers too long. The railroads had been coming through and they were willing to pay good money to detectives who could see that nothing went wrong with their schedules. Bird had went into that and it was the last I'd heard on him. I'd seen him around from time to time and he knew who I was. That meant we'd get into it on sight.

"How'd it happen, Jack? I thought Les was laying out. I had a telegram from him to that effect."

"Hell, he was," Jack said. "Fact is, it was me that picked up your first telegram and taken it out to him and then wired his answer back to you. Me and Amos Bently—you wouldn't know him—had us a room right next to Les's in the hotel there. Then when word got out that men were in town looking for ya'll he'd taken out to a ranch I know about that's just outside of town. The night he got shot I thought he was still out there."

"How'd it come about? How'd they get on to him?"

"I don't know, Will. I truly don't. Me and Amos was sitting in the room there one evening—night before last— and about eleven o'clock we heard a hell of a bunch of gunfire. We run out in the hall and seen it was Les's room and looked in the door and Morton and Bird done had him stretched out. I don't know what he was doing there—I reckoned he'd come back to get something or other—but they'd caught him and gunned him down. When me and Amos got in the room he was stretched out beside the bed with all them bullet holes in him. Will, I swear to God, I believe them two would have gone ahead and killed him if we hadn't come in the room. As it was we had a hell of a job talking them into carrying him over to the infirmary. Bird said he was going to die anyway and what was the sense of going to all that trouble and delaying them getting the body back to Texas. I told them they'd better see to the boy or I'd by God go to the Mexican authorities and raise such a stink that they'd be delayed anyway."

I was listening to him, fiddling with my empty glass. "The law here don't care," I said. "They don't want to mix in."

"I know," Jack said. "And naturally they had them a little bench warrant from the justice over there in Uvalde, but I told them I'd get the word out all over Texas if they didn't do something. They know Les has got plenty of kin and friends."

"He's got one," I said. "I guarantee he's got one friend."

"What do you figure to do, Will?"

"First I'd like to see how Les is."

"You can't go over there. Morton and Bird are sitting up turn and turn about and they'd spot you sure. Hell, there's no way you can get in. They've got 'em a chair parked right in front of the door of his room and they ain't moving. He's

213

worth fifteen hundred dollars to them, you know."

"I know," I said. I took some time to pour us out another drink and then looked over at Jack. "I wonder if you might be good enough to go over and see about him. I'd appreciate it."

"Sure I'll go, Will. I'd planned on it anyway."

"Maybe you could figure out some little way of letting him know I'm in town."

"He ain't awake, Will. He's barely breathing, son."

"Oh," I said.

Jack looked at me. "I know he was a good friend of yours."

"The best," I said.

"Will you want to wait here?"

"How far is it over there?"

"About a half a mile. It'll be just as easy for me to walk rather than taking the trouble to get my horse. There's a saloon right near there. You could wait there if you wanted. It ain't much of a place, though."

"That's all right," I said. "Let's do that."

We got up and left and, as we walked along, I asked Jack which one would be at the hospital. He said Bird had been there in the morning, so he figured it would be Morton. "I think they've got a room at the hotel. Probably Bird is back there sleeping right now."

The streets were dark and nearly empty. It was coming on ten o'clock and nobody was stirring much.

"Jack," I said, "I'm going to get him out of there if I can."

"He can't travel, son. Besides, there ain't no way you can get him past Morton and Bird."

"Over their dead bodies," I said. "That southbound train pulls out first thing in the morning on the return trip and I'm going to take him back with me. I'll get him down there and get him fixed back up."

Jack didn't say anything. Far off I could hear a dog howling in somebody's backyard. It was a very dark night. After a little he looked over at me. "Will, he's hit bad. I want you to know he's in real bad shape."

THE BANK ROBBER

"That's all right," I said. "He's tough."

Jack pointed up the street toward a little square of light that was coming from one of the buildings. "There's the saloon I was telling you about. The infirmary is just up the street and around the block."

We went up to the door and I looked in. The place was completely empty except for the bartender, who was leaning against the wall behind the bar, sleeping.

"This will be all right," I said. "I'll see you in a little." I went on in and Jack went up the street. I took a table and the bartender brought me a drink over. I sat there, staring at the door, and didn't taste my drink for a long time. Finally I drank it down. The bartender started over with the bottle, but I waved him back. "Not yet," I said. He went back behind the bar and seemed to go back to sleep. Waiting for news is a hard way to wait. I sat there staring at the door.

When Jack came back he ducked in quick through the door and then turned around and stuck his head out and looked back up the street. He watched for a considerable time. Jack is a good man all right.

Finally I called to him. "Come on, Jack."

He come over to the table and sat down. He didn't say anything, but he passed his hand across his face like he was tired. The bartender had got himself up when Jack came in and he was bringing over the bottle.

I looked at Jack. "Well?"

"Let's let this man give us a drink first," he said.

I waited while the bartender poured our drinks, not saying anything. When he was gone I looked over at Jack. I said, "Well?" again.

"Let me take a taste of this," Jack said. He drank down part of his whiskey. I was still looking right at him.

"Jack, goddamit!"

He looked at me and then wiped his mouth off. He put his hand over and patted me on the shoulder, clumsily, like a man who ain't used to patting other men on the shoulder.

"Will, Les is dead. He died late this afternoon."

He was still patting me on the shoulder and I suddenly shrugged and his hand fell away. I hadn't tasted my drink,

215

but I all of a gulp took it down. It was cheap whiskey, oily
and raw-tasting. You can only get good American whiskey
in the first-class bars in Mexico.

"I know this is hard on you," Jack said.

I put my glass down. "Is whoever was there still there?"

"It's Morton like I figured and he was still there when I
left. He's seeing to getting the body fixed up to transport
back to Texas."

"You want to do me a favor, Jack?"

"I'll do what I can, Will."

"Get Morton out of that hospital."

"Will, you ought to think on this a little. What's your
rush?"

"That train leaves in the morning," I said. "I intend to
be on it."

"Will, what in hell could I tell Morton that'd bring him
out? They'd be expecting something like this."

"Tell him it's me. That I'm outside and I'm going to
kill him."

Jack shook his head. "Now, Will, I ain't going to do that.
He's been sitting there with a double-barreled shotgun over
his knees and he'd come out and blow your head off."

I remembered the big man I'd seen who'd leaned across
the counter of the bank in Uvalde and blowed Chico to
pieces with a shotgun. I wondered if the two were the same.
It wasn't unlikely.

"Catch him tomorrow," Jack said. "Let yourself settle
down a little."

"No," I said. "If you won't bring him out for me I'll
wait until he comes out on his own. He's got to come out
sometime."

"He might be already gone. With Les dead there's nothing to hold him inside. They can pick up the body in the
morning."

"Then I'm going now," I said. I stood up. "Jack, will
you do me at least one favor? I know you don't want to
get mixed up in this and I don't blame you."

"Ask it, Will."

"Go over to the hotel and keep watch on Bob Bird. I

want to know where to find him when I get through with
Morton. Will you do that for me?"

He answered slowly. "You know I'll do it, Will. I'll trail
him to Kansas if I have to, but you better be careful with
Morton. Don't fight him fair."

"Did they fight Les fair?"

He shook his head and said simply: "You don't get four
bullets in you from two men in a fair fight."

"All right," I said. "Will you see to Bird for me? I'll be
over to the hotel as soon as I finish with Morton."

"I'll see to it."

"Thanks, Jack." I turned around and went out the door.

I was halfway up the street before I remembered I'd
forgotten to pay for the drinks. They really should have
been on me. I'd pay Jack back first chance I got. He'd
understand.

I seen the lights from the infirmary as soon as I turned
the corner. It was a low-beamed adobe building, long and
narrow. As soon as I got to it, I made a circle around it,
checking for doors. There was one in the front and one in
the back, but the one in the front was the only one that
had a light on behind it. I figured Morton had to come
out that way. I got back in the shadows and settled down
to wait. I was terrible scared I'd missed him. I waited a few
minutes, but, finally, I couldn't stand it any longer and I
went up to the door and opened it and looked in. It looked
like an ordinary parlor in a house except there was a long
hall leading right off the middle of the room I was looking
in. Down a bit was a kind of desk with a man sitting at it.
He had a lantern on the table and that was where the light
was coming from. I only had the door opened a crack, so I
couldn't see too good. I looked in, thinking about it as the
place where Les had died. It kind of give me the willies.
I knew I didn't want to die in such a place. It made me
feel bad about old Les. It made me feel goddam bad. I
hated to think of him laying in one of them dark rooms
all wrapped up in a shroud. He'd been a man that liked
his freedom and it damn near killed me thinking about him
all closed up in one of them tiny rooms with a sheet over

his face. I knew he wouldn't have wanted to go that way. I knew he'd rather have taken it out on the prairie with the hot sun burning down. I knew he'd rather have caught one right between the eyes and gone out like a light rather than slowly expiring while a couple of vultures sat outside his door and waited to get the money for his body.

Well, Les had been my friend since I was a boy. Which of us could have predicted I'd just have been lurking outside a hospital in which he'd just died? Which of us could have said, at twelve, out on the lake, that we'd have two of us come to such a bad end? It made me feel awful damn bad.

As I watched, a man suddenly came out of one of the rooms and walked up to the man at the desk. He was a great big man, a little fat. His stomach hung over his belt a bit. He was carrying a shotgun crooked under his arm. He had his hat on and was wearing a hand gun on his hip. I had no doubt it was Morton. He said something to the man at the desk and then laughed. He laughed by throwing his head back and he laughed so hard his belly shook. I guess he was feeling pretty good about collecting his half of fifteen hundred dollars. I stepped back from the door, but left it partially open. I figured he'd be coming out any minute.

CHAPTER 18

A Long Way to Sabinas

I was positioned in the shadows when the door suddenly swung open and Morton stood framed in the light. He stood in the sill a minute, the shotgun under his arm, looking around. He was a cautious man all right. I knew he couldn't see me. He was in the light and I was back in the shadow of a tree leaning up against the trunk. I reached down and made sure my pistol was loose in its holster.

Just as he started out the door, I pushed away from the tree and went toward him. I had my head down a little, but I could see him well enough. He spotted me as soon as I moved and stopped and kind of half brought the shotgun up. I kept walking, acting as if I meant to go on by him and go in the hospital. When he seen my demeanor he kind of relaxed and let the shotgun droop down. I'd put a cigar in my mouth and I nodded as I started by.

"Howdy," I said.

He gave me a sideways look, but didn't say anything.

I suddenly stopped as I was about to pass him. I didn't exactly have my head down, but I wasn't looking him right in the face either. I didn't know if he'd recognize me or not.

When I stopped he suddenly swung around and kind of lifted the shotgun again. I took the cigar out of my mouth and held it out.

"You ain't got a match, have you?"

He looked at me a minute. "No," he finally said, "I ain't."

"Damn!" I said. "Been carrying this around an hour wanting to smoke."

"They'll have one inside," he said. He was kind of half turned back watching me. I was on his side and a little behind him toward the hospital.

"Why the big gun?" I asked him. I motioned toward the shotgun.

"Say, what's your business here?" he asked me. "And what business you got asking about people's shotguns?"

"Oh, none," I said. "I got a pard in there I wanted to see about."

He kind of shifted around to have me more in front of him. "Who?" he asked. "I'm law, so I've got a right to ask."

"Who?"

"Yeah, who."

I wanted him to know who was fixing to kill him and why. I said, "Wait a minute!" and suddenly took two quick steps backward. It lined him up nicely against the light.

"You ever heard of Wilson Young?" I asked him. As soon as I said it he started up with the shotgun, whirling to go into a crouch so he could shoot. I hadn't waited. As soon as I spoke I was drawing. I pulled and shot him twice. My gun made a lot of noise, but I heard him yell, "Oh, no! My God, no!"

At first I thought I'd missed him and I fired again, but he was going to the ground even as I pulled the trigger. He was such a big man that the slugs didn't knock him down as they ordinarily would have. He fell, the shotgun falling out of his hands and hitting the ground. He went down and lay spread-eagle in the dust. I walked over and stood over him a second, noting where I'd hit him. All three bullets had gone home. He wasn't laughing any more. He wasn't ever going to be laughing again and he wasn't going to be transporting any bodies and collecting any fifteen hundred dollars. I figured I'd give him a fairer shake than they'd give Les. I nudged him once with my boot. He didn't move. He was dead all right. I didn't feel bad about it. As a matter of fact I felt damn good. I turned away and walked off.

It was a good little ways downtown to the hotel, but I hurried all I could. As I'd been walking away I'd seen the door of the hospital open and the man who'd been at the desk stick his head out. He'd heard the shots no doubt and was coming to see what was up. It wasn't likely, but there was a chance somebody might jump on a horse and ride down and alert Bird. I wanted to be sure I got there in time. I sure didn't want to miss him.

I remembered one time when me and Les was boys, maybe twelve or thirteen, and we were out hunting jackrabbits. We used to chase them on horseback and try to hit them on the run with a hand gun. It was good sport though not much bother to the jackrabbits, as we mainly just busted a lot of caps without ever hitting one. But this particular time we'd got separated, I think he'd gone one way after a rabbit and I'd gone the other after a different one. I was running my horse pretty hard when he chanced to stumble and fall. It didn't hurt the animal, but it did knock me out and break my leg. When I come to it was getting near dark and my horse had run off and I was miles from home. I didn't know what the hell I was going to do. I was a young shaver and it kind of scared me. I knew Les would eventually go in and tell somebody, but it'd be quite a while before they found me. My leg was swelling up and turning blue and that scared me even more. I figured I was gonna die for sure. Well, I'd been laying there for about thirty minutes, worrying and just about getting ready to cry, when I heard a horse coming up behind me. I switched around and there come old Les, riding along and looking for me. He'd seen my horse hightailing it for home, so he'd known something must have happened and he'd set out to find me. I don't know, I've always kind of appreciated that. It wouldn't have been nothing for a man to do, but old Les was just a kid himself and it was coming on dark. Well, he was always a mighty good man.

When I got near to the hotel I could see Jack out in front. He was pacing back and forth in the street, every now and then giving a look up at a window of the hotel. As soon as he saw me he came walking down toward me.

"Are you all right?"

"Yeah," I said. I didn't feel much like talking. I was feeling pretty bad in my mind.

"Did you see Morton?"

"Yeah," I said. I'd stopped and was looking up at the window Jack had been casing. "Is he up there?"

"Bird? Yeah, he's up there. The room with the light on."

"How do you know?"

"I made me up a question and went up and asked him. He's laying up there in the bed."

"What'd you ask him?"

"Oh, just something about notifying Les's family. Asked him if he was going to."

Jack was awful nervous. I guess he wanted to know what had happened with me and Morton, but he was too polite to just out and ask.

"What'd he say about that?"

"He said, hell no he wasn't going to notify them. Said they could read about it in the papers for all he cared."

"I see," I said.

We walked in toward the hotel and went in the door and stopped in the lobby. "Morton's dead," I said. "I killed him."

Jack just nodded. He wasn't going to say anything about it. I started for the stairs and then turned back to Jack.

"Will you do me one other favor?"

"Name it."

"Will you tend to that about letting Les's daddy know? After I get through with Bird I'm going to be a bit rushed for time and I know Les would have wanted his daddy to know right away."

"I'll see to it," Jack said.

I took out some money. "And will you also see to getting his body shipped back? I expect they've got it ready over at the hospital. All ready for Bird and Morton." I looked up the stairs. "But they won't be shipping any bodies, not right away." I held out a twenty-dollar gold piece. "This ought to cover shipping him on the train."

"Aw hell, Will," Jack said. "I'll get that. It won't be that much."

"I know," I said. "But I want to get it. All right?"

He shrugged and took the money. "I know how you must be feeling, Will."

"I'm fixing to be feeling a lot better."

He put out his hand and touched my arm. "Will, you know Bird."

"I know him," I said.

"He's a tough hombre. He's still got all the bark on."

"That's all right," I said. I turned for the stairs again. "Jack, I'm much obliged for all your help. If I were you I wouldn't hang around here. You don't want to get mixed up in this." I stuck out my hand and he took it and we shook. "I'll lay out somewhere and then catch that early train in the morning."

"I'll see you, Will."

I watched him until he'd walked across the lobby and went outside and then I turned and climbed the stairs. Bird's room was on the second floor. It was the middle one facing on the street. I stopped in front of his door. It was just a little ajar, which wasn't unusual because most of them didn't have latches anyway. I'd loaded my gun on the walk over from the hospital and I loosened it in the holster and then suddenly pushed open the door and stepped into the room.

Bird was laying on the bed with his hands behind his head staring at the ceiling. He had his breeches on, but he was barefoot and in his undershirt. His holster was looped over the bed post. I'd come in so quiet and quick that he didn't have hardly time to jump before I was in and had the door closed behind me. He recognized me right off, but he just kind of raised his head and took his hands down. We stared at each other for a second or two.

I nodded my head toward him. "Was that just about the way Les was settled when you and Morton killed him?"

Bird didn't say anything for a minute. He was watching me close. I knew he was thinking about his holster just right by his shoulder and calculating his chances.

223

Finally he said: "He didn't give us no choice. He made us do it."

"Sure," I said.

"I'm not lying, Young. We had him covered and he pulled on us. We had to shoot him."

"Is that why you had to shoot him four times? I hear them last two looked like you'd jammed the barrel right in him."

"I'm telling you how it was, Young."

I didn't say anything and we stared at each other for a minute. It's not my style to kill an unarmed man, but I wasn't too sure I wasn't about to break that rule in Bird's case. He was still laying on his back, but he'd kind of slowly inched his way up until he was leaning against the headboard a little. I just watched him, hoping he'd make a sudden move.

Finally he seen I was aware of what he was doing and he kind of settled back. "Well?" he asked me. "What are you going to do?"

"Kill you," I said. "Morton's already got his."

He didn't say anything to that. We stared at each other another second or two. I wasn't in any hurry. I wanted to make the bastard sweat a little if he would. But he was a cool customer all right. I hadn't come into the room with any idea I was fooling with a schoolboy. Bird's been around and he can handle himself. But so can I.

Finally he asked me if I just planned to shoot him down.

"There's your gun," I said, nodding toward the bed post. "Yours is in the holster and so is mine."

He gave a little snort. "Oh, goddam, Young! I know who you are. You mean that's all the chance you're going to give me?" He snorted again. "Hell, that ain't no show."

I just looked at him and didn't say anything. He'd pulled himself up a little more, but the gun was still way above him and in an awkward position to make a draw.

"I've heard you were square, Young. I've heard you'd give a man a chance."

"You've got a chance," I said.

"About the same as a calf in a wolf den."

I just kept watching him. I could see it was starting to bother him. Finally he got a little edge in his voice. "Goddamit, if you're going to do it, get on with it. Don't just keep standing there staring at a man!"

"Get up on that bed a little further," I said. "But take it slow."

He looked at me, hard, for a second and then slowly began to inch himself up. There was a bedside table just beside his bed. Hanging from the bed post, the end of his holster was nearly touching the top of the little table. I watched Bird, letting him inch his way along until he was almost sitting straight up. But he was still going to have to reach out and up to make his draw. It wasn't really fair, but it was all I was going to give him.

He'd adjusted himself so that he wasn't quite leaning back. He was almost sitting up. I could see he was tensed. He had his arms flung out at his sides, but he was running the fingers of his right hand up and down the leg of the little bedside table. It pleased me. The way he kept playing with it made me think he was getting nervous. I wanted him to sweat.

"All right," I said. "Hold it right there."

"Here? Just here? My God, Young, this ain't no show. Gimme a chance!"

"That's it," I said.

"My God, man!" He had hold of the leg of the little table, had his fingers around it and was squeezing so hard his knuckles were white. He was getting scared all right.

"You better get ready," I said. I let my hand steal up toward my gun.

We stared at each other. I could see him tensing his muscles.

Then I don't know what happened. His arm suddenly came up and forward and the next thing I knew the little bedside table was flying across the room right at my head. I ducked, drawing as I did, and went down to my knees. Before I could get straightened back up and get off a shot I heard a *boom!* and something hit me high on the shoulder and knocked me back against the door. It had hit me in the right shoulder, my gun hand, and I could feel my arm going numb. I tried to raise my gun. I could see Bird, he was on his knees, on the bed, leveling to get another shot at me. Suddenly his gun exploded again and I felt a bullet hit me in the side. I thumbed my own piece, getting off two shots, but they went wild. I figured it was all up with me. My arm was so numb I couldn't aim. I rolled to my right, switching my gun as I did. Bird fired again, but he hit where I'd been. I laid on my side and snapped off a quick shot at him lefthanded. It was awkward shooting, but it hit him in the stomach and he suddenly sat backward. I was rising when he got himself back up, holding his revolver with both hands, and shot me just under the right collarbone. I pumped two or three shots into him and he went backward and hit the headboard and then slid off the bed.

After the gunshots the room seemed very quiet. My ears were ringing and I was dizzy. I got up on my knees and then got hold of the wall and pulled myself to my feet. The room was spinning and I leaned against the wall trying to get my senses back. I was hurt, hurt bad, and I knew it. I was still holding my revolver and I reached across my body and got it back in the holster. My right arm felt completely useless. I looked across to where Bird lay but the room was so full of smoke I couldn't see. I pushed away from the wall and staggered over to where he was. He was laying half on and half off the bed and he had his mouth open. He'd bought his all right.

"Well, there," I said. "You bastard."

I felt my side and my hand came away smeared with blood. The wound in my side wasn't too bad. It was the wound up under my collarbone that I was worried about. I was scared to look at it.

Then I became conscious of voices out in the hall. I reached across and pulled my pistol out and got it in my left hand. I was going to have to move before the local law came around. I walked over and jerked the door back with my foot. There were about four or five men out in the hall and they kind of fell back when I walked out. They could see I didn't intend to be fooled with.

"Get out of my way," I said. I had my revolver about half up, but not aiming it at anybody in particular. I walked by them and headed for the stairs. "Anybody follows me and I'll kill them."

I stumbled down the stairs and made it across the lobby and went outside. For a second I was confused and didn't know what to do. I could feel myself getting weaker and I knew I was losing a lot of blood. I was in a bad way. I had to hurry. I turned south and started off in a kind of trot. I wasn't going to the train station. I'd go south of town and flag it down the next morning. I'd hide out all night along the tracks. Hell, I'd be all right. I was Wilson Young. I was some hombre.

I ran as best I could, but I couldn't go very fast. I kept getting dizzy. For just an instant everything would suddenly begin to whirl around and I'd feel like I was going to fall down. Then my head would clear and I could go on. I wished for my little filly. I wished mightily for her.

"She'd get me back," I said. I said it aloud, but it took a second to realize I'd spoken out. I thought I was thinking the words.

I'll get back, I told myself. I'll get back to my filly and Sabinas and that Linda. I'll be all right.

I kept running along in a kind of stumbling run. I was running down the middle of the dusty street. I'd gotten away from the square and now I was running down a little street past dark houses. They were all shut up for the night. There wasn't a light showing. I kept running along thinking about the girl. I couldn't think too good, my head kept spinning on me.

Suddenly I stumbled and fell. I ended up down in the dust on my knees. The fall had knocked my revolver out of the holster and it lay in the dust in front of me. I picked it up and looked at it.

I thought about Sabinas and Linda. I thought about it and I felt like crying, felt just like that time when I'd been only thirteen and out on the prairie and it getting dark and my leg hurting.

"The hell I will!" I suddenly said out loud. Far off I could hear a dog howling. I got off my knees and sat down in the dust. I wasn't going back to Sabinas. I wasn't going anywhere. That girl wasn't for me, that life wasn't for me. I was a bank robber. I'd always been a bank robber.

"The hell with it!" I said aloud. I raised my revolver and pointed it at the sky and began firing. It went *boom, boom, boom, boom*. It made a lot of noise in the quiet night. I felt very, very dizzy. I thought how good it would feel just to lay back and take a little nap. I raised my revolver and fired again. The hammer snapped when I pulled the trigger the second time. I was out of shells. I lay back.